THE RIGHT KIND OF WRONG

MONA & KHATARI

Mona Presents
PUBLICATIONS

NEVA DIE Publications

CONTENTS

MONA'S BIO — ix
KHATARI'S BIO — xi
Connect With The Authors — xv
Acknowledgments — xvii
Acknowledgments — xix
Synopsis: — xxi

1. Quincy — 1
2. Quincy — 11
3. Sakina — 19
4. Sakina — 27
5. Quincy — 35
6. Sakina — 49
7. Sakina — 59
8. Quincy — 65
9. Sakina — 75
10. Sakina — 79
11. Quincy — 95
12. Quincy — 103
13. Quincy — 113
14. Sakina — 121
15. Quincy — 133
16. Sakina — 139
17. Quincy — 149
18. Sakina — 155
19. Quincy — 163
20. Sakina — 169
21. Quincy — 179
22. Sakina — 187
23. Quincy — 195
24. Sakina — 207
25. Quincy — 213
26. Sakina — 219

27. Quincy	229
28. Sakina	235
29. Quincy	247
30. Sakina	255
31. Sakina	263
32. Malika	269
33. Quincy	273
34. Sakina	281
35. Quincy	287
36. Sakina	293
37. Quincy	297
38. Sakina	305
39. Lamont	311
40. Quincy	315
41. QUINCY & SAKINA	321
MONA'S CATALOGUE	333
MORE BOOKS BY MONA	335
RELEASES BY KHATARI COMING SOON…	337

Turning Wrong Into Right Was One Hell of A Ride.......

Copyright © 2021 Mona
Copyright ©2021 Khatari
Published by: Mona Presents Publications
Neva Die Publications

All rights reserved. No part of this publication may be reproduced, distributed, or transmitted in any form or by any means, including photocopying recording, or other electronic or mechanical methods, without the prior written permission of the publisher, except in the case of brief quotations embodied in critical reviews and certain other noncommercial uses permitted by copyright law.

This is a work of fiction. Names, characters, businesses, places, events, and incidents are either the products of the author's imagination or used in a fictitious manner. Any resemblance to actual persons, living or dead, or actual events is purely coincidental.

MONA'S BIO

Mona Pens

Mona was born Mona Altidort on March 8, 1973 in Elizabeth, NJ. Although Mona was born herein the United States, she started her early education in her parent's birth place, Cabaret Haiti where she moved to when she was only two years of age. Upon returning to the states at the age of six , Mona was not able to speak a word of English. As time went on she slowly learned English, however she lost her ability to speak French. English became her primary language as creole, not quite French, became her secondary.

Mona's love of writing became apparent at the age of eight. Her ability to create a plot to a story and fictional characterson the spot didn't go unnoticed as she started winning different essays and short story competitions. By the age of 15, she was writing countless short stories, poems and eventually developed her love for writing screen plays.

In 2003 she wrote a short screen play called "Why Me" and from there, her passion grew. Mona is thrilled she's finally able to share her gift with theworld. She currently have more projects she is working on. Mona is a mother of three beautiful girls and currently lives in New Jersey

KHATARI'S BIO

The Bio of Author De'Kari/ Author Khatari

Author Khatari aka De'Kari is a promising author whose work is nothing short of amazing. His work provides readers with an authentic glimpse into street life. He currently writes urban fiction but plans to cross over to other genres. The author was born and raised in Northern California.

The author experienced a challenging childhood. Riddled with abuse, neglect and witnessing violence first-hand, De'Kari's early years were dark and pained. Due to the dysfunction that surrounded him, he was often uprooted and moved from place to place. After various placements with relatives, he found himself in foster care. He eventually turned to the streets which consequently led to a lot of bad choices. In turn those bad choices led to youth authority, jail & prison.

There is more to this author than the street-life. He always had a love for writing. In school he excelled in creative writing. He would always live-out the story as he was writing. Through his most difficult times, he used writing as a way to escape from his surroundings. In addition to writing, he creates poetry, writes songs and does artwork. He loves spending time with family, fishing, sports and helping youth. He is happy that he is finally able to share his writing with others, putting his passion to work!

King Khatari

CONNECT WITH THE AUTHORS

Connect with Mona:
Mona Altidort on Facebook
Mona Promotes on Facebook
Mona Present Publications Business Page
Talks of the heart book club on Facebook
Talks of the heart promotional page on Facebook
Mona_Promotes Business Page
Moluvla_Promotes on IG
@MonaPresents on Twitter
Join My Reading Group: Mona's Chill Zone

Connect with Khatari:
Author Khatari on Facebook
Author King De'Kari on Facebook
Urban.novels.by.dekari on IG
@Dekari67503535 on Twitter
Join My Reading Group: Khatari's Pen is Lethal Group

ACKNOWLEDGMENTS

First off, this goes out to my readers. Thank you so much for your continuous support. Special shout out to Talks of the Heart Book Club and Mona's Chill Zone. Special, special, shot out to Khatari's Lethal Pen reader's group as well as my readers on my Mona Promotes page. All of your supports are greatly appreciated.

I also give special thank you to Ivy Symone! You have become my friend and my mentor. Thank you for all of your advices and teaching me the craft of writing. What can I say, I became a Published Author because of you and six years later I'm still learning from you and I Thank you from the bottom of my heart.

Also, special shout out to my test readers: Danielle Graves Harrison, Gina Harris and Nicole Walker. I can always count on you ladies for your honest feedbacks. Thank You!

Special dedication to my mom. Miss you and love you.

Each and every release will always & forever be dedicated to you.

And special, special, special Thank you to Lesia for your outstanding help & support with this project. Much appreciated!

And…….Last, but of course, not least….To my collab partner…. Mr. Neva Die, a.k.a. Khatari, a.k.a De'kari …What can I say…You are a true talent and I knew I chose right when I asked you to bring this story to life with me and you did that and then some. The story is fire and I thank you and your impeccable work ethic. You pushed, and pushed, and pushed, almost drove me crazy..Lol.. but that's what make you a great talent and I thank you.!!!

And with that said…The Right Kind Of Wrong! Enjoy!

ACKNOWLEDGMENTS

First off, Mona, Thank you for reaching out and giving me this opportunity to do this collaboration with you. Thank you!

Special, special shout out to my readers, the amazing admin of Khatari's Lethal Pen and others that helped to keep the group going.

Special thank you to Lesia for pushing me and helping to make my dream of becoming an author a reality and for all the countless hours you give to support me.

Much respect and props to my cellie and lil homie, Lil E, from the G, who helped me type my parts of the book on these little tablets and demanded that I put his name in the book. Lol

Last, but not least, a special thanks to Ca$h, Lockdown Publications for opening the door for me.

Much love to you all,
Author Khatari aka De'Kari

SYNOPSIS:

Quincy Norton was a successful Real Estate Agent in California living his best life when one betrayal caused a fatal mistake landing him in prison for life. Life as he knew it will never be the same.

Sakina Michelle is a successful Author, book - store owner and mother residing in New Jersey.

Everything appeared right in her life except for the imperfections she hides well and the attraction to the wrong men.

Crossing paths with a convicted felon serving life could be the most wrong of all..but…can it be…

The Right Kind Of Wrong?

CHAPTER 1
QUINCY

May of 2018:

Seventy-Two, Seventy-Three, Seventy-Four, Seventy-Five, finally Fifty sets of Seventy-Five. I was done with my workout. Monday through Friday I would make sure to get it in on the weight pile. California took its actual weights out of its prisons back in the 90's. So, a brotha had to be creative with the calisthenics in order to stay in tip top shape. My daily regimens did their part and a nice healthy diet does the rest. After all, I do Fifty sets of Seventy-Five push-ups followed by Fifty sets of Fifteen on the dip bars every day. On Tuesdays and Thursdays, I also added in my arms and leg routines. Needless to say, I knew I was looking pretty good.

The sun beamed down on my muscled physique adding to my body heat which contributed to the perspiration that cascaded down my body as I poured a bottle of water on top of my bald head. At 6'2" and weighing 285 pounds of rock-hard muscle over a dark brown skin tone, I resembled an NFL football player.

The name is Quincy Norton. I.D. # AF-4175. I am a thirty-year-old African American man currently serving a life sentence for murder. I have been down four years now, first incarcerated at Salinas Valley State Prison in California, a level four maximum security facility. The last couple of years, I was able to stay out of trouble and my points dropped from a level-four down to a level- three and I was then transferred to California State Prison Solano. I've been here now for almost two years.

For the most part, I have stayed to myself and minded my business. I got a few Cats that I messed with here and there, but everyone on the yard knows that I'm from East Menlo Park so I run the Bay Area Carr. It's a long story so don't ask what that name means. I will just say a Carr is a group of people, a click, or a gang, or it could just be a bunch of guys from one area. Everyone from East Menlo Park claimed the Bay Area including myself.

I reached down and placed the empty water bottle onto the ground and grabbed a fresh bottle, while I scanned the yard doing a quick security check. Making sure everything was okay, I took a long guzzle of the refreshing water, before I placed the bottle onto the ground and began my stretches. After every workout, I liked to run three miles and I always stretch before running. Running was a nice way to loosen the muscles and the body back up.

I then picked the bottle of water back up and tucked it away inside of a homemade pouch to carry with me. In prison you never sat something down that you planned on ingesting and leave it unattended. My water comes with me.

Three miles were twelve laps around the yard. I would normally run it in around twenty - two minutes which gave me enough time to think.

Around lap three, "**She**" came into my mind. Like I did not know that was going to happen. She has been on my mind ever since I read her book, **Conscious Over Heart**. It was real, it was touching and heartfelt. Again, I say it was real. Not to mention a tad bit scandalous. No, I am not stupid. I do realize it was a fictional book about imaginary characters, but it was so much deeper than that.

What caught my attention was the woman, as well as the mind and emotions behind the book. It had to be a remarkable sistah behind the scenes that could come up with the concept of forbidden love and to write this book. I felt the authors pain and happiness through the main character. Imagining that she had been through so much in life. Wishing that I could've been there for her while she was going through it. I would've held her tightly and let her know that everything was okay now because I would hold her down. Yeah, strangely, this Author have been heavily in my thoughts since I read her book a few days ago and I could not shake her. I wasn't sure what the hell was happening.

My thoughts were interrupted by a sudden skirmish by the basketball courts. I steadied my vision, trying to get a better look. One could never take anything for granted here. Something little could become something major at the drop of a hat, so I stayed ready for whatever, never taking any chances.

A few seconds later, though, it turned out to be nothing.

I had four laps left to do so I picked up my speed to a nice, steady run and honed in on the finish line. Once again, thoughts of that Author crossed my mind again and I did my best to shake off the thoughts. Lil Mamma had me fantasizing, but I'm not about to jeopardize my safety and security on an author that I barely knew anything about. All I did know was that her name was Authoress Kina, she had more published books available on Amazon and there was a P.O. Box address and picture on the back of the book.

Her picture. And there it was. Her words and writing from her book captured my attention, but her looks had me wondering, shit lusting even.

Damn, I had to stop this shit.

Shaking off my current thoughts, I finished my run just in time for building unlocks. Usually every hour, on the hour, the guard in the tower opened the door to the buildings to let people in and out. They called it hourly unlocks. I picked up my workout stuff and headed towards my building. I was still feeling the heat from my workout session, despite the fact I was shirtless, as I took slow strides. While I walked, I felt eyes on me. Even though they weren't supposed to stare at us, from the corner of my eyes, I noticed two female deputies eyeing me.

The lust in their eyes were obvious and that was quite common in these headquarters; female C.O.'s attractions to the inmates. And I was not exempt to their curiosities, except I didn't fulfill their wishes. I've seen other situations that did not end well and those were the kind of problems I did not need. But, that did not stop the C.O.'s from trying. And the harder their sexual advances were thrown at me, the more I disregarded them. And after four years on lock, with no pussy, shit was not hard to do. Yeah, I still had needs, but I learned how to suppress them.

Now, in the privacy of my cell, when I was alone, shit was a different story.

I smirked as I still felt the female C.O.'s eyes on me as I continued to walk towards my building.

"Q!" I turned to see who it was that called me all of a sudden.

"What's up BJ?" I called out as I recognized my old acquaintance coming in my direction.

BJ was a real old timer. At seventy-plus years of age, he's been in prison for fifty-two years. Majority of those years were spent in the Security Housing Unit or the SHU, where you are locked in your cell for twenty-three hours of the day. And that's on good days, because the law states that you only have to be let out of your cell three hours out of the week for recreation. With nothing but time on their hands, most of the brothas in the SHU worked out and studied harder. BJ was one of them. He may not be as bulky as I was, but he's every bit as muscular and he's in twice as good of shape.

"What's going on youngsta?" I used the word youngsta as a term of endearment.

"Where are you rushing off to like a Bat out of Hell?" He asked me with a funny look on his face.

"Shit youngsta, you know I gotta wash this sweat off of me.

I answered his question as we continued to walk.

"No doubt my brotha. I can understand that getting in the water is essential to the body just as the workout. But tell me something Young Blood, why are you so quick to leave the yard, when you left your CD player on the weight pike?" The funny look that was on his face was now a broad smile.

I checked all my stuff to make sure I had it. I just knew he was wrong. Had to be, because I gathered all my stuff. After checking everything, I realized I was wrong. But before I admitted it, I checked everything a second time. Sure enough, I didn't have my CD player or headphones.

BJ laughed at me and handed me my CD Player.

"I had no idea I did that shit," I said to him, feeling embarrassed that I failed to be on point.

"You know how you did it. I know how too, but I'm not going to tell anybody, Casanova." He started laughing after he said that last part.

BJ was the only person that I told about my feelings for Lil mama. I didn't want to take the risk sharing with anyone else and that would possibly betray my trust. But I didn't have to worry about that with the O.G. B J. He stayed in his lane. Or should I say he knew how to mind his own business and keep business between himself and whoever. No one else.

"Why don't you go on ahead and send that girl a kite," he suggested and I grinned. A kite was a convict's term for letter.

"Writing all that romance, she's probably as lovely as an old Librarian. You know these types of women are the good kind. Because when they finally do get a man, they know exactly how to treat 'em. Doing everything needed to do to keep him satisfied." I wanted to ask him what made him an expert. He has been locked up since he turned nineteen.

But I had way too much respect for BJ to ever ask him a question like that. Besides, his advice was always on point. He's never let me down or failed me yet. Why would I start to doubt him now?

"Last call for unlocks!" The guard in the tower called out signaling that she was getting ready to lock the door.

"Norton you better hurry up if you're going to catch this unlock."

"Special services... Yeah youngsta you're a sure 'nuff ladies' man," BJ teased me before walking off.

"Miss Johnson could you please pop cell twenty-four." I called out as I made it through the rotunda.

"That's C.O. Johnson to you Mr. Norton," She corrected me.

C.O. Johnson, could you please pop my cell?" I corrected in an amused tone, while heading towards my cell.

CO. Johnson and I played this little back and forth game every single day. From conversations that we've had, she knows I was raised by Country folks who taught us how to be respectful and courteous. For the most part, everyone was Miss, Mrs. and Mr. and I often used terms such as please and thank you, yet she seemed to have an issue when I addressed her by Miss. I shook my head at the thought as I walked towards my cell.

And to my satisfaction, the cell door was open by the time I reached it. Quickly, I grabbed my yard clothes, shower gear and a fresh set of undergarments. Next, I made my way down the tier to call next, in one of the showers. Luckily there was only one person in front of me.

As I stood by the shower with my back towards the wall, I scanned the dayroom. As it was in prison, especially if you've been in one of the killing zones, you were always scanning the area. That's how you stayed on point and stayed alive. See, when you're scanning a specific area, you're looking for numerous things. First and foremost, is your immediate area and surroundings. You have to always watch and make sure there are no imminent threat to you or your person. Next, you're looking at the police to see where they are at and what they are doing.

The Southsider's or Surenos and whites are both of our

enemies. We have to watch them because they are constantly plotting and looking for an avenue that will give them an advantage.

Now is where it gets crazy, because the Blacks and Northern Mexicans known as the Nortenos are allies or supposed to be. Even still, we have to watch them as well. I actually have been in more riots with the Northerners than I have with the Southerners (Sureno's). As if all of that wasn't stressful enough, I had to watch my own kind. The Blacks, even with all of these odds against us, were divided. You had Northern and Southern Cali. You had Crips and Bloods, Inland Empire or I E., San Bernardino, Bakersfield, Sacramento, Stockton, Kumi, B.G.F., PLR and the Bay Carr. All California Black groups.

Anyone of these factions at any given time can set it off and become a huge problem. That is why I am constantly scanning the area. Plus, you are looking to see where your potential threats are. If this is not done, then you could easily wind up being a victim of an extreme ass-kicking or even worse, a stabbing.

Finally, my turn came for the shower. I walked in with my boots on and got undressed If you stay ready you don't have to get ready. No matter where I go inside these prison walls, I'm on point. If a riot was to kick off right now, they're not going to say, "leave him alone he's in the shower." No, they are going to see an easy target. Some of the O.G.'s go as far as to shower actually wearing their boots. I stepped in the shower with my boots on but took them off and placed them in the corner. If something was to kick off, I'd put them back on and come out swinging, butt naked.

So, as I stood behind the waistline wall, which was partially exposed, I scanned the area once more to make sure shit was on point. Yeah, the showers were partially exposed so the C.O.'s and staff can keep a close eye on the inmates. In other words, there was no freedom in prison.

While washing up, my mind began to drift towards "**Her**" again. I wondered for the umpteenth time what it would be like just to sit down and have a nice meal with her or to sit and hold a casual conversation. I am a pretty-well versed brotha so we could talk about anything. I bet she's very intelligent. In my mind's eye she was sophisticated and elegant. Yet, she was down to earth and pleasant. Maybe even a tad bit street-savvy. I assumed she had to be based on the contents in her book. She had to be raised in the hood, but reside in a middleclass area for sure. Classy with a bit of street in her. Yeah, my type of woman for sure.

The feeling of someone watching me brought me out of my thoughts. Instantly my antenna went up. I quickly scanned the area moving my eyes only, starting with the greater threat, the Surenos. Looking their way, everything seemed copasetic, so I continued to scan. One by one I eliminated potential threats, not relaxing until I'd made a full assessment. There were no imminent threats, but I still couldn't shake the feeling of being watched.

I looked towards the C.O.'s and quickly found out that they were minding their business. I continued to wash up making it look like I wasn't aware of anything being out of the ordinary.

Who was it? I wondered.

Then my answer was answered. I couldn't believe I caught her, but my eyes didn't deceive me. Up in the guard's tower, Miss or C.O. Johnson was indiscreetly watching me shower. If I wasn't so adamant about finding the source, I would've missed her. She had a book in her hand pretending to be reading. She wasn't paying that book no attention. She was too busy staring at me.

Some dudes would go crazy for an opportunity like this. Not me though. I finished my shower, got dressed and quickly left out of there. I wasn't about to open any doors that I wasn't ready to walk through. Besides, I damn sure wasn't nobody's cheap thrill. There was nothing that miss Johnson could do for me.

I looked at the clock and noticed it was almost One p.m. as I walked towards the tower.

"C.O. Johnson can you open cell twenty-four and cap it please?" I called out to her.

My cell mate or cellie wouldn't be back until four-thirty. This would give me time for my daily nap. Having C.O. Johnson cap my door would make sure that she didn't accidentally open it while I was sleeping.

I noticed the smile she had on her face while I was talking to her. I just smiled to myself and shook my head while I went on inside my cell.

CHAPTER 2
QUINCY

A couple of weeks have gone by. Weeks of me debating back and forth with myself over whether I should write to her or not. My dilemma was simple. I'm not the type of man to put myself out there like that on some Jon B., AL B. Sure, sweet romance type of hype. Especially chasing after a woman, I don't even know.

On the other hand, no matter what I did, I could not seem to get this woman off of my mind. I must admit my curiosity was beginning to get the best of me. On the back of her book, based on a P.O. Box mailing address and her biography, I learned she resided in New Jersey. There was a part of me that wanted to write her a letter of introduction. Who knows, maybe she will respond to the letter. The hesitation comes from the possibility, "What if she doesn't?"

But I'm far from a coward. I refused not to write to her and give it a shot because I'm scared that I may never receive a response. I got everything to gain and nothing to lose. So, last night I made my mind up that I would write the letter. I cannot believe I was making all this fuss, creating my own confusion. My own Pandora's Box.

So my dilemma became even more simple. I was going to write her after all and I guess it was safe to say that I was indeed on some Jon B., Al B. Sure type of shit.

Damn. I didn't know if this woman was even worth all of this fuss.

I shook my head at myself as I just finished up flipping the last batch of pancakes with my spatula. I am an a.m. cook, which means I wake up at three a.m. every morning and come to the kitchen. There were four of us brotha's that cooked whatever the prison was eating each morning. Today was Saturday, so we were having pancakes and sausages. Each of us had an allotted amount that we were supposed cook before we were allowed to eat.

I loved the way the kitchen smelled on pancake day. The smell was none other.

Now it's time for me to make my plate. One of the perks of working on the grill was after you're done cooking breakfast, the boss allowed us to use the grill to cook whatever we preferred. I fried up a few sausages, egg and cheese sandwiches. My Sandwiches were famous around the yard. Some Saturdays I wouldn't eat them; I would pass them out to a few brothas. This was how word spread about my sandwiches. But I was eating these babies today!

Once I was done with all the cooking, I cleaned my grill really good and cleaned my area the way it should be done. Some go half - heartedly, but I chose to put my all in everything that I do. Besides, I really believed it doesn't take a long time to make sure you're doing things right and you are looking right. I genuinely tried to apply that concept in every aspect of my life.

From cleaning to working out, it only takes a little extra time to do it right.

"Norton?" I turned around to the sound of my supervisor's voice.

"Yeah, what's up?" The look on his face told me that he was getting ready to ask me for a favor.

"I just got word that Jackson just got sent to the hole. Do you think you can cover for him?" The look on Ken (my supervisor) face was priceless.

The last thing he wanted to do was ask for a favor. When I come to collect, I always come big. But he did not have a choice, but to ask. Jackson was a dude we all called Swift. He was one of the secondary cooks. With Swift being in the hole, either I helped out or the other two cooks would literally slave trying to make up the slack.

"Come on Ken, man. You know I was trying to get back to watch the game. This was the truth, but I said it just to see Ken squirm.

"I know Norton, but come on man, you're the lead cook and I need you. Come on, I'll make it up to you.

Bingo! This is what I was waiting to hear.

"Yeah, I got you Ken. I will be back in a couple of hours for you," I told him while laughing on the inside.

"Thank you, Norton, man thank you," Ken said in a grateful tone. He turned, and walked back towards his office.

"Q, you know you ain't right cuz." The homie, Lefty, a Crip from Insane Crip came walking up to me.

"I might not be right, but I bet you'll have your ass up in here on the day I cash in that favor," I teased him.

"Cuz, I still owe you big time for sharing that thick, smoked, hickory bacon that he brought you for the last favor."

We did not get bacon in prison. So when Ken asked me what I wanted to cash in on a favor he owed me, I told him some bacon. Now, I would've been cool with about four or five slices of thin, everyday bacon, not Ken though, he took favors seriously. He brought me a slab of thick cut Hillshire Farm Hickory Bacon.

I had a ball in the kitchen that day. I made bacon, egg, hash browns and cheese sandwiches. I also made some bacon, egg, hot link and cheese sandwiches. Hell, I even had enough left over just to eat by itself. Since bacon was one of the things the prison did not provide, it was considered contraband. Therefore, I didn't save any of it. That would have been evidence. It would get Ken fired and mess up a good thing.

"Shit, he's really going to owe me this time for this favor. I'm thinking about telling him I'll pay the cost and have him bring in some prime rib or a nice roast. Boy, I would set this kitchen ablaze with that along with some onions and bell peppers. Swift, I'm telling you Ridah, you ain't even knowing."

"Aww man, cuz, you got to make sure I'm here that day. My old lady used to like to order prime rib whenever I took her out to eat. That stuff is fire!"

Swift was a kitchen worker as well. He was really from the streets. His entire family from his grandparents to his mom and dad are Insane Crips.

We talked for a few more minutes, before I grabbed my belongings, and said my goodbyes. I then went on to search for a C.O. to let me out the kitchen since the doors were closed and locked. Usually, I timed it right and I am done and out the door while the inmates are still eating. It was less of a hassle that way.

Today, I was not so lucky. It took me twenty-odd minutes to

find that C.O. to let me out the kitchen. When he finally let me out, the yard was already open. It could not have been no later than ten am and the yard was live and in full swing as if it was one or two o'clock in the afternoon. The weight pile or the workout area was packed. The basketball courts were live with games, dudes were either walking or running around the track and the hustlah's were hustling. Just a normal day in prison.

I normally rested from my workouts on the weekend to give my body time to rest. So, I gave a head nod to a couple of the die-hards who go seven days a week and kept it moving. I was looking for BJ and knew exactly where I would find him.

True to form, I found BJ at the chess table. He was playing one of his favorite adversaries in chess, Low key. By far, BJ and Low Key were the best chess players on the yard. The yard was full of good players. Some days you may find seven or eight tables filled up with chess matches, which was a lot, considering we only have twelve tables all together for us. No matter how many great players the yard had, BJ and Low Key were the best.

As I stood there watching, I noticed the weather. It looked like it would possibly rain. I thought to myself, rain would be about one of the only things that would break this game up. That and a riot.

"I don't know why you're standing back there all quiet, when you have to know that I smell those delicious sandwiches you made," BJ called out without ever taking his eyes off the chess board.

"You know I wasn't going to interrupt your concentration," I told him.

"I don't know just how you expect me to be able to concentrate when I can smell all of that good food."

"Well let me help your concentration with a couple of these."

I dug in a bag I held in my hands and pulled out a couple of sandwiches. I handed them to him.

"Good looking out, Young Blood."

I responded with a simple head nod. He went on with the game and even though it looked like a damn good game they had going on, I decided to leave. I needed to get inside and write that letter to lil mama before I had to be back in the kitchen. I could feel eyes on me as I walked across the yard, but I refused to trip off of it. I knew it was just a few cats who wished I blessed them with a sandwich or two.

When I got to the building, I pushed the button on the intercom on the wall. It set off a small alarm inside the tower in order to get the tower C.O.'s attention.

"Yes? What do you want?" C.O. Johnson asked through the intercom.

"A.M. cook back from work," I announced.

If it was not for the fact that I had just gotten off of work, I would've had to wait for one of the unlocks to get in.

Without a response, she opened the door. I made my way through the rotunda. There was no need to request popping of my cell door because it was already open. Knowing that C.O. Johnson was looking at me, I made my way to my cell and once inside, I placed my bag down and grabbed my shower stuff.

Next, I went and found an open shower. While inside, I thought about what I wanted to write and say to this woman, I could not seem to stop thinking about. The thoughts could not form clearly in my head, though as I finished my shower. Moments later, I got out, said what's up to a couple of dudes and made my way back to my cell to go and handle my business.

I needed my tools for the trade, so I grabbed a CD and

turned on that dude, **KEM, "The man I used to be."** That was my jam for sure.

After putting all my stuff away and grabbing my notepad and pen, I sat down at a small desk in the small corner of my cell and with limited effort, the words just came to me.

Dear Authoress Kina,

I began this missive of introduction by first stating I pray that this letter finds you in the very best of Gods' loving Mercy, Grace and Favor. I strongly believe in today's society we all could use a lot more help from God than anything else.

As a way to break the ice, I wish I could tell you how many times I wrestled in my mind whether to write this missive or not. I felt like a high schooler attempting to entertain his first crush. At first, I thought my writing would seem like an act of desperation. But finally, I made my mind up and settled on a pure and direct approach at saying hello.

After reading Conscious Over Heart I simply couldn't keep you or your book out of my mind. The book was that amazing.

However, and I hope I am not overstepping my bounds or being too forward by saying, I have a nagging feeling that this book was written with real experiences in mind. If so, I believe, it takes a hell of a woman to be able to deal with a situation like that and still remain a lady. More so, I wouldn't be myself if I didn't attempt to reach out to you in an effort to get to know you.

As for myself, I first want to implore you not to allow my situation or circumstance to define who I am. Because the two couldn't be further from each other. I am a good brotha with good morals and beliefs. I just happened to find myself in an unfavorable situation. However, now is not the time to get into that. Should you choose to bless me with your acquaintance then later on down the line I'll share with you the ins and outs of my situation. Just keep this at the front of your mind, *"There is always a deeper truth than the one that lies on the surface!"*

Anyway, I hope something within this missive has caught your attention and will warrant a response from you. Because I am really looking forward to making your acquaintance and maybe even becoming a friend.

With Sincerest Intentions,

Quincy.

Without proof reading it or rethinking it over or anything else that would give me a chance to second guess myself, I grabbed an envelope, placed the letter inside, sealed it, put a stamp and addressed it.

Now, I have done my part. The rest was up to her. I could not predict the future nor control the sistah's actions or reactions for that matter. But at least I got that monkey off of my back. Here I was sweating a chick that may just toss the letter the moment she reads it. I had to laugh at myself.

I put my writing supplies on the shelf and picked up the remote to my TV Yes, we can order televisions in prison.

The smell of my sandwiches finally got the best of me. I grabbed one and turned on the Houston Rockets vs. Oklahoma City basketball game to catch a little of the Play-Offs before going back to work.

CHAPTER 3
SAKINA

"Can I come over?"

I chuckled before I tore my eyes away from my phone screen and reached over to my Oakwood tone night – stand. I retrieved a Crystal cut wine glass filled with one of my favorite red wine, Merlot. I raised the glass to my lips and took a sip.

"Mmmm." The bitter taste was rather repulsive to most folks, but to me it felt like heaven. Maybe, better than sex, even.

I chuckled again at my thought. Damn. It has been much too long if indulging in this bitter taste of red wine felt better than sex. Oh yeah, much too long, for sure.

Five months. Yes, five months and a hundred and fifty plus days to be exact since I have indulged in sex.

And to be crass; since I've had some dick.

Shaking my head, I took another sip of the chilled wine before I replaced the glass back onto my nightstand. After securing the glass onto the personalized, glass coaster which read; Kina, I resumed attention towards my phone screen.

"Am I beating those cheeks up tonight or what?"

I shook my head once again as I read the message. And just when I was zero point five seconds from giving into his request, he ruined it with his words. Like always, his non-romantic way of initiating sex turned me off like no other.

Can he beat those cheeks up?

Uuugh. That was exactly why the answer was no just like the other countless times he has been requesting to come over within the past two months.

Letting out a sigh, I let my fingers tap the keys on my Samsung Galaxy Android phone.

"Uuuhm, good night," I simply typed and quickly exited Instagram's messenger. Also, a turn off was the means of communication between us in the last two months. He insisted on Instagram only and I was sick of that as well among other things. Him and his mind games.

He called himself punishing me for showing up at his house unannounced five months prior by blocking me from calling him and I showed him I was indeed unbothered by returning the same gesture by blocking him on my Facebook page. I guess he started missing me as of two months prior, since I noticed he started to follow me on Instagram.

At first, I attempted to ignore him on there as well, however, the part of me that still held feelings for him eventually prevailed and allowed him access to me once again.

I reopened the line of communication between us, but once again, he had to have control. I wanted to know the identity of the woman I witnessed him talking to in front of his home and he insisted she was no one I needed to worry about. I, of course was unsatisfied with his explanation and he made a decision of his own by limiting our means of contact to Instagram only.

And once again, I showed him, that a woman always had the upper hand by withholding sex from him.

And now here we were. He was begging like Keith Sweat and I was enjoying watching the foolery. I suspected he was unfaithful with the mystery woman I caught him interacting with, but I could not prove it.

Nevertheless, I was willing to start fresh and give our relationship, well more like our situation another shot, hoping we can finally get it right, but then he sends messages like; "Can I beat those cheeks up?" And instantly I have second thoughts.

Yes, I know, childish and toxic. Our situation.

I was sick of it.

As of this year, altogether, I was sick of him, period. Yet....I could not seem to stay away. Although, I was currently giving him a hard time, deep within, I knew it was only a matter of time, before I gave in to him, like I have done so many times before during our three-year dysfunctional situation.

I shook my head at my dilemma.

Once again, I sighed as I tossed my cell phone onto my bed and reached for the remote control of my "30" inch Samsung: LS24F354FH flat screen television which rested on the coordinating Oakwood tone Chest of my nightstand.

Aiming at the screen, I clicked on the On - Demand button and searched until I located BET's slow jams channel. Without hesitation, I scrolled down the list of videos, labeled in Alphabet of order, until I landed on the letter **S**. After scrolling through the list of some of my favorite R & B singers, I landed on one my favorite of them all. I licked my lips and bit my bottom lip as I clicked on Keith Sweat. Yes, his begging behind was one of my top favorite male R & B singers, begging and all, and in that moment, the way I was feeling, he was my number one favorite.

Although, I was horny out of my mind from dick deprivation, I was also in a surprisingly, romantic mood.

I wanted to be made loved to, not just get fucked and unfortunately, the man I loved, or better yet, the man that I was a fool for, had problems comprehending that, and I was currently sexually frustrated as well as emotionally starved. As horny as I was, I craved romance more than anything and unfortunately, I have been deprived of that within the last three years and even more, prior to that.

Me and men. I always seem to choose the wrong ones.

Sometimes, I felt cursed. Yes, that was the best word to describe my history with men and experience when it boiled down to affairs of the heart.

Letting out a sigh, I clicked on my video of choice by Keith Sweat and the melody sounded off, along with the lyrics. I smiled the way love songs always caused me to as I leaned against my headboard and relaxed. I retrieved the glass of wine from the nightstand and sipped as the video played and the sultry lyrics to: **"There You Go"** soared off.

I was a hopeless romantic for sure and in that moment, no man understood that more than Keith Sweat. It was as if he was singing to me and me only....

"There you go telling me no again, there you go, there you go. Baby, I wanna be more than just your friend, don't you know, don't you know....."

"But you keep telling me things that I really don't wanna hear," I sung the words to the song and within that second, my emotions took over, getting the best of me. I felt the warm tears formed in my eyes and streamed down my cheeks.

"Uuggh." I just had to groan in frustration before I raised the glass, I still held in my hand to my lips and finished off the red wine. Swallowing the chill drink, I reached over and placed the empty glass onto the coaster, resting on the nightstand. After much attempt to wipe the tears from my eyes which were still streaming down my cheeks, I leaned my head against my headboard once again, closed my eyes and exhaled.

The melody and lyrics to "There You Go" filled the room, overshadowing the peace and quietness I strangely resented. Most individuals, especially mothers like myself, embraced and appreciated quiet times, but I'm one of the few who felt the total opposite. When I am all alone, left with my own thoughts and feelings, serious problems occur. And as much as I love red wine and love songs, the combination made my situation just that much worse.

My Imperfection....

Very few were exposed to it. I can count on one hand how many family members had the displeasure of witnessing it and as far as men were concern, none knew of my private struggle. Not even my two sons' father. After ten years together, he still had no knowledge of the real me. As far as he was concern, I was this super woman who can handle anything and let him tell it, "Didn't care about shit."

But I cared when he had trouble keeping his dick in his pants. Ten years of unlimited infidelity, along with disrespect and I was over it. For years I went along with the façade of portraying the perfect family. Outside we appeared to be just that, because that was the image I displayed, but that was farthest from the truth.

And after ten years of the same old bullshit, I left. And before him were more unfulfilling relationships with once again, infidelity front and centered.

And of course, my current situation. Three years of more

nonsense. I shook my head as a wave of sadness washed over me and the questions that always occurred danced in my head.

So, what was it about me that attracted such bad luck with men? Would my luck be different if they knew the real me? Perhaps they sensed my façade? Perhaps they sensed the image I projected was not the real me? At least not all of me? Or did I just attract selfish men who would not know a good woman even if God himself presented one to them?

Just a bunch of why's, why's and more why's, mixed with tears, self – doubt and plain old....

Depression....

For this very reason I hated being alone. Unfortunately, at times I was unable to avoid it. Present moment was the perfect example. My two sons and the best things that ever happened to me were with their father and I call him that loosely, while I had my two bedroom modern size apartment in the small town of Rahway, New Jersey all to myself.

The sudden desire to log on to Instagram once again, crept over me while I reopened my eyes. I reached over for both my cell phone and remote control, contemplating my next move. Should I wallow in my self-pity and sad state or should I log into Instagram and reply yes to my headache of three years? Sadly, the dysfunctional relationship or in better terms, "Situation" he and I shared added to the list of reasons for the depress episodes that takes over me, but once again, I could not stay away from him and eliminate one of my problems.

Perhaps, I didn't want to? Another failed relationship at the age of thirty-five. I was at times, embarrassed by that.

Uuugh.

Letting out another frustrated sigh, I toyed with my decision for what appeared to be a substantial amount of time, before I chose to turn off the television and reached over for my HP laptop and powered it on instead. Clicking on the folder labeled: Kina's Novels, I scrolled down until the curser landed onto0. my current story in progress.

Finally, I aborted the thought of logging back into Instagram and chose to develop the romance story of a woman desperate to discontinue choosing the wrong men by creating a perfect one, sort of a weird science type of venture.

Tonight, I chose to live vicariously through my character while I pretend to be Ms. Perfect myself and fantasy about my Mr. Right.

Yes, I am Sakina Michelle, Author extra Donaire, and no one could bring a story to life quite like me, if I must say so myself. I can attract anyone with my words alone and tonight, my character will do just that: capture Mr. Right.

CHAPTER 4
SAKINA

"You need a man with Sensitivity, you need a man like me."

"Uhhm, must we listen to this sappy song? I swear you and your damn love songs all the time."

I shook my head and laughed at my whining best friend as she did one of the things she did best which was bitch and complain.

"Can you please shut up and let me listen to Ralph?"

"Uuuh, hell no," she boldly replied, and I laughed out loud again.

"Well too damn bad. We're listening to Ralph all the way to the bookstore, biiiiotch!" I shouted and it was her turn to laugh out loud. I reached over and turned up the volume to "Sensitivity" by the group New Edition's lead singer, sexy Ralph Tresvant. I was on cloud nine as I sung the lyrics to one of my favorite love songs by him and all around. From the corner of my eyes I noticed my bestie rolling her eyes and I laughed again over the music.

We were truly like night and day and this particular moment was a reminder. Our choice of music was different to start the list of differences. I was into slow jams, love songs and old school love ballads while she was more of a Hip - Hop head and in tune with hardcore rap. We constantly criticized each other over our taste in music and overall taste in just about every other category on earth. And I do mean everything.

"Uuugh! You drive slow as hell! I swear, it's bad enough I have to listen to these corny, baby making songs all the way to Source of Knowledge, but you just have to drive like Miss Daisy while I'm being tortured," she bellowed and I busted out laughing again.

"Oh God!" I could not stop my laughter.

Yes, she was a fool, but I would not change anything about her for nothing in this world.

Malika Watkins... She was the truth.

Yes, we were different as can be, but we represented the term; Opposites Attract. She was what folks referred to as a hood chick and I was the total opposite. According to my bestie, I was bougie, but I prefer the terms, humble, reserve and assertive. Despite such differences however, we clicked from day one since meeting in college on the Campus of Rutgers University in Newark, New Jersey seventeen years ago. The way we met was rather unusual but set the tone for a lifetime of one hell of a friendship.

She was what I loved to refer to as my very own ride and die. The term befitted since she saved me from a horrific act on campus one evening as I was on my way to my car. Four neighborhood hoodlums were on a rampage that day, burglarizing several homes, when I grabbed their attention. I witnessed their crime in progress involving a home next to the school campus and they were determined to silence me in any way necessary.

Needless to say, I saw my life flashed in front of my eyes before sudden gun shots appeared out of nowhere. The so-called hoodlums showed their true colors as they ran for cover, leaving the scene of the pre-crime as well as me on my knees thanking the lord up above for a second chance at life. Moments later, I was thanking the mysterious stranger for saving my life and she was consoling me. After driving me home, since I was still in distraught, we spent the night getting to know each other, sparking a connection, friendship and sisterhood. And our differences only made our bond that much special.

One would say we were both rather intrigued by each other's different worlds and backgrounds. Well, at least I was, she found me a bit boring and a prude, but her constant ridiculing brought the humor into our existence mixed with a whole lot of fun, trust and loyalty. We became closer than any words it took to define the true definition of the word close and our seventeen-year friendship was the true proof of that. We formed a true sister hood, something I lacked with my own biological sister. And the differences Malika and I shared made things that much interesting and only enhanced our loyalty to each other. She accepted me for who I was and vice-versa.

"Uuugh, I'm going to need a blunt after spending a whole day with your ass."

"Oh, shut up, you don't need a damn blunt." I laughed and she groaned.

"Oh, hell yeah I do. Your corny music, your slow driving ass and a whole day of selling books in a damn bookstore, hell yes, I need two blunts and a big ole bottle of Patron."

I could not stop laughing at her words.

"But you love me though," I said through my laughter. She held her hands in mock surrender and nodded her head in agreement.

"Yeah, yeah, I do love your bougie, white girl acting ass," she joked and once again more laughter erupted.

"Whatever!"

"Whatever my ass and what the hell are you stopping at the post office for?"

She asked just as I pulled into the parking lot of Rahway Postal Office.

"Uggh, can you shut up please? As a matter of fact, I will pay you just to shut up since you won't let me pay you to help me out today at my book signing." I laughed at my own statement and request as I pulled into the first parking space my eyes landed on and shut off the engine to my one-year old BMW SUV.

"Uhh, hell no, you can keep your damn money, because Malika Watkins don't shut up for no damn body, you already know that shit," she replied like only she could and it was my turn to groan.

"Uuugh, please stop referring to yourself in the third person, because you are not that important," I teased her and that was enough to set her off.

"Bisssh, you got me, and the game fucked up. I am that important and then some and if you seem to have forgot, you better google me. Malika Watkins. Malika Watkins. Malika Watkins."

"Oh, shut the hell up!" I laughed as I removed my car key from the ignition and grabbed my wallet, resting near the shift gear.

"Shut the hell up!" she mocked me as we both climbed out of the car. I shut my door closed and as soon as she did the same, I secured the locks with the car remote.

"Whatever, ghetto girl," I joked as I wrapped my arm around her shoulder.

"Yeah, yeah, white girl," she teased me, and I laughed again.

"I don't act white and what the hell does that even mean," I said through my laughter as we made our way towards the post office entrance door.

"You know what that shit mean," she laughed along with me as we entered the post office. I removed my arm from around her shoulder as I reached my P.O. Box.

"Oh, we're here so you can check your P.O. Box. I forgot your ass is a superstar now," she teased, and I stuck my tongue out at her in a teasing manner.

"Yeah, yeah, yeah. I'm hardly a superstar. I'm just a little old local Author."

"Bisssh, you have Eleven published books on Amazon, Two Bestsellers, a screenplay in the works, Five-thousand friends on Facebook, almost Ten-thousand friends on Instagram and the same damn amount on Twitter. Not to mention, the women who writes to you praising how your books inspire them even though it's supposed to be fiction. You're the shit and it's time you realize that."

As soon as she finished the last line to her sentence, I could not help it as I reached over and hugged her. And that was the dynamic of our relationship. She knew me like no other and cheered me on just the same.

"Thank you," I said to her as I pulled back from our embrace.

"Yeah, yeah," she smiled. "Now get off me," she added.

I giggled as I retrieved my mailbox key from my wallet. As

soon as I placed the key in the mail slot and opened the box door, a few envelopes fell to the floor.

"See this shit. Look at how much letters your ass been getting and you're talking about you're not a superstar."

I shook my head as I crouched down and picked up the mail that landed on the floor.

"Whatever. I'll consider myself a superstar when I make New York Time's Bestseller list instead of just on Amazon," I let her know.

"Well, that's next. Just keep writing those bomb ass books, and you'll see."

I smiled at her words.

"Thank you, bestie."

"Yeah, yeah. Let's get the hell out a here, before you're late for your very first one on one book signing."

"You're right," I agreed with her as she helped me gathered the stack of envelopes in the mailbox. Seconds after, I shut the mailbox door closed, we exited the post office.

"I should've checked this box on Monday."

"Yeah, you should've and who the hell is Quincy Norton from California State Prison Solano?

Malika asked as we hurried to my car. The name of the prison or the Name Quincy did not ring a bell, but my focus in that moment was making my book signing on time. I grabbed the stack of letters from Malika's hands and stuffed them in my Tote bag.

"I'll open those letters later. Let's get to this bookstore."

Both Malika and I quickly entered my car and fastened our seatbelts.

"You should let me drive. We'll get there in one damn

minute," Malika stated as I placed the car key in the ignition. And of course I ignored her. Malika drove as if Law Enforcement were after her and, in that moment, I was trying to make it to my book event on time and alive.

CHAPTER 5
QUINCY

One Week Later:

I've been in the Law Library now for almost four hours, looking over different case law and trying to convince Mr. Brown to look at some legal documents I had prepared.

Any time there was a ruling on something in any court, it becomes case law. Such examples are **"The State vs. Mathew Whitaker"** or **"The People vs. John Smith."** Studying case law was indeed boring work, yet, finding something inside of case law was the one way or should I say the fastest way a person could bring themselves home.

The way case law works was simple, if you find a case where the judge ruled a certain way, you could use that to get the judge in your case to rule the same way. Hence if in **State vs. Thompson**, a judge ruled, or the Supreme Court ruled it was self-defense if the victim pulled out a gun and he and the defendant wrestled for it and somehow the defendant took the gun and shot the victim; If your case happened the same way or similar, then **State vs. Thompson** applies to you.

Mr. Brown was the best legal man on the yard, but he didn't help just anyone. He was one of the old convicts that had been down for more than twenty years. He didn't talk to or deal with too many people. He had his circle of people he dealt with and that was it. I wasn't trying to become one of those people. I just needed the O.G. to take a look at my legal work.

"Look here Quincy, you're not like most of the cats behind these walls and I like and respect that about you. You're a good young'n 'Q,' but I can't afford to be caught dealing with you because of your extracurricular activities." He looked me straight in the eyes as he said this: Out of respect, he lowered his voice while talking.

"My extracurricular activities?" I was as lost as a stomped down pimp trying to find a church house.

Mr. Brown leaned in conspiratorially and whispered, "I'm talking about all that dope you're pushing on this yard. Right now, you are being smart about it, but it is only a matter of time before these pigs get wind of it. Honestly young'n I've been down twenty-eight years, been rejected by the parole board twice. I can't afford to be caught up in no bullshit or found guilty by association."

Hearing that he knew of my little hustle threw me for a loop. Even though I knew in prison someone was always watching, I believed my moves were stealth. How in the hell had he learned about my business?

"Two things you should know young'n. One, there are no secrets in prison, no matter what yard you are on or what you are doing, somebody is always watching. Therefore, someone always knows your business. The second thing you should know is that the police know everything that's going on, on this yard, just like we do. Take heed to my words young'n because they will keep you out of the limelight. These people will let you continue to do your thing as long as you keep the violence out of the equation. The moment that the violence starts, they will come for you."

I was dumbfounded but I didn't let it show. Instead of commenting on what he said, I steered the conversation back around to my legal work.

"Mr. Brown, if you are concerned with or have reserved feelings about dealing with me, we can orchestrate things in a way that you'll never have to meet with me or talk to me ever again."

As I studied the expression on his face, I could tell that he was at least considering helping me out. Aside from the other two clerks who worked in the law library with Mr. Brown, there were only two other cats inside of the building with us. We relatively had our privacy. Yet to anyone on the outside looking in, it appeared as if we were discussing the legal book that Mr. Brown was holding in his hand.

"Young'n you know you're just a persistent o'le thing. You know that don't you? I'll tell you what. Give me a little while to think on it. If I do decide to look over your stuff, I'll send someone to you in a little bit." The tone in which he made that statement let me know that the conversation was over. If I were to further persist and try to push the issue, he most likely would've refused to help me on the spot.

I kept it 'G' and thanked the man for his time. Then I walked to the table that I had been utilizing and gathered all my stuff. Minutes later I was politely saying good-bye to all of the clerks as I headed out of the building.

I thought about the jewels that the old man dropped on me as I made my way across the yard. Yeah, I was selling dope, but I was not trying to be no penitentiary baller or some nigga that was trying to hustle in order to fit in with the Jones's on the yard. No that wasn't me.

A couple of years ago I'd come across information on what are known as *after sentence reduction specialist attorneys*. These were not appeal attorneys. These were attorneys whose sole specialty was getting time knocked off your sentence. Nothing was guaranteed, however for those who had the money, those attorneys were known to get chunks of time knocked off your sentence. Personally, I am not the type of dude that will not leave no stone unturned in my pursuit of a particular goal. Especially when it came to my freedom.

Seeing as I don't have anyone on the streets that could help me attain one of those attorneys, I had to get off my ass and get on my feet to get it done myself. So, I began my hustling career. I do not want to be here, do not deserve to be here and don't have a release date in sight. I'm just stuck living a nightmare every day.

I saved up enough money hustling in prison that I was finally able to retain one of them attorneys a couple of months ago. As he explained to me, this was a process that took a great deal of time and more money. If I could keep the money flowing, he would keep knocking away at the time. So, I was going to keep hustling, long as I needed to.

An intense football game was going on when I hit the yard, between the white boys and us. Although it was flag football, the offense and defensive line could hit each other. There was also sideline pops, which meant if you caught somebody running along the sideline you couldn't tackle them, but you could hit their ass hard as fuck out of bounds.

There was a lot of tension in the air as everybody watched the game. If something were to go wrong, it wouldn't be the first time a riot kicked off because of a football game. Silently I hoped nothing kicked off because I had all my legal shit in my hand. If something did kick off, I would be forced to drop all my legal stuff right there and get actively involved.

Brothas we're not trying to hear none of that *"I had my legal shit with me crap"*. If you did not get involved, you were labeled and dealt with later. On the flip side, in a riot, the white boys weren't going to bypass and leave you alone because you had books and paperwork in your hands. They would fuck you up.

Normally I did not carry my paperwork around like this, but I had hopes that I could convince Mr. Brown to look at my legal work. I paid another cat that was good with legal work to write me a Habeas Corpus for relief and that was what I wanted Mr. Brown to look over.

The Blacks were smashing the white boys Thirty-five to Fourteen. I witnessed all that I needed to see on the football field. I gave it to the white boys, even though they were down by Twenty-One points, they still had their heart and pride in the game.

It was almost yard recall, so I headed towards my building. I was rounding the building when all the brothas erupted in cheer. I immediately turned towards the game that was now a good Fifty yards away from where I was. A white boy was laying on the ground withering in pain. The rest of the white boys or the woodpile as they call themselves were making their way over to the football field. Looked like we were about to have us a little situation.

I quickly turned back around. I saw Lex, an O.G. that was in his Sixties. I ran Fifteen feet over to him and told him I would pay him to take my paperwork with him to his cell. Nobody touched dudes that old unless they were down on the battlefield. Immediately I turned back around and started jogging back towards the football field. If it was going to kick off, I wanted to be in the front row, in the trenches with the Thugs. I might be the mind my business, calm, quiet, don't bother anyone type of dude, but if push came to shove, I knew how to handle my business.

As I waded my way through the sea of brothas, I saw the usual suspects; the ones who have been through battles before and were always accounted for whenever something was about to jump off. I quickly made a mental note of everybody that I saw. When I got to the front, I was standing next to the one that laid the white boy on his ass. Two other white boys were lifting him and helping him to his feet. It looked like he had been out of it a little while and was just coming back.

"Just say it Casper. Just say it and we will tear this mothafucker to pieces. Was it a dirty hit?" This white boy named Harley came walking up asking the injured white boy.

You have to give it to the white boys. We outnumbered them something like Five to One and here comes this crazy motherfucker talking about *"tearing this motherfucker to pieces."* To me that was hilarious but that's how the white boys are. You gotta love their heart.

"W- What? What? Naaw brother it was a good hit!" He turned towards Ty, the brother that hit him.

"God damn mighty good hit." With a snaggled-tooth grin, he extended his hand to Ty for a handshake.

It was not until this, that everyone including the C.O.'s

relaxed and breathed a sigh of relief. Just like that, everything was back to normal. That is how it was behind prison walls though. Things could go from okay to an all - out war at the drop of a hat.

Had Casper been a lesser man, he would have said it was a dirty or cheap blow just to save face and we would be getting it in like Gladiators right that very minute. As if they did not want to tempt fate, the C.O.'s announced yard recall.

I entered the building and headed for my cell. There was no need for me to yell out my cell number, because Office Johnson had already popped my door to my cell open. A smile spread across my face as I thought about her watching a nigga shower the other day.

I grabbed my shower shit and was headed for the shower when Wacko walked up on me.

"Q, what's up Cuz?"

"Wack, what's good with it?" I did not feel like talking to anybody, but I stopped to hear him out just out of respect.

"Shit cuz, you know a nigga C-day is the day after tomorrow. Me and the homies got a little something, something planned. But Q, I'm not even about to front Homie, a nigga trynna buy a few of them sandwiches that you be making. I know you don't be selling them like that, but I figured you might fuck with a nigga. It being a niggaz C-day and all." C-day was the way that the Crips said birthday or B-day.

Wacko was a cool dude from Harlem Crip. He was about Ten years older than me. He was not one of them O. G. cats who thought he was still Twenty like most Crips. He was an O. G. who moved like one. I respected him because he was one of the few older Crips that tried to get the youngsters to see that there was more to life than just gangbanging.

"You say it's your birthday huh?"

"Yeah a nigga about to turn Forty." He said it like he was talking about getting the Heavy Weight Championship title.

"I'll tell you what Homie, don't trip, I got you. Now, I am not talking about all of your homies and shit, but I got a few sandwiches for you." He needed to understand that I gave zero fucks about his people, but I would bless him on G.P. (general principle) because it was his birthday.

"Q, thanks Cuz."

"No doubt Ridah."

We shook hands, talked a few moments longer and he went on his way.

Once Wacko left, I went and jumped into the shower.

After the little brief tension on the yard, I really needed a nice hot shower. I needed that hot water to soothe my muscles and wash the tension away. I noticed for the second time that Ms. Johnson was watching a nigga, but I could not waste time with that. I mean, what could she really do for me? Not a damn thing.

She was a tower cop which meant she was almost never on the ground with us. When she came to work, she reported to that tower and when she came down, she went home. So, she could not bring me the bundle so we could get this money. Even if I were thinking with my little head (which I never do), she could not even get close enough to me to let me see how that thang felt. Therefore, I was not going to waste time entertaining sexual, erotic fantasies about this woman getting her rocks off watching me shower.

After washing, I got dressed, and exited the shower.

As I was heading back to my cell, I could see the C.O.'s sorting out the mail. I don't know why but for some reason it made me think about "**Her**" and wondered if she wrote back.

Just as quickly as that thought came to my mind, I had to push it out. Talk about fantasies and daydreams. That girl probably didn't even get my letter and even if she did, why would she want to respond to a letter from a guy in prison? Now that I thought about it, I don't even know why I wrote her that letter in the first place. Yeah, I started thinking how crazy it was of me to not only crush on a chick after reading one book of hers, but to go as far as writing her. She will probably toss that letter in the trash for sure.

Yeah, I was tripping.

Those thoughts invaded my mind as I made my way back to my cell. Once inside, I turned on some Toni Braxton and took care of my hygiene. My cellie was transferred to Vacaville State Prison, so I've had the cell to myself for a few days now, which meant I could take my time and apply my hygiene products properly.

Toni Braxton always made a brotha feel good. I've been listening to her since her first album dropped. I was applying deodorant under my arms when her song *Hands Tied* came on. It was one of my favorite songs, however, it made me think of Monique.

Monique was my ex-wife and the reason I'm sitting in this cell to begin with. Thinking of Monique made me flashback to that one fateful day when my life changed unexpectantly.

Six years ago:

I was a Real Estate Agent and not just an agent, but one of the top selling agents in all of Menlo Park. I had just started branching out and building a clientele with a few celebrities. Selling houses was not just a career but a way of life. Selling was a natural born talent for me, and I did it well. I sold my first house at the age of Twenty and have been on a roll ever since. And now at the age of Twenty-four, I was making six figures and living a pretty lavish lifestyle with my wife Monique.

My work schedule would often vary and was based on set schedules with clients; however, one particular month became extremely busy and I would leave the house as early as 7 A.M. and would not return home until after 6 P.M. One day, I sold three houses and was ecstatic. Deciding to surprise Monique with the good news, I went home early that day without calling. Like I said, I wanted to surprise her, but I would soon find out that the surprise was on me.

The second I pulled up in front of my house, my first inclination that something was wrong was the black Cadillac parked in my driveway. I parked on the street, got out and walked to my front door. When I opened the door, I was greeted by Keith Sweats 'Nobody' being played on my $8,000 Bose home audio system. The music playing, the burning candles and smell of Lavender did not make me trip. After all, I've come home to Monique soaking in the tub like that before.

What made me first start to trip was the pair of size Twelve, Michael Jordan Retro shoes that were by the couch. First of all, I was a size Fifteen shoe, not a Twelve and I have never in my life owned a pair of Jordan's. He has never done anything for our people. All he's ever done was talk bad about the Blacks in less fortunate neighborhoods, so because of this, I will not ever buy anything, Michael Jordan puts out.

Feeling how Ron Isley did when he made the song 'Contagious', I made my way to my bedroom. My heart was pounding in my chest as all sorts of thoughts went through my mind.

Monique and I were married three years. We were young but were head over heels in love. At least I was. There was nothing that I wouldn't do for her. I literally worshiped the ground she walked on. None of that mattered though, when I opened my bedroom door and saw her getting fucked in my bed by some nigga I've never seen before.

Yeah, I was beyond heartbroken and devastated. Even still, I kept it 'G'. There was no need for big scenes, confrontations, and shit. That was for the movies.

I simply turned on the lights interrupting them and turned the music off. Monique was scared and embarrassed. She tried begging and pleading when I told both of them to get out, but I wasn't listening.

Her side dude on the other hand started talking shit like he caught me fucking his chick. I did my best to pay the shit that he was talking no attention, until he walked up in my face. I put him down like I was supposed to. Who the fuck did this sucka think he was? First, he was fucking my wife in my bed, in my house, then to add insult to injury, he had the audacity to talk shit to me for coming home and interrupting them.

As far as I was concerned, they could've left together and got a room or something and finished their business. All that changed when the bitch-ass nigga got in my face. I beat the dog shit out of that dude. I did not even think about it, it just happened.

I messed up, though, when I allowed him to crawl to his clothes. I figured I had proved my point with the ass kicking I delivered to him. So, I let him crawl to his pile of shit over on the other side of the bed. I was thinking that he would shamefully grab his shit and get the fuck out of my house.

What I wasn't expecting him to do was pull a gun out of his pile of *clothes that were on the floor. He turned around and pointed it towards me while he was mumbling under his breath.*

I was nervous, then, I could not even front. After all, I had just kicked the living shit out of this guy. There was no telling what he would do. Out of anger or embarrassment he could shoot me down in my own bedroom. The fact that he was mumbling incoherent shit only made things more unpredictable.

I thought that Monique would've told him to put the gun down or tried to somehow talk him out of whatever state of mind he was psyching himself up for, but, before I knew it, he rushed me, and the barrel of the gun was pressing against the side of my head.

"Bitch-ass nigga, you think you tough, don't you? You think you did something by putting your hands on me? Nigga I will blow your mothafucking head off." In the state that he was in, I had reason to believe that he would do exactly just what he said.

I was the one scared senseless, yet he was shaking and trembling like we were locked inside of a freezing cold meat locker. I knew I had to do something fast before he accidentally killed me.

Out of my peripheral vision, I saw that his finger was not on the trigger. In fact, it was outside of the trigger guard. If I acted, his reaction time would be off, given his mental and emotional state. I took a deep breath and went for the gun and just like I figured, he was caught off guard.

We tussled for control of the gun within a few minutes before I begun getting the upper hand. When I clearly had better control over the gun than he did, last minute act out of desperation, the mothafucka pulled the trigger trying to shoot me. He did not realize that the gun was pointed upwards towards him.

The bullet crashed into his chest cavity piercing his heart. The force of the 45mm bullet hitting him at close range sent him flying backwards a few feet and crashing onto the floor.

I was the one who called the police amid Monique's screams. When the police arrived, I told them exactly what happened. No-one said anything about blame, or my being arrested. It took maybe six hours for them to finish questioning and complete an investigation and for the Coroner to remove the body.

Two weeks later on my day off, while sitting at home relaxing, watching the 49ers and Seahawks game, two detectives came to my door and arrested me on first degree murder charges.

I sat in the county jail for a couple of years before finally going to trial. Never in a million years did I expect to be found guilty. With Monique's testimony it was a clear case of self-defense. At least that's what I thought.

A twelve- man jury found me guilty of second-degree murder and I was sentenced to thirty-three years to life. And that was the end of my life as I once knew it.

I was brushing my teeth as Toni Braxton was wrapping up her song. Before I knew it, a single tear escaped my eye and slid down my cheek. Ironically, the tear was not for how much time I received or even the fact that I was convicted of a crime that I did not commit. I shed the single tear for a lost love. I truly believed that Monique and I was a match made in Heaven. I thought we were happy. At least I know I was very much in love and the crazy part was, after all that I've been through and all the time that has passed.... I still loved her.

That's what hurt me the most. The fact that I should really have a strong distaste in my mouth for this woman, but I did not, was sometimes crazy to me, and I should be blaming her for what happened to me, but I do not blame her at all.

But if she came to me right now wanting to be a couple and work past what happened, I would not be able to do it. But that does not mean that I don't love her. She was just not worth my love.

After finishing up my hygiene, I looked at the clock and realized that I had a couple of hours before count time. I decided to take me a nap until then. I shook off past mental memories of Monique and in that moment, I made a mental note to bury them for life, like the sentence I was currently serving.

CHAPTER 6
SAKINA

"Oh no, you're sold out?"

"When will part three be available?"

"Do you mail to prisons?"

"Yeah, do you mail to prisons? If you do, can I pre-order your series so you can mail to my cousin who's an inmate at Trenton Corrections Facility?"

"How about out of State Prisons? My brother is locked up in Florida. Can you mail there?"

"Okay, everyone, calm down. I have a notebook right here for everyone to jot down their info for updates on the books that were sold out today and for any questions you may have. Please come on over to this table and Thank you for supporting Authoress Kina. And yes, we do mail out to prisons. Any books of Authoress Kina that are carried here in Source of Knowledge Book Store, automatically gets mailed out to prisons randomly every few months, so please come on over to this line so I can get everyone's info."

"Yes, thank you everyone for coming and any book you did

not get to purchase today, can be purchased on my website. Diane will take all of your info and provide everything you need. Thank you so much for coming and supporting me today."

I smiled in return as each individual smiled at me and moved along from in front of the rectangle shaped table where I was seated for the last three hours. They followed instructions and met Diane, the owner of the modern size, black owned establishment at a much smaller, square shaped table several feet away from where Malika and I were posted. Diane and I made a brief eye contact in that moment and I smiled at her as well. She returned the same gesture, before tending to the customers.

"That was bomb. Proud of you, sis."

I refocused my attention towards Malika and my smile broadened. She was right. My first one on one book signing was in fact "Bomb" as she in true Malika fashion worded it. In other words, it was a huge success. My heart smiled, matching the one adorned on my face. I felt proud and truly accomplished. As a five - year published Author, I've attended a few book signing events with other Authors featured, however, today was the first one, featuring me and me only. Readers came out to see and support only me and despite the fact I was a huge ball of nervousness earlier, the event turned out to be more successful than I anticipated. It turned out so well, I sold out every last book I had with me. Everyone last one- hundred and fifty copies of my eleven published books to be exact.

That was like WOW to me. These folks came out just to see me and spent their hard - earned money on me. That notion alone, left me in awe. Some say, as in mostly Malika constantly criticized that I was too humble and failed to realize the depth of my writing talent and today were one of those days. I could not believe the love I received today and sold out in three hours. I was amazed and perhaps I should not be, but I could not help it. I was a humble person by nature. Tooting my own horn never came natural for me, which was why Malika was a necessity in my life. She was a boaster and natural born horn tooter, and, no one did it quite like her.

"And that's what the hell I'm talking about! You sold this bitch out!"

"Oh My God."

I laughed at Malika's sudden outburst and even more at the side-eyes she received from a few nearby folks. And the more I laughed, I shook my head in addition. Malika had no shame in her game. She could care less about decorum or what anyone thought of her. That character trait was both a positive and negative attribute.

Caring what folks thought of you was wasted energy for the simple fact, people will find something wrong no matter what you do, so satisfying yourself is the best life decision. However, on the other hand, Malika's out-spoken, bold and say whatever you want attitude did not always have positive effects on her life. To put it in more simple term, her "Ghetto" ways, were frowned upon in Corporate America.

And to put it in even more simple terms, she could not to find a job after graduating college to save her life. Malika's personality bore a sight resemblance to Angela from Tyler Perry's hit film: Why Did I Get Married? And just like Angela, when she was unable to find a job in the corporate world, she took a different route and started her own business. Similar to Angela's character, she was a wiz in Chemistry and indulged in mixing different products throughout our college years, and after graduating college, she started her own massage oils and candle business, which became a bona fide hit. Surprisingly, she made a killing in the hood, where she currently owns three successful stores as well as an online one. At thirty-five years old she was almost a multi-millionaire and I was damn proud of her. I loved everything she represented, including all of her ghetto ness. We balanced each other out and supported each other one-hundred - percent in all of our endeavors and that was the best foundation of our friendship.

"Oh my god, what? Girl fuck these people. I'm proud of my best friend and I'll scream that shit all in here if I want to," she expressed, and I groaned through my laughter.

"Oh God, please don't. I will pay you not to," I insisted.

"As a matter of fact, you need to let me pay you for helping me out today," I said to her as I reached into my Louis Vuitton tote bag for my matching wallet.

"If you pull out that wallet, I swear I'm fighting your ass for real," she threatened me in an amused tone, despite the fact I knew she was serious as all hell. I laughed again and decided not to test her since I knew she would show her ass for sure. I shook my head and closed my tote bag as I secured the straps onto my shoulder.

"Okay, fine, but at least let me treat you to dinner," I suggested and once again, she replied in true Malika fashion.

"Now food, I'll accept from your ass."

I laughed out loud again.

"Okay then, let me go talk some things over with Diane and then we can pack up and go eat. What are you in the mood for?"

At first, I failed to notice she was suddenly distracted, tapping away on her I-Phone.

"Uhhm hellooooo."

I waved my hand dramatically in front of her face until I regained her attention.

"Oh, my bad, Shawn was texting me and oh, we have to go eat another night. I forgot that me and him have dick night tonight," she replied, and I shook my head again.

"You mean date night?"

"Uhhh, no bissh, I meant what I said. Dick night. See, my nigga wants a baby and I'm trying to make it happen, but with us trying to open a fourth store, we've been busy like shit and fucking kind a took a back burner, so I came up with scheduled dick nights and tonight is our first one," she explained and I was officially done.

"You know what, I'm sorry I asked." I groaned and stood from where we were seated. I was exhausted and being with Malika added to the exhaustion. But it was hard not to love her. I shook my head at her as I watched as she resumed to typing on her phone.

"You need to have yourself a dick night tonight to celebrate your book signing," she suggested without looking up from her phone. I shook my head once again as I reached into my tote bag and retrieved my own phone.

"Uhhh, no, I'm good."

"Uuuh," she mocked me and gave me the response that only she could.

"Your ass is not good. You're horny as fuck. You ain't ride a dick in like five months, so I know your walls are thirsty and feening for some juice."

"Oh Godddd."

"Ohhh Goddd," she mocked me again and added, "my ass."

"I swear I need drinks to deal with your ass," I teased her

with a smirk. Her mouth was something serious and at times I could not take it.

"Then get your drinks and then get you some dick tonight," she voiced again and once more I let out a groan. I was ready to depart from her ass. I did not want to think about any dick since I'm on a strike and drought. At the moment, I was ready to go home, soak in a nice bubble bath with a chill bottle of Merlot.

"Why don't you let me hook your bougie, wine drinking, romance writing, baby making listening songs ass with one of Shawn's friends," Malika suggested and I couldn't help it as I busted out laughing again. I was officially done with her for sure.

"Okay, I'm done with your ass," I replied through my laughter.

"I'm packing up after I talk with Diane and your ass is dismiss," I said to her as I approach and wrapped my arms around her. She welcomed my embrace, right before she, herself, stood onto her feet. After I thanked her for all of her support, I broke our embrace and kissed her cheek.

"Go on and make me a niece and nephew and tell Shawn I said hi."

"I will. I'm about to ride the hell out of his dick. He wants a baby, well a baby I'm giving his ass since I stopped taking my pills."

"Oh Godddd," I groaned again. "Must you?"

"Yes, I must. And you can be enjoying some good dick too and this time I want you to find the right one. That dog baby daddy of yours and that fool Lamont were the wrong ones. I'm trying to get you one through Shawn's friends but you playing with it.

I shook my head in disagreement. I was not in the mood to

discuss the wrong men I've chosen, nor men period.

"Uhhm, I'm done with this conversation. You go home to your husband while I go home to a quiet house since the boys are still with their dad. I'm going to enjoy a nice bubble bath; wine and I think I will do some writing. And oh, I think I'll open and read my fan mails tonight," I let her know with a snap of my fingers as if I had an epiphany. I finally remembered the letters I retrieved from my P.O. Box and tonight was the perfect night for me to indulge in them.

Malika frowned her face in mock disgust, but I opted on ignoring her.

"So, I can't hook you up with one of Shawn's friends?"

She was persistent with it, but the answer was still the same. Her husband Shawn Patson was a good man and perfect for Malika. He was just as hood as she was and together, they resembled a hood Bonnie & Clyde. He was a former street hustler, but he also was as intelligent as Malika with a college background despite the fact he failed to graduate.

He attended the same school as us but dropped out in our Junior year to dominate the drug game, until he caught a drug charge along with other charges and was sentence to ten years in prison. Malika stood by his side and when he came home, he asked for her hand in marriage, partnered in on her businesses and became a hood power couple. He was rough around the edges, but he treated my bestie like a queen and that's all that mattered to me. His friends were just as hood as he was and Malika swore, they were good catches, but I just did not do thugga muffins.

"Uuuh, no, I'm good. I like White collar men," I reminded her, and she sucked her teeth and rolled her eyes like she always did at my admission to my preference in men.

"Yeah and all the white - collar ones were wrong for your ass," she called out to me as I walked away. The conversation was now draining me, and I was ready to end it and prepare to head home. Book signings were exhausting all on their own and I was feeling it something serious. I was ready to go home, relax and planned on doing just that.

"Bye Bestie! Enjoy your night! Call me tomorrow!" I shouted back towards Malika as I headed over towards Diane table.

"Yeah, yeah, yeah, I'm not done with your ass!" Malika shouted back and I laughed as I opted on ignoring her.

After squaring things away with Diane, I collected my book signing items and headed to my car. Malika left an hour prior, once Shawn picked her up since she rode to the book - store with me. I embraced the peace as I was then alone. I placed my items in the trunk of my SUV and shut the door closed. Seconds later, I climbed into the driver's side. Just as I placed the key in the ignition, I felt the vibration of my cell phone. Reaching into my tote bag, seated on the passenger's side, I retrieved the vibrating phone. Viewing the screen, my eyes scanned a familiar phone number. My heart suddenly skipped beats and the familiar number was the cause of it and I instantly cursed myself. This particular number did not deserve a second glance from me nor attention, but against my better judgement, I answered the call anyway.

"What's up Ms. Author?"

I instantly exhaled at the sound of the familiar male voice and in that same moment, I started to feel joy at the fact he finally unblocked my number and called me after five months.

"Uuuugh!" I squealed which was the opposite of what I was feeling and pressed the end button on the phone, ending the call. He did not deserve to know that I was happy he finally called me.

"Uuuugh!" I let out once more. I heard the phone ring again, but I was determined to ignore the call that time. Instead of answering, I reached into my purse and placed the phone inside. Strangely, my eyes fell upon a few envelopes and the return address of the top one, which read, California State Prison Solano caught my attention. That was the prison Malika asked me about earlier.

"California?"

I did not know anyone in California, nor have I ever received a letter from a reader from there, especially from that prison or any prison, period. I made a mental note to open that letter before all the other ones once I settled down. For some strange reason I was curious, who could've written me from a prison all the way from California.

"How did an inmate from a prison in California even had my info to write me?"

I wondered out loud as I started my car and headed towards Rahway.

"Oh, Diane did reveal that she and her staff randomly mailed out books of authors they carry in the bookstore to various prisons," I answered my own question after silently thinking. I did have my mailing info for readers to write me, so that also explained how an inmate could write.

"Quincy?" That was the name I remembered reading on the envelope.

Interesting. I have never had an inmate write me before.

Hmmmm.

CHAPTER 7
SAKINA

"Nights like this, I wished rain - drops would fall."

One of my favorite movies of all time; The Five Heart Beats, was currently playing on VH1 network once I re - entered my modern size bedroom.

An hour and a half ago, I wasted no time filling my marble tile bathtub with lukewarm water and added Shea butter bubble bath from Bath & Body Works after I switched on my flat screen. The movie was playing but I paid it no mind. For some strange reason, I always felt the need to have the television on despite the fact I had no interest in watching anything in particular.

Seconds after, I stripped down to my birthday suit and before I climbed into the tub, I made sure I retrieved a chilled bottle of white Zinfandel wine with one of my Crystal cut glass from my mediocre size kitchen and poured myself a tall glass. Tonight, I was in the mood for a sweeter tasting wine and white Zinfandel was my favorite. I gulped it down with the quickness before I traveled back to my bedroom and placed both bottle and glass onto my Oakwood tone dresser. I headed to my all white interior bathroom and slipped into the warm, bubbled water.

Shit.

It felt like heaven as I soaked and relaxed. I closed my eyes and welcomed the much - needed peace and for once I appreciated it, since for some unexplainable reason, I felt good. My "Issues" did not surface as they normally did when I'm all alone. No, tonight I felt exactly like the image I portrayed to the outside world. I smiled and remained in the same position for what seem like an eternity before I finally let the water out, grabbed a towel and dried my body before I retired to my bedroom.

I smiled as I refocused attention onto my Television screen. All five men from the movie were sexy and the current ballad playing was one of my favorites. I stood in place momentarily and enjoyed the scene until it ended. My interest in the movie ended as well. I found the performances more indulging than the actual scenes from that particular movie. I mean, the performances were outstanding, and I was a sucker for love songs. I was a hopeless romantic but had the worst luck in love, relationships and romance. I sighed as I shook my head at myself.

Turning towards my dresser, I wrapped my hand around the still chill bottle of wine and poured another full glass. I sipped, sipped and sipped. The coolness, mixed with the sweet taste felt so good, I just had to have another.

Repeating the gesture, I poured another. I sipped, first slowly, then I finished off the glass..

Yes, that time it felt better than good.

Once again, I repeated the gesture and on my fourth glass, I decided to slow it down.

I suddenly caught a glimpse of my reflection in the mirror. I turned forward as I placed the empty wine glass on the dresser. I felt so mello, I could've care less I wasn't using a coaster. In almost slow motion, I unwrapped the gray, terry cloth towel from around my body and held it in my hand.

Eyeing my naked frame in the mirror, my eyes lingered, almost in admiration. My body wasn't model or video material, but I personally felt I was a special kind of sexy. I was not slim, nor was I thick. I was more of what some referred to as slim - thick. Suddenly I felt confident, self-assured and strong. Normally I did not experience such feelings about myself when I was alone, but after the love I received today, it placed me in a mood I failed to experience too often. Besides my two loving sons and Malika, I did not receive love too often.

At least from my perception that is how it appeared in my eyes. Once my beloved mother passed away five years prior, and once again with the exception of my sons and Malika, there really was no loving me. At least, not the way I wanted to be loved. The way I needed to be loved. I had limited family members who cared enough to check on me and the biological sister who I was raised and shared DNA with hated the ground I walked on.

And at times, I indeed hated myself.

Self-love…. Self-esteem …. I needed motivation. The love from my two sons, Earle Jr. and Kyle and once again, the love I received today from folks I didn't even know was part of my motivation. The support I received from Malika was another part. And strangely, the letter I received from readers were one of the hugest parts of motivation for me. Strangers from other states and even from around the globe brought on a feeling of self-confidence that I've come to depend on. Really, depended on it as if my life was on the line.

Yes, my inadequacies... They were complex beyond comprehension. I was a complicated person, period. A complicated woman...

But I hid it well...Love from strangers I felt came easily for the simple fact...They had no realization of the real Sakina. With the exception of Malika and the Almighty up above himself, no one knew the real me. And the real me, I felt was not quite likable or loveable. And with the opposite sex, I hid them best.

But yet, they seem to still treat me like shit. At least from my perception. But then again.... maybe it was just that. Like shit.

In that moment, I heard my phone vibrating in my purse. Turning away from the mirror and in all my naked glory, I walked over to my nightstand where my purse was resting and reached into it. As I grabbed my phone, my eyes landed on the stack of mail. One particular envelope was the first to catch my attention.

Quincy Norton

"Who in the hell is that?"

Curiosity gained the best of me as I scooped up the envelope along with my phone and took a seat on my bed. Still naked as can be, I leaned again my bed's headboard and made myself comfortable.

In that exact moment, my phone vibrated again. Viewing the screen, the same number from earlier flashed across the screen.

My headache of three years.

I exhaled which was much needed. I felt exactly like the women from the movie Waiting to Exhale.

All four of the characters were looking for love in all the wrong places and indeed they found it. Ironically, that was the story of my life.

Sighing again, I mustered the courage to end the call as I did earlier. Although, this time, I was much weaker. The bottle of wine I consumed was working it's magic and betraying my strong will in the process. I was horny as hell to begin with after five months without sex, but the wine made my situation twenty times worse.

I've done good, avoiding him physically for the past five months, but tonight was the night of all nights that I might fail tremendously. The incoming call ended but seconds later, it resumed. In that same moment, I felt my pussy lips twitching as if he was calling out to it from the other end of the phone line.

And again, the phone vibrated. And of course, again, my pussy lips twitched.

"Uuugh!"

I let out and silently begged God for strength.

The call stopped once again, and I let out a sigh of relief. I shook my head. Yes, I missed the hell out of him, but he was no good for me. He was like carbs and sweets. Just all kind of wrongs for you but just can't help and feast on it any damn way.

"I need a distraction to be able to ignore his calls."

Admitting that out loud was like a cry for help and someone up above was listening because my eyes landed on the envelope I held in my other hand. Curiosity gained the best of me again as I placed my phone aside onto my bed and proceeded to opening the long white envelope.

I bit my bottom lip in anticipation as I went on to read what appeared to be a brief letter from Quincy Norton.

Hmmm. Who was he? An inmate writing me. That's a first. He better not be a killer or a rapist, shit, or both.

CHAPTER 8
QUINCY

"Building six prepare for yard release! Yard release in ten minutes!" Officer Johnson called out over the loudspeaker.

I had on my charcoal grey sweat suit with my all white Nikes. My head was glistening from my fresh shave twenty minutes before and I was smelling like Issey Miyake Muslim oil. I was so fresh and so clean to go nowhere, except to the yard.

When you look at it, it was kind of funny because a good percentage of the population will try their best to look and smell top-notch. Even though we don't have anywhere to go and no ladies to impress. Yet a playa was gonna be a playa no matter where he was at. Just like a boss was gonna be a boss. Period.

Until you've seen brotha's in prison, you never quite seen ingeniousness. All we were given to wear, was our state-issued prison blues (elastic blue parachute pants and a blue V-neck shirt) and we can purchase white, light grey or charcoal grey sweats. That's it! Yet, looking at how cats don't rock their outfits differently and the cats that altered and mended their shit, a person would think that we had a catalog of different clothing to choose from.

"I repeat, yard release in five minutes. Building six, yard release in five minutes." The crackling noise in the intercom made C.O. Johnson sound like the wicked witch in one of them movies.

I went to the back side of my cell and felt along the wall under my shelf. When I felt what I was reaching for, I lifted slightly and pulled. A homemade shelf inside of the wall slid out and I picked up my two knives off the shelf. I slid them into the knife sleeves that I had sewed into my clothes.

Next, I put my shelf back into the wall where it blended perfectly like it wasn't there. It was an old-school trick that I learned from my old cellmate who, he, himself, was an O.G. First, I had to buy a thick screw so I could chisel out the cement wall. That shit took two days and gave me blisters for weeks. When I'd gotten too deep inside the wall to reach with the screw, I said 'fuck-it' and paid the homie on the paint crew to steal a chisel for a day and let me use it.

Once everything was chiseled nice and good, I built my shelf out of the cardboard from a case the top Ramen noodles came in. The final move was to pay the lil homie to come paint my entire cell. Someone could be looking right in the direction of the hide-away shelf and never see it.

"Building six! Yard release! Yard release at this time!" Those were the words we all were waiting on.

I waited patiently for my cell door to open. When them doors cracked open, that ass had better be ready. You didn't want to get caught with your door open and not be ready. Plenty of dudes have died that way, from other cats running up in their cells on them and stabbing their ass.

I finally made my way to where the Bay Area hung out. These were my folks, my people, my comrades, my brothers. This was the Bay Carr, it consisted of cats from every section of the Bay Area. On one prison yard, you had many Carr's, gangs, clicks or groups. Whatever term you wanted to use to classify us. In California's prison system we called clicks Carr's.

"The moon gonna be blue tonight cause 'Q' is on the yard." That was Coleman. He's a dark-skinned, mild mannered, brotha from Pittsburgh, California. He got double-life for murdering three mothafucka's that raped his eleven-year-old daughter.

"If it is blue it's because you put magic on it like you do those pinochle cards." Everyone around started laughing. Coleman by for was one of the best pinochle players on the yard.

"Naaw, Coleman just aint that observant. Everybody knows that the only time brah comes to the yard is on his days off or on holidays. Today is Q's day off." I looked at Murder B who'd just spoke and smiled. Murder B was from East Oakland. The Murder Dubbs to be exact. That's where he got the name Murder B from. Though he could play pinochle, his past time was poker.

"B, let me find out you plotting on me. Shit, you got a nigga whole schedule down," I joked.

"Naaw big homie, I just pay attention to my surroundings and stay on my security tip," Murda B called out as he counted out his poker chips, getting ready for his game.

"Take uncle BJ for instance..."

"What's up unc?" He called out to BJ, who'd just walked up. I don't know how Murda B saw him with his head down counting chips.

"Now unc is gonna be on the yard all day, every day, from the moment we come out until the moment we go in. The only time he's not going to be out here is if it's raining, unless there's tension in the air, then he's gonna be out here in his raincoat with that big ass sword that he got.

"That's right nephew. They already got me locked away in this prison for life, why would I go and further incarcerate myself by locking myself into that cage voluntarily. No-siree-Bob! That's not my job. Far as that rain, that cold weather hurts these old bones. So, if I have to come out, somebody is for sure going to pay for it." BJ spoke matter-of-factly.

All of us laughed because of the way he said it. Yet we all knew that he was dead serious about everything he just said. I turned towards BJ and gave him a one arm gangsta hug.

For the next five minutes or so we all took turns talking shit and cracking jokes. We were waiting for all of the buildings to finish releasing for yard.

Once everyone was let out, we had a brief meeting. This was when we put each other up on everything that was going on in the yard. It's really the most important part of the day. The only reason I can get away with missing a meeting is when I don't come to the yard because I am at work. Then I would have my lil homie J give me the rundown, if it appears the Crips had a little internal conflict going on between the Northern Crips or NC's and the Harlem Crips. The shit didn't involve us, but it was good info.

A cat would hate to get caught up in their area if anything kicked off. That's a quick way to get wrapped up and sent to the hole on a beef that was not even yours. When the meeting was over, I walked a couple of laps with BJ as I always do, whenever I was on the yard. While we were walking, I saw my little homie, Chuck walking out of his building. I needed to talk to the lil Homie, but I thought about it and decided I would stick to the script and have J holler at him instead. After all, our security measures were put in place for a reason, I wasn't about to jeopardize that.

I killed a couple of hours chilling with a few of the fellas and watching one of the pokers and chess games. I couldn't help but to think about how boring prison really was. Don't get me wrong, niggas find shit to do, but for the most part you woke up, went to breakfast, went to the yard, came back to your cell, and waited for count. After count, you went to dinner, night yard and that was it. Do it all over again the next day. The only differences were if you had a job or if you took a class or something. Lately I've been giving some thought to signing up for a class or two when the new semester started.

"What's up Q?" Ju-Ju came and stood next to me while I was watching the chess game.

"What's up Ju-Ju? what your lil hustling ass up to? You stay with something on the fire, so I know you got something cooking. Talk to me.". Ju-Ju was a little hustling mothafucka. Whatever you were looking for, he either had it or he could get it for you.

"You know me. I got that fire water, that's why I came over to holla at you. I know how much you like to fuck with the Jesus Juice." Ju-Juu was a little animated mothafucka, funny as hell, but it was really hard to be incognito when dealing with him.

"Oh yeah? How much you got?" He nodded his head at the laundry bag that was in his hand and said, "I got two full water bottles left."

"And what you talking?"

"For you big brah, give me twenty dollars."

"Are you sure? Cause you know I respect the hustle."

"Yeah I'm sure big brah. I also know if I was ever in need or if I ever took a loss, all I got to do is ask and you got me. So right now, I got you."

"You know it lil brah, real niggas do real shit. Hands down, straight with no chase. I tell you what, just leave your laundry bag right there on the ground. I'll give it back to you along with your money tonight at yard.

"Alight big brah, bet!" Ju-Ju didn't say anything else, but spinned around and rushed off. No doubt rushing to his next hustle.

Inside of the laundry bag were two water bottles filled with White Lightening. White Lightening was the penitentiary's version of moonshine. It was pure alcohol. The cooks would first make pruno which was wine. Once it's done, they boil all the alcohol out of the pruno, catching the evaporated alcohol in a bag. It's so strong, so pure that you can pour a drip on the table and set it aflame.

When the next building unlock occurred, I grabbed the laundry bag and beaded back to my cell. The first thing I did after washing my hands was take my cell phone out of its hiding spot and sent my lil homie J a text message. It was simply an emoji of a happy face.

This was my way of letting him know everything was all good with the shipment that came in last night.

I was about to put my phone back up, since I had set times that I used it, but since I already had it out, I went online and double checked the arrival date of the three books I ordered earlier. I had received notification from Amazon that the items had shipped, and I couldn't help it. I found myself smiling and shit.

I don't know what it was about lil mama, but something got

me really wanting to get to know her. I know I was doubting myself earlier, doubting why she would even want to hear from a brotha in prison, doubting that she would even read my letter, but I now had to put myself in check. Second guessing myself was not even my style.

So, now I was back to my original mindset. I was loving this woman's pen game and after viewing her picture and bio, I was curious about her. So, after surfing Amazon.com, I learned that she has written a total of ten other books. Three of the books were follow up and sequels to her book, '**Conscious Over Heart**,' so I ordered the part two to start with along with two other titles, using my Pay pal account. I made sure to choose next day delivery since I was eager as hell to read the next set of lil mama's books.

And now here I was smiling again, because according to Amazon's tracking info, the books were scheduled to arrive first thing tomorrow morning. I prayed that I would receive them on the same day at count time.

I put the phone back in my tuck-spot and turned on the TV. I turned the volume all the way down and turned on the radio. Next, I cracked one of the water bottles and got my sip on. Ju-Ju was right, it was some fire. I had no intention on getting drunk, it just crept up on me. Well I should not say drunk, but I'm in the building and I'm feeling myself, which was only one step away from being drunk.

My man Red came by with some raw chicken that he stole out of the kitchen, which was perfect timing because I wasn't going to the Chow Hall in this condition. I don't ever go outside intoxicated unless I have to.

By the time count came, I washed my face with cold water and brushed my teeth. I pulled my phone out again and called the little homie Chester and told him that I needed him to drop this money and laundry bag off to Juju tonight. I made sure to let him know that I had a plate of food for his big ass when he got back in.

With that taken care of, I went to work, Chef-Boy-R-Dee style! I pulled out my hot pot and threw some lard into it before plugging it in. While that was warming up, I grabbed my seasoning, flour and got busy on the chicken after I washed it off.

An hour later I sat down to a plate of fried chicken with a side of white rice, all smothered in gravy with onions. I washed it down with a tumbler of Kool-Aide laced with more White Lightening.

At yard release, Chester stopped by the cell and picked up his plate and the laundry bag for Juju.

"Q, I swear to God, Rogue, eating the shit you be cooking be making a mothafucka forget that he was locked up," he said to me, when the cell door opened, and he smelled the food. The term Rogue is reference to buddy or a friend.

Chester was Nicaraguan and Black. He was "6 ft.4 in." tall and nearly 280 lbs. He could eat like four brotha's his size.

"It's all good Ridah! Just make sure Ju-Ju gets his shit."

"I got you Rogue," Chester shouted out before he went on about his way.

Finally taking some time to lay back, I decided to go on to Amazon and read the sneak peeks of the two books I ordered. First, I clicked on **For Your Eyes Only**. I could not wait for the full book so I could get my read on and have more of a glimpse into Sakina's mind. I wanted to get to know more about her and how she thinks. Soon as I am done with the sneak peek for this book, I will click on the sneak peek of **Just for The Touch of You**.

Her titles alone piqued my interest more for her than they already were.

Damn.

For a woman to have me drawn to her just from her words alone had to be some kind of woman. At least that's what my fantasy of her consist of.

I'm wondering more and more, what she was really like.

CHAPTER 9
SAKINA

Like wow. After five minutes of reading his letter, I must say I was blown away. That has to be one of the most - sweetest and sincere gestures I have ever experienced from a man. His letter actually made me feel good and there it goes again. Me needing motivation to feel good about myself. And his letter did just that. I felt better than good. He had me feeling like a superstar of some sort. And I must say I was quite flattered that he not only took the time to read my book but took even more time to reach out and write to me.

Why did he? No other inmate has written to me since my five - year career as a Published author. I've had plenty reach out to me on Facebook but to actually write to me was definitely a first.

And the letter itself. His boldness to even write to me.
His words.
His delivery.
The articulation of his words.
I wondered if he was a writer.

The thought crossed my mind as I decided to read the letter once again.

Hmmm.

I must say I was quite impressed with Mr. Quincy. I detected a trait of charm just from his words.

A charming thug.

Wait, was he a thug?

I guess it was wrong to assume he was one based on the fact he was incarcerated.

Speaking of being incarcerated, I wonder what his story was.

Curiosity suddenly took over me as I reached for my cellphone. I clicked on my web engine and typed: California's Public Records. I was fully aware that all inmate's records in the county jails and prison systems were available to the public.

Biting my bottom lip, I suddenly felt anxious as I typed in the name Quincy Norton on California's website page. Seconds later, his arrest record appeared. I then felt my heart - beat increased once I viewed the words arrested for murder and conviction: Life.

Murder? Life?

And just like that, the giddiness I felt moments earlier, disappeared. Mr. Quincy Norton no longer appealed to me and the good feeling I felt from his letter no longer existed.

As a matter of fact, I'm great on pretending that his letter never existed.

I do not like judging folks, but the last thing I needed in my life was interaction with a convicted murderer. And yes, I have a long history of dealing with the wrong men, but at least they were upstanding citizens with clean records. They were just crappy boyfriends and all wrong for me.

And the worse of all for me was a convict who took a human life and was posted behind bars for the rest of his life.

Oh no, I was okay with my wrong men who held careers and were free from the prison system. Speaking of such, my current headache was once again calling as I noticed his number flashed across my screen. Deciding to finally answer his call, I pressed the talk button, forcing the web session on the public record's page to close.

In that same moment, I crumbled up Quincy Norton's letter and had every intention on tossing it in the garbage.

"What's up Ms. Author? So, you finally decided to answer my call?"

I sighed at his voice. My headache of three years. I felt bittersweet feelings. I was happy to hear from him, but I also knew letting him back into my life was temporary happiness.

Hurting each other. That's what we did best. Well, the second thing we did best…

Yes, he was all wrong for me, but he was an established man with a fifteen-year career as a New Jersey Police Officer. He also owned his own home, possessed an impressive bank account, as well as a prestigious reputation.

He was presentable on paper and in public. I also looked good on his arms and vice-versa. He was just about every woman's dream and to top it off, he was a beast in the bedroom.

Yes, he was the right kind of wrong.

Right?

Still crumbling up Quincy Norton's letter, I answered my headache's question, opening the door, granting him entrance back into my life and eventually in between my legs.

"Uhhm, yes I did."

"That's what's up. So, can I come over and beat those cheeks up or what?"

I cringe at his words as I always did, but like a fool, I was going to let him right back in…. like I always did.

Because, he was the right kind of wrong?

"Sure, come on over," I replied to his question.

"Alright, I'll be right there. Get that pussy wet for me."

And with that, the call ended.

I exhaled as I watched my phone screen turned black. The crumbled letter in my other hand caught my attention and I silently wondered which right kind of wrong could possibly be the healthiest for me or any woman.

CHAPTER 10
SAKINA

An Hour Later:

Sex ain't better than love (oh)
Sex ain't, sex ain't (oh)
Better than love
I been outchea in these streets and I done learned
Every girl I gave my loving to was only a substitute
I been outchea in these streets and I done learned
Even though she's in my arms this ain't where my heart belongs
Sex in the air no lovin' here: Soon as I get through, I'm outta there
And it feels so bad but it feels so good
Wishing I could care girl I never could
But then I fell into your love

**Didn't let me touch the ground: Now I see it clear that your heart is there
And all these other women they just can't compare
Girl I know**

Trey Songz "Sex Ain't Better Than Love" was currently playing on the On-Demand music station and he sung the lyrics with his sultry, panty dropping voice like only he could.

He was trying to convince whomever that sex was not better than love and I totally disagreed in that moment.

"Shittttt."

I felt as if my eyes were on the verge of rolling to the back of my head as my headache of three years was doing the damn thing with his fire tongue. I was not myself for the time being so if my lingo was slightly different, then blame it on the two more glasses of wine I consumed thirty minutes prior once he arrived at my apartment. He was not much of a drinker, especially wine per say and that was fine, fine, fine.

More for me, was how I felt. As much alcohol as possible was indeed necessary when dealing with him.

"Shittt, shitttt."

Even though, he was the most tolerable when we were not engaged in conversation; in other words, only when we were fucking to put it in simple terms. Despite the fact our "Situation" was complicated, and I indeed loved him, fifty percent of the times I did not quite like him as a person. Yes, he was intelligent, funny and quite estoute. He was a very conscious black man who I have actually learned a lot from. He loved schooling on

African American history and was very informative. He was smart and knew his shit and that side of him I did like. He kept me on my toes. He also was funny. Some days he did make me laugh and brought a smile on my face. My heart often smiled when thoughts of him occurred.

At times he complimented me like only he could. He thought I was pretty, sexy and had the best pussy he ever had, let him tell it. Yes, he fed my ego that required feeding on a consistent basis. Part of me kept him around for those reasons alone and of course the top reason was going down in that very second.

"Aaaah shiiiit. Aaaah Lamont."

Grabbing his head for support, I screamed out his name and climaxed as his tongue tortured my clitoris.

Yes, his head game was one for the books. Honestly, I could not get rid of him no matter how many times I've tried, and I have actually wanted to. No matter how hard I tried to stay away from him, my heart, my body and of course my pussy always betrayed me.

And present moment was prime example. After our call ended an hour ago, I sat in place contemplating cancelling our booty call session. After I agreed for him to come over, part of me regretted it. I knew nothing good would come of letting him back into my life, buttttt......He was like a drug and dammit I was addicted. A bona fide addict.

Lamont Pacer. NJPD extraordinaire.

I did love him, but, unfortunately, as good as he made me feel, character wise and sexually, it was only temporary. It never lasted long. No one affected me quite like he did. And sadly no one hurt me like he did either. The other fifty percent, no I did not always care for him as a person. He has affected me in ways no human should even let another human affect them.

When Lauren Hill sung; **As painful as this thing has been, I just can't be with no one else, I keep letting you back in, how can I explain myself? No one's hurt me more than you and no one ever will.**

I felt that shit.

But, like the foolish woman that I was and yes, a fool in love, shit, maybe a fool in lust, I let him right back in.

Like I said, I resembled an addict……

Smack. Smack.

Two smacks were delivered to the side of my right ass cheek once he raised his head from in between my legs. Positioned onto his knees, he gazed down at me. His eyes were hooded and laced with obvious lust. Yes, after five months of staying clear of one another and after the way he just ate my pussy, even the way he has been begging to come and "beat those cheeks up," I knew he felt what I felt.

We missed the hell out of each other. He was unable to stay away for long either.

Yes, we were the poster board for toxic relationships but in that present moment, my pussy could've cared less.

Licking my lips, I returned his intense gaze. Staring into each other's eyes was a form of foreplay for him. He did it often. I was not sure why, but it was his thing. At times I felt as if he was trying to tell me something through his eyes since expressing himself verbally was a challenge. But of course, no expression ever came. We have engaged in all kind of conversations within the past three years, but he never could express his true feelings for me.

So, instead, I drew my own conclusions. I assumed he didn't care for me much besides the bedroom and aside from our friendship. I could be wrong but with him I just could never be sure.

Suddenly, he reached over, and placed his right hand onto my right breast. Our eyes stayed locked as he squeezed it.

"Sssss," I hissed. He then started twirling my nipple with his thumb and index finger and I lost it. My breasts were the most sensitive part of my body and no one knew that better than him.

"Ssss, aaah, Lamont," I hissed, groaned and could not take it anymore.

I felt warm fluid in between my legs oozing out as if a volcano erupted. I arched my back as he repeated the same gesture onto my left breast.

"Aaaa, fuckkk. Aaah shittt, Lamonttttt," I screamed out in sheer ecstasy. He twirled, pinched and squeezed both nipples until I begged for mercy.

"Aaaaah, pleaseeee baby stop."

And as soon as I pleaded those words, he entered me.

Damn.

I exhaled as his dick maneuvered through my wetness.

Shit.

After five months with no sex, his penetration through my tight walls almost felt similar to the night I lost my virginity all those years ago. At thirty-five years of age, the night I became a woman felt like ancient years prior. I've had a few lovers since then, but all long - term relationships. My two sons' father was the longest at ten years and for the last three years, I've entered this "Situation" with Lamont. Besides these last five months, I have never gone long without the dick, so I didn't know my walls could tightened up the way it has. But here we were, and Lamont was stretching me open as if it was my very first time.

And in the midst of it, he appeared to appreciate the tightness and after a few seconds as well as strokes, it was evident.

"Goddamn Kina. Pussy tight as hell, you kept it tight for daddy huh? Ohh shittt, Kina. I miss the fuck out this pussy."

Oh yes, he talked his shit and the more he did, his pace increased, and his strokes deepened. He was in beast mode and I felt what was sure to be my first of many orgasms for the night surfacing.

Damn.

I attempted to close my eyes in that moment, but he was not having it.

A sudden deep stroke halted such movement and his eyes were still deeply pierced into mine as his stroke pace increased.

"Keep those eyes open as I punish this pussy," he demanded as he thrusted into my throbbing center. I was soaked and wet in that moment and that only enhanced his performance. He was on a natural high as beads of sweats formed onto his forehead and just when I didn't think it was possible…

He stroked me deeper…..

He fucked me harder……

And as he twirled my nipples one last time, I arched my back once again, opened my legs wider, giving him better access and threw the pussy back at him.

For a few seconds we thrusted simultaneously, before I could no longer restrain my orgasmic peak.

"Aaaah, gooddddddddd!"

"Shittttt," he groaned as well as he matched my timing and reached his peak along with mine.

"Shitt, Kina, I hope you're not fertile, baby," he added as he climaxed. I felt our juices intertwine as his strokes slowed down.

He reached down and kissed my lips, however, as my high decreased, my body tensed.

And there it was.

Hurting each other.

The second thing we did best after we were done with our first.

Of course, he did majority of the hurting, and his words after sex always crushed my soul.

After he pulled his still semi erection from inside of me, I felt like shit. And no one achieved that better than him.

"Je suis plus fort que la plupart, Je suis plus fort que la plupart."

"Oh, here comes the Creole."

I sighed, ignoring Lamont's sarcastic comment as I stood up from the bed and headed towards my bedroom door. Grabbing my thigh-length, purple, satin, robe, which hung from a hook on my bedroom door, I quickly exited the room. I once again recited the little French chant I always did when I struggled to prevent an emotional break down and show the side of me, I care for no one to see. The side my mom always taught me not to let the world see. Especially men.

"When folks know your weakness, they either use it against you or use it to control you."

My mom would always remind me and that was one of the realest lessons she ever taught me. Till this day I lived by that motto.

No one saw nor knew of my weak and fragile side as well as my secret struggle with depression, except for Malika, my sister, and my mother of course.

My late mother...

Evelyn Michelle... She was a strong, proud, Haitian woman. She was also my rock and the epitome of what a real woman should be. I learned strength and how to be a strong woman from her. Growing up, I can honestly say that I have never seen her cry once. Not one single tear. Not when my father married another woman on her and moved back to their birth country of Cabaret, Haiti, leaving us broke and struggling and certainly not when my younger sister, Shamille turned to a life of crime, catching a fifteen year burglary charge. No, not once did I ever witness my mom breakdown or lose control.

Now, I was unaware what she endured emotionally behind closed doors, but to me and the outside world, she represented the word strong with a capital "S." She believed in shielding her children from any form of worry and pain, so the fact that Shamille and I were hurting from our father's abandonment, my mom opted on remaining strong. During that time, I was only twelve and Shamille was ten, but we knew she was hurting. We also assumed she was holding up simply on the strength of us, but I later discovered she did so for a whole other reason.

"I rather die right this very second than to give you the satisfaction of crying over you."

I secretly overheard her say to one of my father's picture one day. And at the age twelve, I clearly understood and from that day forward, the respect I held for my mom was on a whole other level. And I strived to be that same kind of woman.

And from the moment my father left, she strived on teaching my sister and I strength, poise, how to keep it classy and never give a man any of your energy. She also taught us the importance of showing your strength to the outside world at all times.

"Never show your vulnerable side. Folks will use it to their advantage."

She would continuously say, and I believed her. I held dear to heart everything she ever taught me and I carried her teachings throughout my life and when I lost her to breast cancer five years ago, I promised her I would be the same kind of mother to my two sons that she was to me and my sister.

And I kept that promise. I knew she was smiling down at the woman I strived to be. Making her proud, even after death, was important to me since she died of a partial broken heart from my sister's disappointment.

Shamille became the total opposite of what we were raised to be, and my mother did not handle it well. She was so disappointed, she disowned my sister and out of anger, Shamille rejected any further love or support I offered her during her case and once she was sentence to fifteen years.

Sadly, I have not spoken to my sister in six years and such reality added to my cause of depression. But, of course, I hid my pain well. With the exception of Malika, no one knows of the multiple cause of hurt that I endured.

My sister's wrong decisions with men, which ruined her life, my mother's death and finally, my unhealthy, toxic relationships caused me to self-destruct, but in different ways from Shamille.

And unlike my sister, I hid my weaknesses, my imperfections and my toxic ways from the world quite well.

And of course, from the men in my life. No matter how much their actions and mistreatments of me crushed my soul, they will never know.

And I put that on my mom.

"Je suis plus fort que la plupart, Je suis plus fort que la plupart."

Reciting the prayer once more, I reached a doorway in the back corridors of my apartment. Pushing the door open to my home office, I entered and swiftly shut the door closed and secured the locks.

By then, the robe was fully draped on my body. Tying the belt to shield my naked form, I made my way to a small, Cherry wood tone office desk with a black, leather medium size chair. I sat down on the leather interior, and reached over to the desk and pulled open the top draw.

Letting out a sigh, I retrieved a small box along with a small bottle of Poland Spring water. Licking my lips, I leaned over and lifted the lid of the already opened box which read Argo Corn Starch.

I shook my head at myself and once again let out a sigh as I untwisted the cap to the bottle of water and poured some into the box. My eyes lit up like a kid in a candy store as I watched the Corn Starch form into a bulky knot.

Using my hand, I reached into the box and grabbed the bulk of starch and brought it to my lips. Licking it first, I placed it in my mouth, and I swore it felt like heaven. The feeling of the chunky, powdery, edible in my mouth was indescribable. This must be what crack heads felt like every time they indulged in a hit.

Except, Corn Starch won't ruin my life. Only one's body, since it was known to cause excessive weight gain, but I've managed to prevent such thing from taking place in the last ten years.

Yes, I have this nasty habit of eating Corn Starch and I do so as if I was a drug addict. Such bad habit developed thirteen years prior when I was pregnant with my eldest son and developed anemia and grew worse eleven years ago with the pregnancy of my second son. I have tried to quit, since my doctor encouraged it many times, but it was a habit I just could not seem to break.

Strangely, it relaxed me and besides the French prayer, it was necessary to prevent a break down. Remaining poise and unbothered to folks were a must. I could not disappointment my mom's memory.

And I won't. A strong and in control woman I must portray at all times. But for the time being, I needed some assistance.

And besides the French prayer, my bottle of wines and of course Corn Starch, were the help I needed.

Right when I took another chunk from the box and placed it in my mouth, a knock was heard on the office door.

"Kina, baby, come back to bed. I didn't mean shit by what I said."

I sighed and closed my eyes. I chewed on the ball of Starch and savored the taste. Right after I swallowed, I felt better than ever.

"Kina, what the hell did I say that was so wrong?"

I exhaled as my eyes remained shut.

"Come on baby, let me hit that tight ass pussy again. That shit felt good as hell."

And once again I exhaled.

After a few moments of silence, I was hoping he caught my drift and got the point.

"You want me to leave?"

I smiled in that moment.

And he did get the point, thank God. One thing about him, he knew when to give me my space. Or perhaps that was easy to do when you were not in love with a woman. At least I assumed he was not. I mean, how could he be? No man in love behaved the way he did or say the things he said.

"Yes," I called out loud enough for him to hear.

"Okay, but when you calm down, I think it's time we talk. Like have a serious talk. I'll call you later."

And with those words expressed, I heard his footsteps down the hallway. Shortly after that, I heard his footsteps again and seconds later, I heard the front door to my apartment opened and closed shut.

For a split second, I started to get excited. I thought maybe, he was finally going to say some good shit. Some rightful words. Maybe finally be the man I have always wanted and needed, but then I remembered...

That we have been here before. He has expressed those words before. And same as always, he delivered nothing but disappointment. I refused to set myself up for another one though. I also refused to have him come close to see my less than control side. Five months prior, he did see a glimpse of it when I showed up at his door unannounced and caught him talking with another woman outside of his house. Yes, I showed him a glimpse of my weak side, but never again and that's a given.

Deciding to give my Corn Starch mini feast a break, I secured the box shut and placed it along with the bottle of water inside of my desk. I kept it in there just in case Malika snooped in my kitchen cabinet and discovered my stash. She knew of my fetish, but, despised it and disposed of it anytime she found one. I appreciated her for caring about me, but I just was not ready to quit.

And of course, now that I thought about it, deep inside, I was not ready to leave Lamont alone completely.

And perhaps that was showing weakness after all. I knew he was wrong for me, but my heart wanted him to be right so bad.

After returning to my bedroom, I removed my robe and slid comfortably under my comforter. A movie was currently playing on my flat screen, but I gave it no attention. My mind was on Lamont and our sex session from earlier. It was damn near perfect until he ruined it with his words.

Suddenly, the words he uttered as he reached his peak uttered in my head.

"Shitt, Kina, I hope you're not fertile, baby."

Once again, I felt sadness. After my second son, I desired a third child but was never able to conceive one. My ex Earle was worse than Lamont could ever be and out of all my exes, he was the worse for me. God must have thought so as well, hence the fact I failed conceiving a third child. Earle's cheating and disrespect reached a whole other level that remaining unbothered almost became impossible. After a decade with him, I no longer wanted him but at one point, desired only his sperm since I wanted all three of my children by the same man. But, once again, God knew best, because conception was no longer in the cards for me. At least, that is what I have grown to convince myself.

And with Lamont, I have also convinced myself of that theory so much so, that within our first year of seeing each other, I became comfortable and never practiced safe sex, nor was I on any birth control.

Yes, foolish, I know. In three years, a committed relationship was never established, so having unprotected sex with a man who I cannot even confirm is my man was beyond foolish.

Shaking my head at myself, I exhaled.

What was I doing? At thirty-five years old, I needed to get it together and figure out my love life with a quickness.

Just as I was lost in my thoughts, my cell phone was heard vibrating. I looked over on my nightstand where it was charging. I had a feeling it was Lamont, so I opted on ignoring the call.

As I attempted to turn my head away, something caught my eye.

"The inmate's letter," I said out loud.

Yes, I knew he had a name, but after learning what he was incarcerated for, I just couldn't see past that. I mean I did appreciate his kind words regarding my book and that he took the time to read it, but sorry, I did not care to pen pal with a convicted murderer. I mean I had no idea what the details were surrounding his conviction, but did it matter?

The man killed someone. He took a life. Not to mention he was doing life as a result of his action. Why in the hell would I even converse with someone like that or give him the time of day?

No, there was no need to. The only inmate I would ever give the time of day to was my sister. Besides inmates who followed me on Facebook and have read my books and supported me, this Quincy Norton person can go on about his business.

Giving the crumbled - up letter one more glance, I made a mental note to toss it in the garbage, first thing in the morning. Tearing my eyes away, I closed them, attempting to get some sleep but I knew such task would be impossible. I suffered from insomnia and tonight the struggle was real.

But I was determined to try since I had a busy day tomorrow as well as week and even month. I had three book releases approaching and I was beyond exited. Promoting over - load was on my agenda which could be quite exhausting.

Speaking of such, I decided to temporarily forget the idea of sleep and reached for my phone off the nightstand. Deciding to upload some new promotional flyers with never before seen pictures of myself along with my upcoming releases, I went into promo mode instead of opting to sleep.

Being a Published Author was the most fulfilling position I've ever filled in my life besides becoming a mother and nothing felt more - right than that.

CHAPTER 11
QUINCY

Two Days Later:

I finally put Kina's book down. She was truly a gifted sistah. On top of that, she was fine as fuck!!! I don't know how I let my mind wonder off, but it did. I pulled out my cell phone and pulled up a picture that I found of hers when I googled her name. There was a picture of her in the back of her first book, but it was a simple headshot. The picture that showed up on Google also lead me to her Facebook page where I discovered more pictures. Gotdamn, this sistah was something else. Her cum-fuck me eyes were the perfect complement to the sexiest pair of lips that I have ever laid my eyes on.

It was not long before my mind started playing a movie of her kissing all over my chest while my hands caressed and explored her Heavenly body. The sounds of her moans echoing inside of my mind put me in a severe state of arousal. Naaw let me say that shit how it really was....My dick was rock ass hard! I felt my shaft throbbing inside of my boxers begging to be released.

Inside of my mind her kisses were as soft as butterfly wings fluttering in the spring. I could not resist the urge any longer. I pulled my boxers down and relieved my throbbing erection.

Before I got carried away and forgot where I was, I reached up and pulled my courtesy curtain closed. That way if one of the C.O.'s walked by, they would not be able to see me.

Laying back down, I imagined what it would feel like to have Kina's body on top of mine, feeling the heat of passion coming off her body and infusing itself with mine. Our kisses were reeled with raw, animalistic passion. The kind that Love novels are written about. She sensed my hunger. No longer capable of waiting, I picked her up and glided her gently down on all ten inches of rock - hard steel. It took a moment for her walls to adjust to my size. The entire time, our lips were locked devouring one another.

The moment she began to slowly slide up and down my shaft, my hand moved in complete unison up and down matching her pace. Before long, she and I are carrying out multiple sex scenes like we were the characters in her books. This shit was beyond mind blowing. Our sexing was so intense. The both of us sweat as we panted and grunted, making sounds foreign to man. They were closer to that of wild animals than humans.

Inside of my cell, I could not help it, I was actually moaning and groaning, as I am visioning my strokes speeding up to match Kina's as she was fully taking all of me like a champ. I could see her bouncing up and down on my dick as if I was made specifically just for her.

I placed the phone down by my side. I did not need the photo of her any longer. The vision that were playing in my mind was like animated 3-D. I've jacked off plenty of times in my day, but never have I experienced anything remotely like this before.

She cried out that she was getting ready to cum. I gripped her ass cheeks tightly and violently began thrusting my hips upwards towards her. We're going so hard at it, that her poor headboard was begging for mercy as it crashes loudly against her wall. I felt the strain in my stomach and the tightening in my balls just as her walls contracted around me. Still I pumped hard and fast. Even as she cries out, I take one of her nipples into my mouth and gently bit down while giving her all that I got. She howled like a She-Wolf howling at the moon as she releases, showering my shaft, causing me to release.

The semen shooted out the tip of my shaft like a water hose. It sprayed a thick arch raining down all over my neck and torso. Damn, that was intense. I came so hard it caused me to lift a full eight inches off of the mattress.

Satisfied and drained, I just laid there panting with a huge smile on my face. I don't know why but it was like I could sense Kina laying on top of me exhausted, smiling, and looking into my eyes as happy as could be. I could see the look of satisfaction on her face. The sparkle in her eye tells me that she was as happy as I was that I reached out to her and wrote that letter.

I laid on my bunk for a good ten minutes while I tried to recuperate. Once I felt that I'd waited long enough, I got up, grabbed my wash - cloth and soap dish then stepped to the sink/toilet combination and washed up.

Just that fast, the fantasy was over, and I was back to reality. Back to being locked up serving a life sentence for some bullshit.

After I was done washing up, I returned to the side of my bunk and noticed my cell phone flashing, indicating a call was coming in. I knew who it was even before I picked it up. First I checked on my safety and security making sure that the C.O.'s were not anywhere on the tier before I answered the call.

Laying back down on my bunk, I answered the phone.

"What's up Ridah?" I spoke just as soon as I answered the phone.

"What's up with the Big Homie? I'm not interrupting no quality time session right now am I?" J asked in a lowered tone.

We had to whisper when we talked on the phones because voices carried inside of these walls. Especially at night when the entire building was quiet.

"Naaw you're good Ridah. I was just taking care of some B.I. on the net. What's good with it though?"

"Big Homie, let me find out that you're all on Monique's social media sites, cyber stalking her."

I laughed but if only J knew how close he was to the truth, except my ex-wife Monique wasn't my target. Little nigga would be talking shit about me for the rest of the year if he did know. I actually had to laugh at myself. Here I am fantasizing about a chick that I have not even met before.

In a way I was on some stalker shit, but when a dude has been locked up with nothing but other dudes, you had to use your imagination in order to keep your stress down and your dick clean. Real talk. A lot of what I consider weak-willed niggas let the time and lonesomeness get to them. Before long, they find themselves sneaking around in dark corners sleeping with the homosexuals getting their dick dirty and selling their souls to the devil.

But that could never be me. I rather die without sex for the rest of my life than to go out like that. So fantasying was my number one option and as of lately, lil mama, Authoress Kina, was the leading lady in my fantasies. It wasn't even about her books or writing anymore.

" Q, Rogue did you hear what I said? " J brought me back from my thoughts with that question.

"Naaw, I thought I heard some keys. What you say?"

"I said that I just dropped a nickel into your lunch box and I'm running out of books to read." That was code to let me know that he just put $5,000 into my PayPal account. He also let me know that our workers were running out of product.

"Right Rogue, bet. I'll make sure to send the book mobile by your way so you can select a few titles to read." I let him know that I would be sending him a fresh package by one of our mules tomorrow.

"Aight, bet that Big Homie. In the morning."

"In the morning Ridah." We did not tell each other good night in prison. That was too mushy and soft. Instead we said *in the morning* or *mjemwa usaku* which was Swahili for good night.

When I got off the phone with J, I pulled up my PayPal account and checked my history. Right there, was the $5,000 that the little homie was talking about. It was transferred from his account to my account. I scrolled down to check my balance next. **$87,652.**

Every last dollar was made selling dope behind these prison walls. I was not selling dope because I was trying to become the next penitentiary Nino Brown. I was on a strict hunt to leave no stone unturned in my quest securing my freedom and getting the fuck out of prison.

Not widely known, there was a small group of law firms with lawyers who specialize in "After sentencing time reduction." Meaning, they specialized in knocking your time down in chunks. Sometimes that may be small chunks like one or two years. Sometimes it's in big chunks like twenty-five years. These lawyers were very good and just as expensive.

An O.G. named Paul Oliver put me up on these types of lawyers when I first got to Salinas Valley. Paul was your typical O.G. the kind that stayed out of everyone else's business by minding their own. He was serving a life sentence for killing a security guard at a bank robbery. When I first met Paul, he had already been down a little over fifteen years. Somehow his wife managed to get her hands on $300,00 which she used to hire one of these specialty lawyers who eventually got him out of prison seven months ago. It took some time for them to get it all done but they did.

Paul's story was the inspiration and motivation that I needed. True, I am in here fucking up my life by selling drugs, especially since I wasn't a drug dealer on the streets, but like I said, I did not have anyone out on the streets looking out for or taking care of me. Besides, my younger sister Cynthia, I did not have much family, so, I had to do what I had to do and make my own way unless I wanted to die behind these prison walls.

At $900 an hour, I was making my way through an attorney by the name of Sheldon. I spent three full months searching the internet for the right lawyer. Sheldon ended up impressing me the most.

Once I was done checking on the financial aspect of things, I made two brief phone calls. The first was to my safe house. I let him know to drop a package off to the mule in the morning. A package for us was one ounce each of weed, heroin, and crystal meth. The second call was to the mile letting him know to be expecting the package.

I ran a smooth ship with no kinks and kept things simple. One ounce of meth had **28** grams in it. If you cut it in half, you will get **Two** -yard grams which if you cut each yard of gram into fours, you end up with four $50. That's 300 fifty papers which equals to $16,800 you make off one ounce. When you apply the same formula to the heroin, you end up making $10,000 and $5,000 off of the weed, giving us $30,000 every time we bust a move. I take $15,000, J keeps $10,000 and the last $5,000 was split between the safe house and the mule. Aside from me and J, no-one knew what anyone else makes, so there could not be any envy in the machine. Plus, every five times we bust a move, I threw them a package just for themselves. If you don't feed your wolves, they will turn on you, and I fully believed in that phrase.

After all my business was done, I put my phone down and laid back on the bunk thinking about the beautiful Sakina. I decided that I would write her another letter in the morning. I didn't want to press her, but at the same time, I wanted her to know the first letter was not a fluke. I was serious about mine.

CHAPTER 12
QUINCY

My alarm went off at two-thirty a.m. I rolled over and reached for my stash of tobacco and rolled a cigarette of Bugler tobacco. Next, I boiled some water in my hot pot and made some coffee. This was my morning routine. While I was waiting on my water to boil, I brushed my teeth and got dressed. Then I sat on my bunk to enjoy my coffee and cigarette before the C.O. popped my door open for me to go to work.

Twenty something minutes later I was walking across the yard headed for the kitchen. The night air was crisp and cool. The night sky was clear and full of stars. They sparkled under the full moon like diamonds under a chandelier. I could not help but think that Sakina could use a night like this for the perfect scene in one of her books.

C.O. Schafer let me and the rest of the guys who were outside waiting into the kitchen. We had to sit and be counted to make sure nobody tried to skedaddle up out of here first. Then we could move about in the kitchen. I did not like to waste time lollygagging around, bullshitting like most of the guys did. So, I went straight to my station and started getting prepared for my morning task.

Today all I had to do was make a large pot of grits. Grits was the easy day of the week, it was followed by toast, which was the hardest day of the week. On toast days I had to take a hundred loaves of bread and turn them into toast, four slices at a time. That shit took forever, and I was constantly burning my hands on the janky ass toaster that the prison had.

Forty minutes after I began, I was done with my work for the shift. To make my time go by faster, I spent the rest of the shift walking around helping different niggas that were behind with their task. Everybody was used to me helping. They knew I was not doing it out of being nice, but because that was just the type of dude that I was. If a job got to be done, then let's get it done. Especially since they had some C.O.'s that would hold the entire crew up from leaving at the end of the day if one-person was not done with his work. Therefore, I liked to get in and get the jobs over with.

Halfway through the morning shift, I had already drunk my third cup of coffee and I needed to take a mean piss. There were two bathrooms inside of the kitchen. The main bathroom was IP in the front as everybody used it. The second one was smaller and at the back of the kitchen. It was also more secluded. I liked using this bathroom because it was about ten times cleaner.

Feeling like I was about to piss on myself, I burst into the bathroom. Sudden movement to my left caught my attention. The nigga Too Sweet was standing off in the corner with some other homosexual nigga down on his knees in front of him.

Apparently, I interrupted something that I was not supposed to. The sudden movement that had caught my attention was the two of them jumping from being caught.

Now ordinarily, I would have turned right around and made my exit, but I could not hold my piss any longer. It was a good thing that I did not leave. I rushed over to one of the urinals and handled my business. While I was doing my thang, I kept my eye on Too Sweet. He and I had a couple of run-ins in the past and I was not about to give him the upper advantage over me at no time. Back when boxing was still legal in prison, Too Sweet had been the heavyweight champion at several prisons.

The more my eyes scanned the situation, the more I began to pick up on the fact that something was wrong. I just didn't know what. I caught Too Sweet nervously watching me out the corner of his eye which only confirmed my suspicion that something was not right. I finished releasing my bladder and decided to confront the situation head on. I turned around and openly assessed the situation.

It did not take long for me to realize that it was not a homosexual down on his knees in front of Too Sweet. It was a new kid that just started working in the kitchen a week ago. I think his name was Jahad Antione, but they called him Sushi. His left eye was swollen shut and his lips were busted, a clear sign that at least he had put up a fight. The bruises were easily noticeable on his high yellow skin.

Too Sweet was one of the predatory homosexuals mothafuckas. He didn't like doing his thang with normal homosexuals. He liked to rape young innocent heterosexual males who would struggle and put up a fight but ultimately lose.

I looked from Sushi to Too Sweet with a look of fire written on my face. Behind the veil of nervousness, I could see a challenging stare inside of Too Sweet's eyes. I could clearly see a desperate plea for help on the kid's face. He could not be a day over eighteen. I openly despised Too Sweet and everything that he stood for. Not the fact that he was a homosexual, because my take on that was to each his own. But this nigga was a pure predator. A rapist! A Booty Bandit.

"Lil homie if you not trying be where you at right now, this is your opportunity to get off of your knees and get on up out of this bathroom." I wasn't looking at Sushi. I stared Too Sweet right in his eyes while I spoke.

"Bitch you better stay right where the fuck you're at if you know what's good for you!" Too Sweet spoke with pure venom. His eyes never left mine as he spoke.

"Q, didn't I tell yo ass about getting involved in my business?"

"Nigga fuck what you're talking! This youngsta's from the Bay which makes this Bay Business. My business! Now unless you're trying die up in this bathroom, I suggest you let the kid up and go find yourself another victim."

"Q, you and I both know you don't wanna tussle with me toe to toe and I know you don't got your knives up in this kitchen with you. So, unless you wanna take this little nigga's place, you better get the fuck up outta here and stay up out my business."

Everybody on the yard knew that Too Sweet wasn't a killah. He might beat you to death possibly, but he was not for the knife play.

Me, on the other hand, I treated it like my Capital One Express Card. I never left my cell without it. From inside of my waistband under my jacket, I pulled out ten inches of cold hard steel. This was not the life I chose, but I had to do what was necessary to protect myself while living in hell.

"Try me Bitch and I'll gut you like a stuffed pig! Kid this is your last chance, I swear on my life if this mothafucka touch you he'll die right here. Now if you're not trying to be here, get up and get out."

This time, the kid hesitantly stood up. Fire shot from Too Sweet's eyes. His stare was deadly as he watched the kid walk out. Just as everybody knew about his hand play, niggas knew about and respected my knife play. They knew that if I pulled, I was ready to use it.

After the kid left, Too Sweet and I just stood there staring at each other until I walked out.

"Our day is coming Q., trust and believe that." Those were his words as I walked out.

In prison you either learned fast or you became a victim and I would never be any bodies victim! I had knives all over the prison. If I was going to an area that I could not take a knife, nine times out of ten I already had one there. But I was not the only one. Most cats that have been down for a long time did the same thing. That was why the police always found so many knives during random searches.

The rest of my shift went by incident free. Although it went by slow because I kept expecting Too Sweet to do some coward shit. The kid found me right before the shift was over and kept thanking me. I told him that it was nothing and reminded him to be more careful. Plus, I let him know that I wouldn't put his business out in the streets. This relieved him a little. After saying thanks again, he walked off. Before he did, I reminded him to watch his back. Too Sweet would no doubt try again. He could not let a victim get away. That was how sick fucks were.

Back in my cell, I put all thoughts of Too Sweet and the kid out of my mind. Not before sending the lil homie J a text letting him know the business without putting the youngsta out there.

Then I rolled a cigarette, put my phone back up and wrote Sakina another letter and a poem. I don't know why, but I kept having the urging feeling that I would not hear from her and that she would not respond to my letter. The feeling was getting stronger and stronger, but that was okay, because I had never been one to give up easily. I was persistent when I needed to be. And catching the attention of this talented sistah was more than enough reason to be persistent. Once the poem was written, I decided to read it out loud before writing the letter.

The Right Kind of Wrong (Poem)
Most often we as people tend to judge a book by its cover. We focus on what we think we see instead of taking the time see the truth hidden underneath.
Assumptions are the biggest forms of misconceptions that are known to man. We'd rather embrace the lie in our face than to give the benefit of the doubt to our fellow man.
I, myself, used to assume instead of taking the time to gather all the facts. That is until GOD opened my eyes by allowing me to end up here where I'm at.
Take a diamond for instance, its buried beneath tons of rock and coal. How about that nasty caterpillar it becomes a beautiful butterfly once that cocoon ages. Deep beneath the sea, inside of an oyster shell, you'll find a remarkable shiny pearl. Some of the most beautiful flowers on earth are in some of the most dangerous places in the world.

I dare not ask you to go out on a limb, especially since you don't know me. I simply ask that you allow me the opportunity to express to you that I am so much more than what you think.

So much more than the man who was found guilty and sent to prison. I guarantee that you will believe that I am a damn good man if you took the time to listen.

I'm A God fearing, self-respecting black man who always places family first. Never once did I complain about the hand I was dealt because I know things could've been worst.

I don't make excuses for my actions; I just simply refuse to allow my actions to define the person I am within. I know what I was found guilty of, but I promise you, saving my own life is why I am in the Pen.

The Right Kind of Wrong.

By: Q. Norton.

It was not until the tears caused my wet cheeks to itch; did I realize that I was crying. Damn, it has been a long time since I've allowed myself to shed real tears. Yeah, I allowed one tear to fall recently, thinking about Monique, but this was different. In fact, the last day that I cried was the day that I was found guilty. It also happened to be the only day that my ex-wife Monique came to the court room and the last day that I laid eyes on her.

My tears back then had nothing to do with the fact that I was found guilty. They were because I had been betrayed and let down. Betrayed by my wife, best friend and soul mate. Betrayed by the very system I believed in and supported. Betrayed by my

Heavenly Father who I thought would vindicate me of all the charges I faced.

I may not have been the most prized catch, but I was a hell of a man and an even better husband. Or at least I thought I was. My career as a Real Estate Agent was demanding, so my business hours were very long, and it at times caused me to have limited time at home, but I took care of home like a man should. I kept the bills paid, food on the table and was able to give Monique the type of lifestyle that she had always dreamed of.

When I was home, I gave my wife and her now eleven-year-old son Damone, all the love and attention that I could. Damone went to one of the most prestigious schools in California so we did not get much time when we were all available. However, when we did, I made sure that we were able to make the best of it. Topping everything off, I was a faithful and devoted husband.

When I was a free man, I supported law enforcement and our local judicial system. Sad that it took me being accused as a criminal to learn just how corrupt our legal system truly was.

Writing that poem opened old wounds that were not as old as I thought. Like how much I missed little Damone. I never thought Monique would just up and ex him out of my life the way she did. I haven't seen my little buddy in over six years. Monique had him young and when I met her at the age of twenty, I passed no judgement on her. I fell in love with her and raised her son as if he was my own. The way she had disregarded me out of his life as if I was never his only father figure was the most hurtful of all.

I needed to get out and get my life back together. Maybe not the life that I once had but a life. With my mood then changed, I decided to write Sakina at another time. I went to my case of water bottles and reached for one. I pulled out the bottle and turned on some Sade before sitting down and rolling a cigarette. As she sang *Smooth Operator,* I drank the white lightening and smoked my cigarette. Yeah, Monique was a smooth operator alright.

CHAPTER 13
QUINCY

That poem I wrote Sakina sat on the shelf for four days, before I was in the right state of mind to finally write her that second letter. I normally don't get caught up in my emotions like I did but I never got a chance to grieve for the life that I lost.

From day one, prison was a crash course in **" Learn the laws of the jungle and how to survive or die."** I've had a hard-exterior wall built up from the moment I got off the bus. I've been so caught up in the hustle and bustle of things that I never had the time to focus on my reality for what it was. Just as a callous forms over a soft or sore spot. I subconsciously placed a callous over my life and the wounds that life had given me.

The sounds of Angela Winbush's *Angel* played low on my boom box as I laid across my bunk looking up at nothing in particular. I was thinking and tend to stay in my head a lot. It was an old habit of mine. I was constantly dissecting something to its simplest form or analyzing one thing or another.

We were on lockdown once again for some bullshit. Lockdown meant that everyone was confined to their cells. The only movement were essential workers, which were the workers needed for the prison to at least operate its bare essentials. Such workers were cooks, clerks, medical personnel, etc. The administration would lock the prison down for a wide range of things. Most of the time it was for some bullshit though. Like this lockdown. They are claiming that they found a bullet on the yard. Tell me where in the fuck would an inmate get a bullet without a gun? The only people remotely with access to bullets were the C.O.'s, but they wanted to tell us that they found a bullet. Okay then where the fuck is the gun? Did you find the gun too? Never mind, let me fall back.

Angela finished singing and Patti LaBelle came on singing *Love, Need, and Want You*. This song brought me out of my stupor and made me make the decision to get up and write Sakina's letter. I don't know, but there was something about Patti LaBelle's voice that made every moment the right one. I decided to embrace the moment and let my pen flow.

In the hustle and bustle of things, I never had the time to focus on my reality for what it was. But, now that I have, I was more determined than ever to change my situation. And my pursuit of this woman was symbolic in some sort of way.

She represented: New Beginnings.

Dearest Authoress,

At the risk of appearing thirsty, I decided to follow up my first missive with this one. I've never been a timid or tentative individual. I figure if I am going to fail at something it's going to be while giving my all and not because I was scared to try. I don't know if you read my first missive or even if you received it. Given my circumstance I understand why you didn't respond to it if you did.

Allow me to ask you a question or two while giving you something to ponder. Have you ever felt in your heart that something was completely wrong even the law or society told you that it was right? Or have you ever done something that your heart and your conscious told you was right, but society told you it was wrong?

When we mass categorize, we tend to forget that each individual circumstance is uniquely different. Kina, I'm sorry, Sakina, I'm not sure which name you prefer, I urge you not to focus too much on where I am at. Just for one second, try not to even focus on why I am here, because the answer to either of the above won't change. Instead, I want you to maybe ask yourself what will cause a person to do what was done. Because accidents happen every day. Before this occurred, I've never been in trouble with the law or anything remotely close to it. I worked hard all my life to become someone that my family could become proud of and I succeed at that.

I am from the heart of the Hood by way of East Menlo Park, but I am far from a Thug or a Goon. I am a man. A man in every sense of the word. So, when I was attacked by someone in my house, I defended myself and ended up here. I did not go looking for trouble, trouble came and bothered me. I came home from work one day to find my wife in our bed with another man. An altercation took place and he pulled out a gun on me. At some point, I managed to place my hand on the gun and at the same time, he pulled the trigger in an attempt to shoot me, but the gun was pointing towards him. Next thing I knew, I was charged and convicted of murder. And now here I am, surving life for simply defending myself.

I don't know why I am sharing so much with you. I am normally a private man. It's just that I feel a certain trial connection pulling me to you. Thus far I've read four of your books and with each book I read I *feel that pull getting stronger. My soul is telling me to get to know you even if it isn't romantically. I feel the Heavens have brought you into my life for a reason. What I do know is that I want to explore that reason. I can sense your energy and fire through your words, and I can feel your spirit. I like what I feel. If I'm not being too forward, I found a picture of you on Facebook and I LOVE what I see. You are truly one fine sistah. But I am sure that you are fully aware of that.*

Honestly though before casting judgement on me, please read the poem that I wrote for you and Google my name. Learn the man that I am. See me for who I was and who I am. I am not a convict. I am not a criminal. I am not a murderer!!! I am simply a man that fell in love with the wrong woman and that decision cost me everything. But my life isn't over. Just that chapter of it. And if you are the woman that I think you are........then all of that happened just so I could come here and find your book so that I could meet you.

With warmest wishes,

Q.

I'm not even about to sit here and lie. I could've put way more game into that letter. Yet, that wasn't my goal at all. I don't want to serenade her with words. I'm looking to catch her attention with my openness and sincerity. Even if that means exposing a part of my weak side. Leaving me partially vulnerable.

I do not mind putting myself out there a little bit. Behind these walls, I had to have my hard exterior on for so long, that it was actually refreshing to reveal a small portion of the real me that lies beneath this armor that I wear.

For a minute, I thought about pulling my cell phone out of my temporary tuck spot just so I could look at Sakina's photos. She was

THE RIGHT KIND OF WRONG

that sexy and I was that hooked. Then I thought better of it. Taking unnecessary risks, is when you get caught, and that was the last thing I needed. Not only was I not trying to replace my phone with the $2,500 cost, but I was not trying to get the write-up for having a phone. The One hundred and twenty-five days that they took from you was not the problem. The eight points that they added to your classification score was. I was not trying to be on a level-four forever. I am trying to drop my points down to a level-three.

Just when I listened to reason, I heard people sounding the alarm.

"Kakoo-ey on the yard! Kakoo-ey on the yard!" All across the yard, dudes were yelling the alarm. Kakoo-ey was the name for the Goon Squad. The Goon Squad was prisons equivalent to the S.W.A.T. team on the streets. Whenever Kakoo-ey hit the yard, they were coming to tear some shit up. Instantly, I kicked into gear. You had to be speedy and efficient in prison if you didn't want to get caught.

I rushed and grabbed my latex glove. I dropped the phone inside of it and tied it into a knot. I repeated that two more times. I kept my heater on at all times and a large jar of Blue Magic hair grease right next to it. This kept the grease warm and melted like water. I took the latex glove with my phone inside and secured it inside of the jar of grease. It also had a toilet paper roll inside, rigged up so that the grease wouldn't touch the glove.

Once the phone was nice and secured inside of the jar, I filled a bowl up with ice cold water. I sat the large jar of grease in the bowl with cold water running down on it. It cooled the grease off immediately. The grease began thickening instantaneously. Around forty something seconds later, it was as smooth as the day they originally made the jar of grease. It looked fresh out of the store.

As I straightened everything back up, someone inside the building yelled that kakoo-ey had come into the building. My hygiene shelf was completely loaded with hygiene. I always kept about one hundred dollars - worth of hygiene on my shelf. Unless a dude had X-ray vision, he wasn't about to find my shit.

I laid back on my bunk and faked like I was interested in whatever was playing on my TV. The Goon Squad ended up going right next door to me.

My neighbor was a cat named Silk out of San Francisco. He was a quiet, low key cat who sold a bit weed. You would never think he was selling enough to get the Goon Squads attention. Somebody probably snitched on him. I learned one thing about prison a long time ago; It's about ten to fifteen snitches on the under in every building.

I made a mental note to be more careful, as I listened while they ran through his shit. From what I could hear through the vent, they were in his cell looking for a phone. After searching for thirty something minutes and not finding anything, I heard one of them say to the other that he should try calling Silk's number. The fact they knew his number did not surprise me. It was normal for dudes in here to have each other's number for whatever reason. What I did not understand was why dudes would save each other's phone numbers in their phone under contacts. If the Goon Squad busted one dude for his phone, they could potentially bust a bunch of others whose phone number was in that phone. All they would have to do then was go around and pick them like wild cherries.

I'd be damn if I didn't hear the sounds of *Scarface's Mary Mary* playing on the ring tone. When they could not find the phone as a last resort, they tried calling the number and hit, pay dirt. There were many rules to having a phone in prison, but the main thing was are making sure you turned it off when you're done using it. Making sure your ringer was always turned off was just as important. That way, you never had to worry about the C.O.'s walking by, at the exact same time that little mothafucka started ringing.

Once they got what they had came for, they left. Just like that. With the Goon Squad, it was rarely a fishing expedition. They came looking for something specific and when they found what they were looking for, they would leave. As I watched them escorted the homie to the hole, also known as Administrative Segregation, I silently thanked God for giving me the foresight not to have dudes with my number. Only a handful of cats had my phone number and I instructed them not to have my shit saved in their phones. As a habit, we all went one step further with our security. We would delete our call logs every time we used the phone. Always staying a step ahead.

Safety First!

Here I was, Johnny Citizen when I was at home on the streets, before this case, and now, I was moving and thinking like I was an A-1 highly trained and mastered convict.

Life, was truly something.

Finally, I decided it was time for me to take it down for the night. Once again, I did not bother to proofread the letter I wrote to Sakina, nor the poem. I simply placed both in an envelope, addressed it, sealed it with a stamp and sat it on the desk to be sent off the next day. Like I said before, the ball was in her court, except this time I was not going to leave it completely up to her to score the goal. I felt something pulling me towards this woman and I was determined to find out exactly what that was.

I wondered about her and what she was like. Exterior wise, she was beautiful, but I was starting to wonder more and more if she was just as beautiful internally.

I quickly sent a silent prayer, wishing for the best because God knows, I could use some much - needed good wishes come true.

CHAPTER 14
SAKINA

A Week Later:

"In the name of the Father, the Son, the Holy Spirit, Amen."

"And Amen. Thank you everyone for attending our final rehearsal. I will see each and every one of you on Sunday morning and parents don't forget, the boys and girls are to be dressed in their Sunday best in all white. Have a lovely evening."

"Same to you," I said in return along with the rest of the parents. I watched as a few mothers gave Sister Farah a warm hug before making their exit. A few remained behind as they conversed with each other. The children did the same, including my two sons, Earle Jr. and Kyle.

I smiled as I watched them interact with the remaining children. We were currently at Immaculate Conception Catholic Church attending the last rehearsal for their upcoming First Communion.

Yes, I chose to raise my sons in the Catholic Faith the same way my mom raised me and my sister. Although as an adult, I do not consider myself Catholic nor do I follow any religion, I do believe in God, in the resurrection of Christ and the Holy Father. I also believe in a higher power and the afterlife.

It baffled me when some folks state they do not believe in God. It is almost like, a tragedy to me. Nowadays, you must believe in something. This was a crazy world we lived in and living in it was a struggle all on its own and to exist without believing in something was like walking through life without having a dream.

Having a dream is a must. Living with a purpose is a must. Believing is a must.

Yes, I believed in God and I made sure my sons believed as well. In fact, I opted on raising them to be God fearing, respectable, strong black men, with integrity, strong morals, and having their first communion performed was only the beginning. I planned on instilling everything in them that my mom did with me and my sister, and I prayed that they carried the teachings throughout their life.

I wanted them to be over achievers, and everything this world we lived in often created an assumption that they could not achieved.

"Never be a victim or product of your surroundings or your environment. Always be the best man that you can be," I would always express to them and I prayed and prayed that they were listening to me.

"Mom, you're ready?"

My eldest, Earle Jr.'s voice caught my attention. He was now standing in front of me as I was seated in the front row of Immaculate Conception's church. He extended his hand out to me as a gesture to help guide me to my feet and I smiled.

He was the making of a true momma's boy and I felt no shame in admitting so. I felt sorry for any of his future girlfriends because that boy loved his momma like no other. Already, I could tell he would be the type to compare me and the way I do things pissing off the special lady in his life. I am talking from the way I cook, down to the way I do laundry.

I silently chuckled as the thought amused me.

"Come on mom," he said to me once more. Extending my hand with his, I stood to my feet. Just then, my youngest son, Kyle joined us.

My smiled broadened as my eyes averted back and forth between the two. I made some handsome boys. If I did not achieve anything else right in this world, birthing these two boys was the most righteous.

Earle Jr. and Kyle Harrison were my pride and joy and the only blessings that resulted from the toxic relationship I endured with their father.

Earle Raekon Harrison was not my first love; however, he was my first real heartbreak. Upon meeting at the New York Times newspaper office, in New York City, where I was fulfilling a paid internship at the age of twenty-one and he was employed in the mail room, we instantly clicked. He was not quite a winner in the looks department, but he was a gentleman, sweet and quite the charmer. I was impressed and fell for his charming ways, but of course, as our relationship progressed, I discovered all that charm was very a façade.

Who I thought was my prince charming, turned into a frog with a quickness. It did not take long for Earle to show his true colors, however I made the hugest mistake in life by ignoring the early signs of red flags.

I should've remembered the old phrase; when someone

show you who they are, believe them. Instead, I gave Earle the benefit of the doubt and by the time I decided to believe him after all and leave him alone, I discovered I was eight weeks pregnant with our first son. After convincing me to give our relationship a real chance, Earle and I moved into our first apartment together. By the time I was pregnant with our second son, I was moved into my own place. He started to show more of his true colors, and I had to show him that I was not the one, but unfortunately, that did not last long.

By the time our second son was born, we reunited, and I was back living with him but shortly after, the infidelity along with more disrespect reached an all-time high. Initially, I was determined to give my kids the family dynamic that was taken from me and my sister when our father left, but after women started calling our home phone, I decided my sanity was more important.

Although, I remained in the relationship for ten years totaled, we did so in separate homes. He continued living in our old apartment, and I moved into a two - bedroom apartment where my boys and I have been living comfortably for about ten years now.

Once I ended our relationship three and a half years ago for good, I never looked back. And no, we were not friends. He was a toxic boyfriend, a toxic lover and an even more toxic individual. In order to maintain my sanity, I chose to communicate only on a co-parenting level and even that was a challenge.

Yes, of all my relationships, he was my greatest regret, with the exception of my two beloved sons. They were the best part and I would not change them for anything in this world.

"Is dad still picking us up to get our suits and a hair - cut?"

My youngest, Kyle asked as we headed towards the church's double doors.

I quickly prayed that Earle was in fact waiting outside to pick them up as scheduled. Our visitation agreement was set up for his weekend visits, but at times he would disappoint them. He had no respect for the joint custody agreement filed between us. At times he would pick up the boys whenever he felt like it, which left them often disappointed.

And of course, I was left to do damaged control. I prayed once again, silently that this time was not the case. This weekend was special for the boys and they were looking forward to picking up their suits and have their hair cut. I could easily take them, but such tasks they enjoyed more with their dad than with their mother.

"I hope he's outside," Kyle voiced as we pushed the door open.

The May sunshine instantly hit our vision.

"Dad!" Kyle shouted out as he ran towards a black on black, Lincoln Navigator truck. Earle came through and I was happy.

I smiled as I watched Kyle climbed into the truck excitedly. I was not even offended that he failed to hug me before he left for the weekend with his father. While Earle Jr. was a momma's boy, Kyle was more of a daddy's boy. But all in all, both loved their parents and I was proud of that. Despite the fact, Earle was not a consistent dad, their love and respect for him remained in - tact. And although I wished for more consistency, I was still glad Earle was an active father and I guess I was grateful.

"I love you mom, I'll see you on Sunday," Earle Jr. said to me suddenly. Before I could respond, he wrapped his arms around my waist and hugged me lovingly. My heart smiled in that moment as I hugged him in return.

"I love you too, baby, I'll see you on Sunday," I replied to him and placed a kiss on his cheek. He smiled and ran his way towards the waiting truck. He climbed into the front seat and secured his seat belt. Kyle finally acknowledge me and waved.

"Sorry mom! I love you!"

"I love you too!" I laughed as I waved in return.

I started making my way towards my own vehicle which was parked directly in front of Earle's. Right before I reached the driver's side, I felt a pair of eyes on me from the corner of my eyes and I rolled mine. He was staring on the low, something he always did when we came into contact with each other.

His eyes lingered over my slim, thick frame, which was cladded in a form fitting, Navy blue dress slacks, with an equally form fitting, short sleeved white blouse. I discreetly snickered as I used my car remote and unlocked the driver's side door. As I grabbed the door handle and pulled it open, our eyes locked. I noticed the lust in his eyes and amusingly, the remorse, and I fought the urge to bust out laughing. Typical men. They always missed what they could no longer have but failed to appreciate when they had it.

Tearing my eyes away, I placed the key in the ignition and secured my seatbelt. I then made eye contact with my sons as I switched my car gear and slowly maneuvered into the roadway. I smiled and waved at them once more as I focused on the road.

Still smiling, I felt good in that moment. My two sons always put me in an uplifting mood. They were the only male species in my life who never disappointed me, and I truly believed they were the only ones who never will.

I could not stop smiling as I headed towards my hometown of Rahway. My first stop was the post office to check my P.O.

Box right before I headed home. Later, I was scheduled to attend a ladies' night out with Malika.

An hour later and I was finally home. Malika called my phone three times, but I chose to relax first, before I entertained her. I loved the hell out of her, but Malika could be a bit over whelming at times and preparing my mental before I linked with her was a must. We were not scheduled to meet up for a few more hours, so I wondered what the reason was for her three phone calls.

Hmmm. I wondered what she needed as I kicked off the pair of black leather open back Michael Kors stilettoes, I sported, the second I entered my apartment.

My feet were killing me from the stylist footwear, but they were so damn cute, the pain was worth it. Yes, I possessed a shoe fetish, up to the point, I could care less if the shoe were uncomfortable, I was going to wear it no matter what. I shook my head at myself as I left the stilettoes in the middle of my mediocre size living room. My bare feet against the cream - colored plush carpet decorated on the apartment's polished hard-wood floors felt damn good.

I made my way towards my bedroom. Still holding my purse along with the stack of mail I retrieved my P.O. Box, I walked at a slow pace, until I reached my grand bedroom. I placed my purse on the night - stand and dropped the mail onto the bed.

I looked around my bedroom as I unfastened the button to the crisp white blouse I wore. The décor represented my expensive taste, as well as my frugal tendencies. I loved nice and the finer things in life, but refused to pay some of the prices they cost. Most expensive labels I owned, I either, purchased on sale, or were gifted to me by Malika. Yes, I possessed a bit of a cheap side and I held no apologies for it.

I have been working since I was fifteen years old, so working hard came naturally for me. My mother was a hard worker as well and instilled the same attribute in me and my sister. Well, at least in me. My sister allowed a man to turn her to a life of crime to obtain money where I chose hard work to obtain my nice size bank account. In addition, I was able to provide a comfortable, semi lavish life - style for me and my sons. Earle did not pay child – support, but he did share equal expenses for the boys with me. My children had the best of everything, and I would not have it any other way.

I was a successful Author with my own business, which generated a six - figure income monthly. I was young, healthy and did not need anyone or a man for anything.

I lived a pretty content life. I should be happy, but happiness did not come easily for me.

Letting out a sigh, I finally unfastened the last button to my blouse and removed the fabric, allowing it to fall to the floor. Next, I unzipped the zipper to my dress slacks and removed them as well. I felt relived and relaxed in only a black, lace, two-piece set. Pulling back the designer comforter, adorned on my bed, I climbed in and pulled the comforter over my body. I opted on relaxing momentarily before I prepared for a night of dinner and drinks with Malika.

I felt fatigued in that moment and attempted to shut my eyes when I remembered the stack of mail, I retrieved from my P.O. Box. Reaching over, I snatched up the envelops and scanned through them.

"Letters from fans," I said out loud. That proud feeling of

accomplishment washed over me as I continued scanning over the countless mail from readers. I was still amazed that so many strangers felt the need to write little ole me. As successful as I have been as a Self-Published Author, I was still in humble mode. I chose to be that way, for it kept me grounded. I was still grateful for all my blessings.

"Uuugh, I will read these tomorrow. Too many to read now."

And they were that many. I was literally to the fifteenth envelop when a familiar name caught my eyes.

Quincy Norton.

Wow. Him again?

I could not believe he wrote me again. Persistent, I see. Suddenly, I recalled trashing his first letter and a tinge of guilt washed over me.

But then I remembered that he was serving life for murder.

"Uuughhh, what does his murdering ass want?"

Curiosity suddenly got the best of me as I decided to read his letter and save the other ones for tomorrow. Sitting up and resting my head against my bed's headboard, I tore open the envelope and prepared to read the letter, only to noticed there were two letters in the envelope.

Wow. Two letters?

Choosing to open the one I felt the strongest about, I unfolded the white sheet of paper and prepared to get my read on and see what this inmate could possibly want with me.

A poem?????? The Right Kind Of Wrong?

Like Wow. That was the sentiment I felt after I read Quincy, better yet, Q's poem. The Right Kind Of Wrong? Such an interesting title.

And the poem itself. He was indeed talented. His poem blew me away. My heart was skipping beats as my eyes scanned over his beautiful words once again.

Licking my lips, I felt anxious as I placed the white sheet of paper down with the loveliest poem I've ever read and reached for the second paper. I was then more curious than ever as I unfolded the white sheet of paper.

Tears fell onto the sheet of paper before I even realized they formed in my eyes in the first place. My eyes burned and my heart fluttered with a new - found excitement I have not felt in a long time. Reaching up, I utilized my right hand and wiped my tears away and once again, read the most beautiful, letter of expression I ever had the pleasure of reading. I've never in my life known for a man to express himself so well.

Yes, he now had my full and undivided attention. And he was dead wrong.

Thirsty was the last word on this God green earth I would use to describe this letter he so beautifully penned to me. I felt newfound tears formed in my eyes as my eyes scanned over his words. I was not sure why I was so emotional. Maybe it was for the simple fact, no man ever went above and beyond to get my attention.

Three years ago, I thought Lamont showing up at my office and mini bookstore, after coming across one of my books at a bank that one of my readers accidentally left behind was a sweet gesture, but this right here was on a whole other level.

Quincy Norton. Q Norton?

Suddenly I felt guilty for pre - judging him. I felt even worse as I thought of the way I threw his first letter away.

"I'm so sorry," I found myself saying out loud. Finally, I

decided to do more research and find out the true identity of Mr. Quincy Norton.

Getting out of bed, I went to my dresser and grabbed a hold of my laptop and reached into my purse for my phone. I decided to call Malika and ask for her much needed advice on this newfound situation, but one thing was for sure… There was a reason this man came across my books and felt the need to reach out to me the way he has, and I intended to find out just what that reason was.

CHAPTER 15
QUINCY

After the Goon Squad came to the yard, everybody was nervous as fuck. Even though I knew they were not going to come back anytime soon, I was a bit nervous myself. I had to calm my nerves and handled my business. Word had spread earlier today that the Squad hit several cells on the yard today. I had to check and see if I took any losses.

When I powered up my phone, I noticed that I had a couple of messages. Before making any calls, I decided to check my messages first. The first text was from my lawyer informing me that he was coming to see me within the next couple of weeks. The second message was from my little sister Cynthia who was attending Bryn Mawr University in Pennsylvania. She had a school break coming up next month and she was supposed to come see me. Apparently, her and a group of her friends decided to go to Florida for her break instead. She promised she would come and see me soon and I was okay with that.

Still, I missed my little sister, but I couldn't be mad at her for wanting to live her life. I remembered being her age and I definitely remember what the college party life was like. The wild parties and the last-minute unforgettable parties. I went to the University of Southern California and majored in Real Estate, but never graduated. Once I started selling houses and making money, obtaining my degree took a back burner.

I took my Real Estate license and passed on my first try. Yeah, when it came to intelligence or better yet, ambition, I was no spring chicken.

And my ambition went a long way, because right after receiving my license, I lucked up and signed with one of the most prestigious Real Estate firm in my hometown. I became one of the top selling real estate agent in the tri-state area. I was able to provide a pretty lavish life - style for me and my family and life was great.

Yes, a Real-Estate agent. And a successful one to be exact and I did it between the ages of twenty-one and twenty-four.

I became lost in thought for a moment as I thought about the days, I lived not only the life of luxury, but a legit and honest one.

That was another lifetime ago, another life.

Going back to my messages, the third one was from J. It was short and to the point but full of detail; right on point; "Grandma said to let you know a storm came through back east, but all of the kids made it home safely. Everyone says hi, they love you and will be there to see you after the bad weather passes."

He was telling me that everybody had everything put up, or at least had time to put everything up before the raids started, so, we did not get caught slipping or take any losses. He also let me know that everybody had already checked in and had given him a report.

I quickly sent my lil brah a message letting him know that everything was everything on my end and we will touch base as soon as the lockdown was lifted. Which should not be too much longer since it appeared that the Goon Squad achieved their mission. The word on the wire was that they hit four buildings and took down eight different dudes.

At least now we had confirmation on what the bogus lockdown was about. I looked up at the sky and smiled. Last night something told me to hit J and tell him that I thought the lockdown was just an excuse cause the Goon Squad was about to make a move. My intuition was right on time. I put my phone away and got down on my knees to talk to my creator.

Thanking him for protecting me and keeping me safe while I walk sure footed through this jungle of treachery trying to find my way back home. God knew I do not like some of the things that I was doing in the name of survival. I also knew that he said, **"faith without works were futile."** He knew that I did not kill that man and I was only defending myself when he attacked me. I only prayed that God gives me some credit or lead the way in what I am doing because of my innocence and because of the fact that I never, not once turned my back on God blaming him for my situation. Hopefully that will count for something and he will continue to keep me safe while I momentarily sinned. I just wanted to regain my freedom, my life, and my spirit.

After I said my prayers, I washed up in the sink.

Strangely, out of nowhere, images of Sakina's sexy ass crossed my mind arousing me immediately. I swore, I could not stop thinking or fantasizing about her. I was starting to think about her every day and shit, every night. I'm talking every damn night, but we were not having any of that tonight though. I just jacked off a couple of nights ago thinking about her. The more pictures I viewed of her on her Facebook page, the more my physical attraction grew towards her. And each night, she was the leading lady in my fantasies, but tonight, I had to shake her.

I had discipline. I needed discipline and in prison that was a must. I had to remain focus so I can stay on survival mode. That was a must and I was determined.

But I swear to God, Sakina was starting to get to me. I was not sure why. Plenty of chicks hit me up on Facebook since I created a page a few years ago. I mean some of the baddest females I have ever seen in my life, but most only had looks going for them.

I liked a woman with substance. A woman who can stimulate my mind as well as my dick. And for some strange reason and also from her books, I had a feeling Miss Authoress Kina can do just that. Shit, both, really. I could tell from her writing she was intelligent and then, there was her beauty. Lil mama had the sexiest pair of lips that I have ever seen. I know I commented on her lips before, but, shit, they turned me on something serious.

Every time I viewed her pictures on Facebook, I could not stop staring at them. All I kept thinking about was what it would be like to kiss them. They looked kissable as hell to me. I don't know why but I kept picturing berries every time I studied her lips. Shit, I was willing to bet that her kisses tasted like the forbidden Ambrosia. The nectar of the Gods. Even her name Sakina sounded angelic. I wondered how she would feel to know that I fantasized about her daily. If she knew that the prospect of possibly getting with her was the motivation that I needed to handle my business appropriately and efficiently so that I could come home to her.

Damn. I was tripping. Or was I? This was like a love at first sight kind of thing.

And let's say, my wish came true and God blessed me a miracle and I did come home, what would I come home to?

I had no wife, no children, no home, no career, hardly any friends. No woman.

But.. Sakina Michelle. Yes, that was her full name. That was the name on her Facebook page.

Sakina. What would I be coming home to? She was an Author, yes. And from what I could see on her Facebook page, a successful one, but who was she really? And was she even single?

And if she did take the time to read my letter and was intrigued enough to respond, I was wondering for the first time would I actually be intrigued with the woman that she turned out to be as much as I am with the woman that I'm fantasizing about in my head. Will she turn out to be just as fantastic or would she just be basic.

Or even worse than that, what if she turned out to be a bopper or a hood rat.

Women thought that they were the only ones who seek beyond a person's physical attributes. That they were the only ones who looked deep within a person for their true traits and qualities. I cannot speak for other guys, but I myself, tried to relate with a sistah on an intellectual level, first and foremost. I can let the conversation go its natural course when I'm talking to a young lady of interest. Or I can navigate the course such conversation will take. My point was, I am a very learned individual and could hold my own with just about anyone on just about any subject under the sun.

I love a nice strong woman who can hold a good conversation and actually have her own opinion and views that she was not afraid to share. That was why I love me a strong Black Queen.

And I was wondering if Authoress Kina could be that for me. My Queen.

I shook off thoughts of this woman before I went back on my word to be disciplined tonight and decided to pull my phone back out and send my little sister a message letting her know that I was cool with her going to have fun with her friends. And to also let her know, that I understood it all and that I had been the same way when I was in school. I also wanted to inform her that my lawyer was making lead way with the case.

If things went according to plan, there very well may be a light at the end of this dark tunnel. I did not want to get her hopes up too high or go into too much detail in a text message. So, I just told her that he found a legal loophole that may pertain to my case. Besides, he had not completely broken it all down to me yet. I ended the message letting her know that she could reach out to me whenever she wanted to.

After sending Cynthia the message, I activated my web browser and went to Sakina's Facebook page, after all. Yeah, temptation got the best of me. I had to stare into her deep welcoming eyes before I went to bed. Lately, that has become my nightly routine. I believe in the power of positive mental projection. I was making sure that this beautiful sistah was going to be mine. Then I went to sleep with thoughts of nothing but her on my mind.

CHAPTER 16
SAKINA

"I know you're fucking lying!"

"Really?"

"Bitch! Yes, really! Tell me that's not that nigga!"

I shook my head and laughed at Malika's dramatics.

"You are such a fool," I laughed continuously.

"Nah, seriously, tell me that's not him!"

"Okay, you're going to crash, screaming and acting a fool while you're trying to drive and look at my laptop. Hurry up, go home and change and get your butt over here. I'll be waiting for you."

Before Malika could protest, I hurriedly ended the phone call. I placed my cell-phone onto my bed and resumed attention back to my laptop screen.

In that moment, I bit my bottom lip, in I guess you can say in a seductive manner. Seductive was exactly what I was feeling as my eyes roamed over the figure on the screen. I was currently on Facebook viewing one of the most handsome, shit, finest black man I've ever laid eyes on.

I wasn't as dramatic as Malika, but my sentiments were just as close to hers.

In Malika's words, 'That nigga was fiiiineeee.'

Yes, Mr. Quincy Norton was quite a sight for sore eyes.

I was currently on his Facebook page and have been on there for the past thirty minutes. After reading his heartfelt letter and poem, I went ahead and called Malika. I told her all about the first letter and admitted that I crumbled it up and discarded it. After she cursed me out and called me the dumbest heifer on earth, I went on and read the second later as well as the poem to her.

And after she asked the question, I was wondering as well, I found myself on his Facebook page, curious to what he looked like. I was hoping his page was not private and thankfully, it was not indeed, because I had full access to his photos. Many folks chose to make their page private, but as an author, I was one who chose to leave mine open to the public. I had both a personal and Authors page as well as an Author's business page, but I still decided to leave full access to my once personal page. Besides a few of my sons' photos as well as Malika's, my page was flooded with flyers and collages of my books as well as my pictures. I chose to present myself as an open book and the readers loved it.

And besides a few perverts commenting on my pictures daily, I had no regrets to my decision. I had more admirers and mostly readers. Even men were quite respectable.

I was currently on my Author's page and was truly thankful Quincy Norton's page was public.

"Oh, Thank you Jesus."

I had to express my gratitude out loud as I viewed countless pictures of him. To say he was fine and handsome was actually an understatement. I felt my body heat arising and my eyes burned in what I just knew was lust as they roamed over what appeared to be an over six feet tall, muscular, hard body built Adonis with smooth dark toned complexion and a silk, clean bald head.

Yes, once again in Malika's true fashion, he was the shit.

Malika was not exaggerating with her reaction. The minute we came cross Quincy's first picture, she screamed out like a pure fool and I did not blame her. We were both surprised to say the least. Never did I expect for Quincy to look like such a...I swear there were limited words to describe his features.

His mug shot picture I briefly viewed almost two weeks ago on California's public page, did not do him justice. But then again, most mug shots never did.

"Damn."

I could not stop staring and after I looked over all the photos gracing his page, I was without a doubt lusting. And after I scrolled all through his page and discovered he loved to write poems and inspirational quotes, I was damn near crushing.

You'll never meet a nigga quite like me. The decision is up to you. Will I be your reality or just a fantasy?

Rather than judge me...get to know me....

Q... Cali's own....

Damn.

His brief bio or quote under his profile photo grasped my attention and dammit I was now intrigued. I loved poems and a man who wrote and knew how to execute them, was after my own heart.

"I can't believe it, I ain't had a crush in years."

I laughed to myself after quoting the lyrics to one of my favorite rap songs by **L.L. Cool J: Hey Lover**

Wow. I haven't felt like this in years for sure. I felt like a teen experiencing my very first crush.

I shook my head at myself. What was I doing? I was actually gushing over a poem, a letter and…… Scrolling through his photos again, I felt my center slightly throbbed.

Damn.

In that moment, I decided what I was feeling was a bit deserved.

Quincy Norton.

His letters, his poem, the way he reached out to me, the way he went out to explain himself…. then his Facebook page. I was granted a glimpse of the man he was or could possibly be and I must say, I was a bit intrigued.

I was more than intrigued.

I'm not sure what was happening, but my interest was piqued.

I was now more curious than ever, and I've decided that I was going to conduct a full background check on this mysterious man who has gone all out to grab my attention.

I now had a feeling he was more than just an inmate and a convicted killer, and I was going to find out exactly who Quincy Norton was.

"Why not start with this?"

As soon as the words left my mouth, I did something I've never done before.

I made a bold move regarding a man.

Using the wireless mouse to my laptop, I clicked on the friend request button. My heart skipped a beat as I grew nervous at what I have done. I exhaled as I wondered how long would it take before he accepted my friend request.

Seconds later, I exited Facebook and went on to the Google page.

I typed in his name and waited to see what information would be revealed. As I waited for his response on Facebook, I planned on starting my search and Google was always my best friend and number one search option.

Later That Night:

Yeahhh, babyyy, is you drunk, is you had enough? Are you here looking for love? All eyes on you....... She was the baddest...He was the realest....

"That's my shit!!"

Uuugh.... was my current sentiment but I kept it to myself.

Malika was on her fifth Coke & Hennessey and acting like a pure fool. As much as I loved her, I was a bit embarrassed by her at times. Our differences sometimes worked my nerves. By nature, she was outspoken and a real live wire, but with alcohol intake, she was loud and borderline obnoxious.

We were currently seated at the VIP section at a popular bar & lounge in her hometown of Newark, New Jersey. Malika was a full bred hood chick. At times, one would never guess she possessed the intelligence of a borderline genius and was a college graduate.

Newark, also known as brick city, was one of the roughest, urban cities in New Jersey and Malika represented it to the fullest.

While I enjoyed more of a quiet and classier setting, she preferred noisy and crowded environments. Like, the place she loved to hangout, a shooting was more than likely to occur. Folks end up shot, literally.

"All eyes on us!"

She sung out the lyrics to **"All Eyes On Us" by Nicki Minaj and Meek Mill** and I had to finally let out a chuckle. Yes, she was a bit too much at times, but she was as real as they came. There was no façade about her, and I loved as well as respected her for it.

"Okay, let me chill for a minute," she announced suddenly, and I was thankful.

She also knew when she was doing too much, and I loved her for that as well. It made our weekly girl's night out more tolerable.

"Nowwww, let's talk about that nigga Q!" she exclaimed, and I groaned internally once again.

"You started telling me about what you found on Google when we got here, but I became sidetracked by the drinks and chicken wings. Now, who did his ass killed?"

I nodded my head, before taking a sip of my drink of choice, an Apple Martini. I allowed the drink to warm my system oh soo good, before I went on to fill her in all about Quincy Norton.

"Hold the fuck up! That nigga was a big time Real Estate agent in California? And he ended up killing a guy who he found fucking his wife in their home? In their bed?"

I nodded my head for confirmation and in true Malika fashion, she expressed her opinion like only she could.

"Ohhh hell nah! His slut wife should've caught a bullet too!"

I shook my head and laughed out loud.

"Stop," I urged her, but it was no damn use.

"Nah, that was fucked up! It don't get no grimier than that. I can't stand bitches like that, who have a good man but don't appreciate it."

Once again, I nodded my head in agreement. I agreed with her to the fullest. Some women have everything I've always yearned for in a man but take it for granted.

Suddenly my thought traveled to Quincy. From what I discovered on Google, he appeared to have been an upstanding citizen and a good ass man. He possessed a college background with a good work and career background. He was only married for a short time and had no children.

I was amazed how he had no priors but was given life for defending himself. According to Google, he shot his ex-wife's lover in self-defense after the man attacked him. It all seemed so unfair.

I shook my head at the thought of it all. Malika's voice then broke into my thoughts.

"That's fucked up, he got life. Who the fuck was his lawyer?"

"I think his lawyer's name was mentioned in the article I found on google but I can't fully remember," I admitted.

"Damn man, that is fucked up," Malika expressed, and I totally agreed.

"So, what happens now?" Malika asked and my eyes pierced through her.

"What do you mean?"

She laughed and replied, "Sakina, stop playing with me. You didn't do all that googling of that man's story for nothing. Your ass is curious about him."

She pointed her index finger at me as she stated the factual and I couldn't even lie.

Exhaling, I had to admit Malika was right.

"Okay, okay. His letters, his poem, his obvious interest to read my books and contact me, yes, I'm very curious. And discovering the truth behind his incarceration, I'm more than just curious."

"Okayy and what exactly is your ass curious about?" Malika challenged and really, I had no response to her question. I honestly did not know.

But I did know this....

"Well, I now know I pre - judged him and was dead wrong about him. I also know that he is way more than just a killer and a convict and he really don't deserve to be in there."

"You're right about that," Malika agreed.

I sighed before taking another sip of my drink.

"Okay, so are you going to write him back?"

I thought about her question for a few seconds before I decided to confess to her.

"I did better than that. I sent him a friend request earlier when I was on my Author's page on Facebook."

"I watched as Malika's lips formed into a small grin. I just knew she was about to be dramatic again and I groaned once more.

"Ha ha bitch! You're trying to get that jailhouse dick! And let me tell you, it's the best dick on earth!"

She shouted and I thanked God that the lounge music was on blast drowning out her loud - mouth.

"Uuuugh, God, you need Jesus," I laughed as I went on to sip more of my drink. We conversed more about Quincy and the possibility of what ifs.

I was having a great time as I felt my cell phone's vibration from within my purse. The second I retrieved the phone and viewed my screen and read the incoming text message that just came through, my good mood almost was ruined.

A message from Lamont instantly threatened to place a damper on my night. He requested for a conversation after I ended my night with Malika and I already knew what that meant.

But he was about to be disappointed, for I just wasn't in the mood tonight. I ignored his text and prepared to enjoy the rest of my night instead.

CHAPTER 17
QUINCY

It had been a couple of days since we came off lockdown and things were pretty much back to normal or should I say back to the way they usually were. I made sure that I made my appearance on the yard the moment that it opened back up. Which was right on time because the Homie had a batch of white lightening ready for me.

J and I were able to chop it up without everyone all up in our business. The lil homie had been doing his thang even while we were on lockdown. He told me he was ready for another drop. He also told me that my money was already in my account. That was music to a young playa's ears. This wasn't a game to me. I was playing for my freedom which means I was playing for keeps. It was about time for me to give my lawyer another payment. Not only was I already on point with his next payment but I had an additional payment tucked away in the cuts just in case.

"Aww shit! Rogue there them niggas go!" J called out while looking over my shoulder.

I turned to see what the little homie was talking about. Over by the handball courts two Northern Mexicans were getting on one of their homeboys. They called it a removal. Meaning the gang decided that someone had to be forcibly removed from the yard.

No sooner had I turned around and noticed what was going on, the alarm started ringing and the tower guard came over the loudspeaker telling everybody to get on the ground.

Some dudes got down immediately. Most of us stood and watched the commotion for a little while longer before finally complying with the order. This being a four yard, you had to make sure you were safe before getting down.

"Well, I guess we're going to be on lockdown." Somebody yelled out as we finally got to the ground. When I looked to my left, I saw Chuck a few feet away from me shaking his head.

"Nigga where in the fuck did you come from?" Chuck was always sneaking up on people.

"See there you go. It don't cost nothing for you to stay up out of mine," he joked. We all began laughing. This was one of our little inside jokes, meaning stay out of my business. Chuck was a cool homeboy. He was from Menlo Park like J and me. The three of us have been knowing each other ever since grade school. I was a little older than them.

"Little nigga you are my business so I'm not in yours, I'm in mines. You better tell that nigga something J." I joked back.

"I ain't gonna tell that nigga shit! You know that nigga Chuck is burnt. They got to make a new category for his level of craziness." J added.

"Well nigga, since my business is your business, I guess it's alright for me to tell you then. I was coming from your bitch house; I mean our bitch house. I was testing out that new California King yo trick ass just bought.".". Everybody died laughing at Chuck's joke,

Just then, a bunch of C.O.'s rushed the yard in response to the alarm. We kept on doing us, cracking jokes and talking shit. The fight was no longer of any interest to us. Fights and stabbings were such a constant occurrence that was beyond the initial shock of "it's going down." The commotions were no longer important to those of us that have been here for a long time.

A loud weird sound was heard echoing across the yard. It was the call that the gurney was coming onto the yard. I looked up and sure enough they were coming on the yard with the gurney. By this time, the Goon Squad made their way to the yard. Their presence was probably due to gang related or there was a knife involved.

"Ooh look! He leaking like a once a month prostitute." Chuck was always saying the damnedest things.

When I looked at the dude whom they lifted and was putting onto the stretcher, the amount of blood that I saw on his clothes confirmed Chuck's suspicion. They were stabbing him while they were jumping him. He was bleeding something serious. They must have stabbed him with some serious sharp object. See, in prison, you see all types of knives. From small pencil pokers to the real big ten-inch pieces of steel that we call bone crushers. Then you got your slicers which are basically knives made with razor blades. Slicers leave an ugly ass scar but for the most part, them, and the little pencil pokers were harmless.

Even though the slicers leave an ugly scar, they still do not leave the amount of blood that was all over the Mexican's clothes. Because he was stabbed, we were laid out on the ground for what felt like hours, even though it was only like forty-five minutes. The valley sun was beaming down on us like the furnace of hell. It was pure torture.

I was happy as a kid at Christmas time when they finally recalled the yard. We were sent back to our housing units one unit at a time. When it was time for my building, I said my peace to the homies and quickly made my way to my building.

A couple of hours later I was feeling relaxed and refreshed after washing up and changing my clothes. I was chilling on my bunk watching Real Housewives of Atlanta when an idea came to mind. I got up and walked to the cell door to check my security. Then I walked over to my spot and pulled my phone out and jumped on Facebook.

When I pulled up Sakina's page, I sent her a friend request first. Then I opened up the instant messenger and fed her with both verbal barrels:

Most dudes don't know what they want, they spend their lives running around blind. Some are lucky enough to find out exactly what it is they want in life but can't ascertain it. I've patiently waited all my life for what I wanted, settling for less until it came. Now that I have finally found you, I am coming for what is mine. Here's a gift for you:

Night of perfection....

The night was dark and cold, moonless with a chilled kiss from the wind's lips. A night quite like this, when I first stumbled across one of Heaven's most precious gifts.

Amazed beyond belief, I was shocked to complete silence memorized like never before." If only.....".

I began to wish until a whisper from Heavens lips said, "My child she is yours!". My first thoughts were surely I must be losing my mind, until the voice spoke louder. She is your Queen to be. Let no man separate what I have joined together at this very hour.

It became oblivious to the night chills, captivated by her beauty, intrigued by her smile. Her succulent lips, that skin with honey golden kiss, I was star struck gazing into her eyes for a while.

I remember my heart thumping rapidly in my chest, lungs constricting as if I couldn't breathe. A comforting warmth enveloped my body as I envisioned her standing next to me.

Exquisitely elegant, she's everything I've been searching for and so much more. The answer to my prayers, my completeness. My sweet Sakina it is you whom I've been searching for.

Night of perfection...

Yeah, I knew I was going somewhat overboard with this chick. But something has me convinced that she was well worth it. I'm not just talking about her beauty. She's beyond reproach in the looks department. Every time I thought of her name or looked at one of her pictures it was like a longing deep within was filled.

I go hard for my paper and the happiness that paper brings; that false happiness that material means can provide us with. Why couldn't I go just as hard if not harder for real happiness? I let Gilligan's work with their ego's and their pride. Real men tap into their emotions and listen to their hearts. My heart was talking to me. I be damned if I was not going to listen.

Chapter 18
Sakina

It was two days later on a Monday morning and I was feeling exhausted. It had been one hell of a weekend and I was emotionally drained. After partying it up with Malika well into the break of dawn, sleep should've been on my agenda on a Saturday morning but that was impossible. The whole day was spent preparing for my sons' first communion the next day which was an absolute success. Earle Jr. and Kyle officially fulfilled their first communion and I could not have been prouder.

After hours of celebration on Sunday and spending quality times with my boys, followed by writing into the break of dawn on this Monday morning, I could barely keep my eyes open.

I was currently seated at my office desk in my office and bookstore located only blocks from my home and I was tempted to call an early day. My bed was calling me and ignoring it was getting harder and harder. Earle Jr. and Kyle were in school and I knew I would have nothing but peace and quiet.

So far it was a slow morning in the office. It was already ten a.m. and not one customer have come in yet. I was baffled because Mondays usually are the busiest day. Every Friday, I normally restock on books since Monday would normally draw in a large crowd. By late afternoon, I would be sold out, especially on my books.

Looking around, I suddenly felt proud of my accomplishment. Owning my very own bookstore was always a dream since I became a published Author and three and a half years ago after quitting my ten - year position as a legal secretary, I finally made it happen.

Sakina's Reads & Things was located in the heart of Rahway, New Jersey, not too far from my home. I carried mostly my books as well as bookmarks, t-shirts and other promotional items, but I carried a selective amount of Author's books as well. It was currently a modern size store, based in a three - story office building, so the amount of books I was able to store were limited but my goal was to upgrade and move into a larger space, in another year or so. Business was doing exceptionally well, and I was super proud of myself.

Suddenly feeling alive, I focused my attention onto my desktop computer. I decided to stay in the office after all and try to stay busy. Taking naps in the middle of the day, no matter how tired I felt, just was not part of my character. I was a mover, no matter what.

Logging onto Facebook, I went straight to my Author's page. Suddenly, my heart skipped a beat as I wondered if Quincy accepted my friend's request. Surprisingly, seconds later, I discovered he in fact, did not and I could not help but feel a bit disappointed.

Why wouldn't he accept my friend request?

Damn why did I care? What the hell was happening?

Letting out a sigh and decided on pretending not to let the thought of him consume me, I went to my inbox and checked all of my messages. After responding to each, I looked over a few posts on my page. I was bored after a few moments. There was nothing interesting going on, so I decided to log off and check out my main page.

Sakina Michelle was once my personal page which I decided to make public so my readers can have full access to me.

Seconds later I was logged in. No sooner after looking over my friend's request, I noticed it: A friend request from Quincy Norton.

Oh damn. No wonder he did not see my friend request from my Author's page. He followed this particular one instead.

Suddenly I felt excited. My heart began to beat rapidly, and bead of sweats were forming on my forehead. I was nervous and was not even sure why. I just knew I was happy he reached out to me via mail and now via Facebook. He was obviously on a mission and I was flattered.

This was the attention I strived for. A person showing me I was thought of. I was needed…somewhat wanted. It was as if I needed it. I was not sure this was healthy on my part, but it has been a part of my character for so long I did not know how to do without it.

I don't know what it was, but it was as if this Quincy Norton knew what I needed and was acting accordingly. This man just knew what to do and now my interest and curiosity of him was more piqued than ever.

Biting my bottom lip, still feeling nervous, I used the computer mouse and clicked the accept button under the friend request. After doing so, I sat in silence, not sure what to do next. Finally, I decided to go out on a limb and leave him a message. I felt it was only right to thank him for supporting me as an Author and reading my books. I also wanted to express my gratitude for his letters, kind words and heartfelt poem.

I went ahead and proceeded to the inbox, but my heart felt as if it was caught in my chest as I instantly noticed a message from Quincy.

Wow...

I was in awe once again and wasted no time reading what he wrote.

"Now that I've finally found you, I am coming after what is mine."

His words echoed in my read as I read it repeatedly. In that moment, I wasn't sure what to believe. To some folks, this might appear bizarre. This man appears to be crushing just from reading my books. He made a bold move by writing to me and now he has reached out to me through Facebook and has boldly placed a claim on me.

"Now that I've finally found you, I am coming after what is mine."

I read the words again and felt excitement and confusion all in one. Was he for real or was he just gaming? I've heard stories of some of these jail guys. They knew how to finesse with their words to get what they wanted.

I just was not sure what was really happening here. Was this guy playing with me or was he sincere? Was he that fascinated by my books, my writing and me? I mean I noticed the different women on his page complimenting and openly flirting with him. Some, I noticed were some beautiful women, so what exactly was it about me that has sparked this man's interest. And it was crazy, I'm questioning his interest and intentions now, but I did send him a friend request.

I had some interest myself, right?

I was still in a state of confusion as I read over his words once more. I started to contemplate responding when suddenly, the bell to my store door chimed off. I looked up and in walked, my headache of three years.

I shook my head as I watched Lamont swaggered over to my desk. He came directly over to me and before I could respond, he crouched down and placed a kiss on my cheek.

"Good morning," he greeted.

"Good morning," I replied. I made eye contact with him hoping his attention would not be drawn to my computer screen. Although, I felt I owed him no explanation, since we never established a committed relationship, I also did not want to give him any ammunition to point fingers at me to justify his actions. He was good at that.

"How can I help you Lamont," I said to him in a stern tone. The sooner he stated his reason for his visit, the sooner I can get him to leave so I can go back to my inbox. Strangely, I felt anxious to return to the message convo with Quincy. I was still torn on responding but I wanted to be alone as I decided.

"Well, first I bought you a cup of coffee from Dunkin Donuts."

Lamont placed the large cup of coffee in front of me on my desk. I did not notice the cup in his hand when he first came in, but I was actually thankful. The way I was feeling earlier, coffee would be a good thing for my system.

"Its French Vanilla, light and sweet, just the way you like," he stated.

"Thank you," I said to him and I was truly grateful. I was unhappy with him but at times, he did have his moments. To say he was all bad would be the hugest fib ever spoken.

"You're welcome," he replied back.

"And my second reason for coming here is," he started to say as he took a seat in a chair on the other side of my desk across from me.

He leaned forward in his seat as he stared directly in my eyes. I could not help but admire his features. Aside from his toxic and at times ugly ways, I could not deny that he was in fact close to what one would label as handsome.

From his bald, polished, neatly shaven head, to his chestnut skin tone, to his dark, thick eyebrows, and full lips, he wasn't bad on the eyes.

And as he sat there in his Rahway Police Department uniform, he reminded me of my physical attraction to him. At forty years old he could easily pass for the tender age of thirty and he was sexy with it. Status wise, he was a great catch, but in my heart, I knew he could never be what I fully needed and wanted in a man. He was all wrong for me, despite the fact I wanted him to be right so bad.

"What is your second reason Lamont?" I asked even though I honestly did not care. I knew whatever came out of his mouth would be the same old bullshit and I was sick of it.

"Well, I was trying to meet up with you this weekend to talk with you, but I see you ignored me."

"No, you wanted to meet up Friday night to have sex and I'm done with that. I'm ending our intimate and personal relationship. I'm tired of constant disappointment. I deserve better, so I'm done with you. Maybe one day we can be friends but as of now I need space from you."

I thought my words would affect him and maybe he would argue and digress as he always did, but surprisingly it did not. Instead, his next set of words were ones I've never heard before.

"I know you deserve better. You've always deserved better

and now I'm ready to give it to you. I don't want us to go our separate ways. I love you Sakina."

WTF....

I was speechless but more so because in that same moment, I noticed from the corner of my eyes, that a message just came in from Quincy and I was able to read the words clear as day.

Quincy: Good morning beautiful. Thank you for accepting my friend request. You have me feeling like the luckiest man in the world right now. How is your morning so far?

CHAPTER 19
QUINCY

First and foremost, beautiful, and for the second time today, thank you for accepting my fiend request. In my mind, that gesture meant that I have piqued your interest or at least triggered your curiosity. Which is a good thing because I am very intrigued by you. I hope you do not feel offended, but I took my time to do a little research on you. Afterall I could not be infatuated with just a lovely name and a beautiful face. The more that I found out about you, the more I became interested and the more I liked you.

I am sure you have some concerns about my being incarcerated. I do not blame you, any woman would. Which brings me to why I am writing you this message. I just want you to get to know the real Quincy. Not who you may think I am or who the public tries to portray me to be. But the man that I truly am.

I am a God fearing self-respecting dignified African American male. I was born to drug addicted parents who abandoned me at an early age. Forced to live with my grandparents who instilled moral dignity, self-respect, hard work and the fair treatment of others in me as well. Growing up I was a handful but no more than the average child. I love and respected both of my grandparents and followed their rules.

After my grandfather died, it was my grandmother who taught me what it means to be a man. She taught me all the virtues that a woman should have for herself and taught me how to look for those virtues in a young lady. Most people say that a woman cannot teach a boy how to become a man, but I beg to differ. She taught me very well. Despite my current location and situation, I am a damn good man. I refuse to let anything that deals with my incarceration define me. Instead, it motivates me in a way like never before. My main motivation is to get myself from behind these walls and back into society. My second motivation is to be able to find it in my heart to forgive my ex-wife for what she did to me. To this date I have no reason why she did what she did to me. In the beginning of my incarceration all I wanted to know was why.

Now I am realizing that it does not matter because what is done is done and cannot be undone. I am also motivated to forgive myself. Even though it was an accident and I was only defending myself, taking a life is a pretty heavy thing and it weighs down on my conscious like one would not believe. I struggle with this the most. I was always taught to better and uplift my fellow man. My conscious haunted me every day for what seemed like forever after the incident.

Even now the thought of taking someone's life or extinguishing their flame burdens my soul. No-one thinks about this though. About what I went through or possibly may still be going through. Think about it, Sakina I am human as well. I am a good man. And because I am a good man, I have a heart with live emotions. If you take anything away from this message let it be the fact that I am human too. I am a good-hearted man with a wholesome and loving heart.

Oh! Before I forget, congratulations on your store. I saw more of your pictures once you accepted my friend request. That is a very big and positive move that you made, and you should truly be proud of yourself. Congratulations. I knew you were a very intelligent and goal - oriented person. It is good to know that my assessment was right regarding you which means that I am on point about you. You will see Goddess. You are special and delicate but more importantly you are royalty. And I will always treat u as such. If only you will give me the opportunity.

With the warmest of wishes and champagne kisses.

Q.

"I pressed the send button on the Facebook messenger and instantly became an official stalker. I mean a true brother was going after what he wanted while popping my collar full fledge. But the sistah has yet to respond to anything I have sent her. So far, I have read five of her books, tracked down her social media sites, googled her four times, written her two letters, and messaged her twice. Tell me Jenny, keep it 100 with me now, you know how we do it. Am I a stalker or what?"

She laughed at me, probing a grin of my own.

I was in the private office of Dr. Lynette Suarez, licensed psychologist. I have been counseling with her a little over a year now and met with her every Monday afternoons. I knick-named her "Jenny from the Hood" because she is a young Latina only a few years older than me and I can tell she grew up in or around the hood. She was cool peoples and I respect her as such.

"Norton, because you've taken interest in a female, that does not make you a stalker. Nor does the fact that you wanted to know a little more about this particular female before dealing with her on a more direct level. That's perfectly understandable." She had her everyday nothing could go wrong personality as she spoke those words.

"I hear what you're saying Jenny, but sometimes I feel like that creep outside your window in the bushes. Like I'm doing something wrong. You know I've never had to go anywhere near this to catch a ladies' attention."

"Which is one of the reasons why your actions may seem taboo to you. It maybe you subconsciously believing that you shouldn't have to chase a woman, and in doing so, you develop doubt of self. Another key reason you're feeling the way you do, could be because of your ex....."

This time I cut her off. "Here we go with that again," I mumbled.

"No Norton, you need to hear this. Week in and week out, you talk all that macho talk. Well you need to be macho enough to listen sometimes. You cannot begin to heal until you finally accept and deal with what she did to you. Until you face the betrayal that landed you here in prison, you will not be able to trust another woman. In essence, what you are doing to yourself is creating negative scenarios where none exist to give yourself reasons to terminate the relationship before it even fully begins to develop. Assault victims do this all the time. It's a defense mechanism - victims create so that they won't be hurt again."

After saying this she sat there looking at me waiting on a response. Yet daring me to challenge her.

This was why I like Dr. Suarez aka Jenny from the Hood. She was not intimidated by my controlling offense nor by my size.

The first time I met with her she asked me did I really want help or if I was another inmate that wanted to get out of his cell. I told her that I honestly did not know if I needed any mental health treatment or not. I also told her that if together, she and I felt like I did needed help, then I was ready to accept any and all the help that she was willing to give.

Even with the pact that she and I made that day, it took me meeting with her for an hour a day once a week before I began to trust her. Which was right around the time I started calling her Jenny from the Hood. Our entire time meeting, I have never disrespected her by crossing the line over - stepping my bounds. Even though Jenny is fine ..... *Naw she is fucking beautiful. That take her home and meet your mama I wanna wife her beautiful.*

"Listen Jenny, you got it all wrong, I'm not running from anything. I'm tracking this woman down like the Repo man looking for a stolen car."

"And yet, still you are sitting in my office trying to tell yourself and me that you're somehow wrong for trying to convince a lovely woman that you are a good man. You are sabotaging a potentially good thing because one woman's betrayal is giving you a hard time trusting another. I hate to tell you this, but your ex-wife isn't the first woman to do something devious to a man. And she probably will not be the last. However, she is in a very small percentile of people who will fully and intentionally harm others. Now considering, that you are tracking this new woman down, and not the other way around, I would say the chance of her being one of those people are extremely rare. Plus, given her response to you, or lack thereof, makes the risk even lower. If she would've had any intentions on applying any ill will towards you, she would not have taken so long to respond to you. She would've done so immediately."

While she spoke, Dr. Suarez jotted something down on her trusted notepad.

I could not show her that she had struck a nerve with her assessment. So instead I came at her with; "So you mean to tell me that you think she is a catch worth keeping? From everything that I told you about her?" This was music to my ears.

"Yes, judging from what you have shared with me, I think you have found a very lovely young lady. I also think that she may be somewhat vulnerable. Maybe there is some hurt from her past which would explain her hesitance towards you. However, I think that if you continue to pursue her as smoothly as you are, that she will come around sooner than later."

"Okay, you say that now, but if you are wrong, it's going to be your shoulder that I will be in here crying and drooling on."

"Okay Mr. Norton, that is it. Our time is up. If it comes to you needing a shoulder to lean on, I will be here for you." She told me once she stopped laughing.

"Damn, the good times are never long enough." I stood up ready to make my exit.

"See you next week."

After saying good-bye to Jenny, I left her office intending to go straight to my cell. I had something in store for Sakina's sexy lil ass. Of course, I believe the good doctor was on point. So, it was time to turn things up a notch. I was about to go on *Full Beast Mode*. Time to turn it up and show her some things. Show her why I was elite.

CHAPTER 20
SAKINA

Later That Night:

"Damn, Kina baby, this pussy, shitttt. Open your eyes and look at me baby."

Now that I've finally found you, I am coming after what is mine.

"Kina, look at me baby."

Now that I've finally found you, I am coming after what is mine.

"Aaah shiit, Kina baby, look at me baby."

And looking at him was what I tried to do, but....

Good morning beautiful. Thank you for accepting my friend request. You have me feeling like the luckiest man in the world right now. How is your morning so far?

"Damn baby, you got the best pussy."

Now that I've finally found you, I am coming after what is mine.

"Shitt Kina baby look at me, I'm about to bust. Fuckkkk. Can I bust in this pussy?"

And just like that, those set of words brought me back to reality. I reopened my eyes and stared into Lamont's eyes. They bore the same expression as always whenever he was reaching his sexual peak. And once again, staring into his eyes was a must for him. And yes, I granted him that except his other request was a no.

"No, pull out, Lamont," I demanded as I slid both of my hands in between our bodies, palming his stomach.

"Fuckkk babyyy," he groaned. I could hear the hint of frustration in his tone, but I could care less. Ejaculating inside of me was no longer an option for him.

"Pull out!" I demanded once again, and he finally oblige.

"Shittttttt."

He breathed heavily as he let loose on my sheets and rolled over onto his back.

"Lower your voice before you wake up E.J. and Kyle," I warned him before I climbed out of the bed and stood swiftly to my feet. I reached over on the foot of my bed and grabbed the satin, grey, thigh length robe I wore before our sex session began an hour earlier.

"You okay?" I heard him asked me as I tied and secured the robe's belt. I silently exhaled.

No, strangely, I was not okay. At least not the kind of okay for a woman who had just received some good dick. When it boiled down to sex and laying down the pipe, so to say, Lamont was a beast at it and after his love confession this morning in my office and finally having a sudden desire to commit and have an actual relationship with me, our love making should have escalated to another level.

Right?

However, that was not the case. Since his confession, the energy has been off for me.

Energies.

I was big on them. Energies and vibes. If they were not right, neither was I, and when I was not right then nothing was right. Like nothing at all.

But of course, I could not let Lamont know or see that. A least I chose not to. That side of me he never sees and never will. No man has, not even my children's father.

"You okay?"

I heard Lamont asked again as I headed out of my bedroom door, but I opted on ignoring him.

"Damn, now I can't bust inside of you even though I confessed I loved you and that I want us to give this relationship shit a real try," I heard him say right before I closed my bedroom door.

I shook my head and sighed. I suddenly felt irritated.

Quickly, I headed towards the bathroom. As soon as I entered the room and shut the door, I leaned against it and said a silent prayer. I was feeling anxiety like never before. I was unsure why I was experiencing such emotion. All I did know, ever since Lamont confessed all that he did to me this morning, I have not felt right and that was strange.

After three years of wanting nothing but for him to commit, the words he finally expressed should've been like music to my ears, but…. oddly, it was not.

Like why?

I closed my eyes in that moment and there it was. The answer to my question. The reason why the vibe was off with Lamont's love confession and sudden need to be committed.

The reason why I've been on edge. The reason why even though Lamont spent the whole day with me and suddenly felt the need to interact as a family and took me and my sons out to dinner, I still felt incomplete. And most of all, the reason why even during a steamy sex session, my mind was somewhere else.

On someone else....

Now that I've finally found you, I am coming after what is mine.

Quincy Norton.

The second he sent me a message on Facebook at the same time Lamont made his confession, I could not get him off my mind. I mean, couldn't get him off of my mind at all, even during the sex session with Lamont. There he was, putting in some of his best moves if I must say so myself, and strangely, Quincy's words from his letter and Facebook messenger echoed in my head repeatedly. I could not get him off my mind and the fact that I was unable to reply to his message with Lamont sitting across from me, strangely bothered me. I was in fact disturbed by it and so much so, that I have been irritable all day.

I should have been happy and on cloud nine over Lamont's sweet gestures throughout the day, but I could not help but feeling...well.... irritated. I wanted to log onto Facebook and reply to Quincy, but the opportunity never presented itself. Lamont have been by my side all day and I wanted to be happy, but....

Quincy.

He is having an effect on me and I cannot explain what was happening. And the fact that I was thinking about him during sex with Lamont was like whoah.

Why did that happen?

I was not a cheater but thinking about another man during sex with my current one felt as if I was doing just that. Cheating.

Lamont was not perfect, and we had our issues, and I still felt he has been with another woman, but me dealing with multiple men was not me at all and emotional interaction, I feel was far worse than physical. And Quincy Norton was coming at me emotionally like no man had ever done before. And... I was not opposed to it.

Shit.

I had to get it together. I was really becoming a basket case over a guy who was in prison and serving life. Yes, his story was indeed fascinating, and he appeared to be so much greater than just a convict, but the reality of it all simply was, he was incarcerated and serving life.

Yes, I needed to get it together.

Shaking my head at my own dilemma, I reopened my eyes. Letting out a sigh, I walked over to the bathtub and turned on the shower. I was still feeling a bit stressed and opted on taking a quick shower to relieve some of it as well as washing away Lamont's scent.

Thirty minutes later, I was done with a much - needed shower but I was far from relaxed. Lamont was sound asleep when I returned to my bedroom, which was of great relief to me. My nerves were still on edge and he was more than likely to get on all of them including the last one. I could not take his complaint over his sudden need to ejaculate inside of me.

Where the hell did that come from suddenly?

He was always concern with me getting pregnant and now all of a sudden, he had no issue to unload his seed inside of me. Taking a quick glance at him as I slipped on a pair of black

Calvin Klein signature tank top with the matching boy short, I made a mental note to make an appointment with my Gynecologist and get on some birth control. Although I convinced myself I could no longer conceive anymore children, I now did not want to risk any chances.

Damn.

When did my feelings for him became so torn? I loved this man for the last three years. All I have ever wanted and prayed for was for him to come correct and do right by me. Now that he was finally doing so, something was off.

Biting my bottom lip, my stress level was arising. I tore my eyes away from Lamont and quietly left my room. I quietly checked on my sons who were sound asleep before I headed towards the kitchen.

I wanted to call Malika to vent but since it was so late and well after midnight to be exact, I opted on another form of relaxation.

Opening the door to the refrigerator, I grabbed a half - filled bottle of Moscato and shut the door closed. I then reached towards a stack of paper plates on a nearby counter - top and grabbed a hold of a plate. I left the kitchen and headed straight towards my home office.

Seconds later, I was comfortably seated in my office chair. I turned on my computer desktop and as I waited for the bootup process, I reached into the desktop draw and reached for my favorite stash.

Corn Starch.

My bad habit was also a true stress releaser and I needed it tonight like a crack head needed a quick fix.

However, tonight, a couple spoons intake was not enough for me. I needed to fully indulged.

I licked my lips in anticipation as I lifted the lid to the box, retrieved the plastic spoon and poured a substantial amount of corn starch onto the paper plate. I wasted no time reaching for the bottle of water I also kept in the draw, unscrewed the top and poured some water into the powdery substance.

As soon as it formed into the perfect lump just the way I like, I utilized the plastic spoon and scooped up a chunk and placed it my mouth.

I closed my eyes momentarily and savored the taste before I swallowed. I repeated the gesture with a few more spoons. Seconds after, I popped the cork to the already opened bottle of Moscato and took it straight to the head.

Normally I would sip from a glass like a true sophisticate, but tonight I was not in that type of mood. The well put together Sakina image I always portrayed just was not in me tonight. Instead, I chose to let my anxiety take over the best of me as I downed Corn Starch and Moscato.

I could not quite explain this side of me or the other similar sides or my love for Corn Starch, but there was no real explanation. It was just a part of me, that I chose to keep hidden except from Malika. Lamont have never seen this side of me, nor my depress states and he never will. My sons father never did nor any of my exes.

All Lamont or any other man will ever see is me looking good, strong, laughing and having the time of my life.

I shook my head at the private oath I have made to myself and I silently thanked my mother. She taught me well. Not once have I ever witnessed her break down over my dad and I have learned well from her.

Letting out a sigh, I downed more Moscato and decided to give the Corn Starch a rest. Consuming too much of it mixed with the wine will not settle well with my system. Putting away any evidence of the Starch, including the paper plate in the draw, I relaxed in the office chair and focused attention towards my desktop computer.

I planned on locking myself in my office for as long as possible until these feelings I was experiencing passed. I hope Lamont remained asleep until dawn or until I pulled myself together.

Besides, this was the perfect opportunity to finally do what I have been wanting to do all day.

I logged onto my main page on Facebook and pulled up my messages. I planned on finally responding to Quincy, but my heart skipped a beat when I noticed a second message he sent from earlier today.

Wow..

He messaged me twice today. I was amazed this man was reaching out and pursuing in such a dramatic way. First, his letters, poems and now these very heartfelt messages.

With the warmest of wishes and champagne kisses.
Q.

My eyes read over his very long and descriptive second message and the final line brought on a sudden smile I could not hide. A man who had a way with words was after my own heart.

I scanned over what he wrote, and I was now more intrigued with Quincy Norton than ever. I loved the way he was opening himself to me so candidly. He was putting himself out there towards a woman he did not even know, and I really was wondering, why?

Like what was it about me besides what he has seen on my Facebook page and what he has read in my book that made him decide to go so hard with me? Or has he done this with other women he has met on Facebook?

Shaking off the thought, I chose to focus on the obvious.

His interest in me.

If it was real, only time will tell. In the meantime, I think I will entertain him.

Utilizing the computer mouse, I went ahead and gave him my own response.

Hello Quincy,

I apologize for not replying to your first message this morning. I was at work and became quite busy. First and foremost, I want to thank you for your support and interest in my books and work. As an Author who loves her craft, all readers support and interest means everything to me. So, once again I thank you. I also want to thank you for the beautiful poems you've mailed to me. I love poetry and your words are truly something. You have been so candid with expressing yourself, I'm not sure what to say nor how to respond but I just want you to know, that I'm reading and I'm paying attention. And since you are being so candid, let me admit, that I did pre - judge you when I received the first letter, but I am truly sorry. And I thank you for opening yourself to me the way you've had. I just want you to know......

I'm Listening.... I'm Paying attention.... I'm Seeing....

So.... Keep talking.... Keep Sharing.... Keep Showing......

Have A Good Night...

Sakina but you can call me Kina

Once I clicked the sent button, I felt something I haven't felt all day.

I smiled as I sat there staring at his messages…his words…

I was also searching for the green light next to his name, indicating that he was in fact online but there was none. I was secretly hoping he was in fact online. I felt the sudden urge to talk to him, like engage in a real conversation. I figured talking on the phone was not possible due to his situation, but I was willing to settle for Facebook messenger.

Letting out a sigh, I finally logged off Facebook and shut down my computer. I decided to call it a night as I stood, still holding the bottle of Moscato. Thinking about Lamont in my bed, probed my desire to take it with me.

As I made my way back to my bedroom, I finally understood what I have been feeling all day.

I was feeling torn… because I was interested in Quincy Norton.

But…Was it right? Was it wrong? It was definitely unrealistic because he was serving life and there was no future with an incarcerated inmate serving life, but was it wrong to wonder? To daydream? Was he wrong for me? We were from two different worlds, but could he be the man of my dreams?

The Right Kind Of Wrong For Me?

CHAPTER 21
QUINCY

Earlier That Day:

"Q!" I was crossing the yard just leaving Dr. Suarez' office and beelining straight to my cell. I heard whoever was calling me, but I had plans and was not trying to have these plans interrupted.

"Q! Brah, check it out."

Knowing that whoever was calling me was unavoidable, I cut my eyes to the right to see Tae Tae beelining towards my direction. He looked like he had something serious on his mind, so I made my way towards him.

"What's up Ridah?" I asked once we finally met.

"Rogue where you been? A nigga been looking for you all over the place."

"It's Monday Ridah. Niggas know I meet with my therapist on Mondays. Why? What's up? "I asked him, wondering what was so urgent.

"Rogue it went down earlier. You know that kid that was trynna say that he was Village Mobb. Turned out his family was from the Gardens."

"You mean that West Indies kid. The one that just started in the kitchen? I think his name is Sushi or something like that." I knew it was him just as well as I had a good idea about what I was about to hear.

"Yeah that's him. They just brought him out on the gurney looking bad. Word is that after Too Sweet raped him, he beat the boy nearly to death. Niggas is feeling some kind of way. JuJu already told everybody that when the faggott comes out of the kitchen he's on him. Chuck said he's on him too and I'm not even about to lie, I'm going to be there stumping the shit out of that faggott."

I could see in Tae Tae eyes that he was ready to get it popping, but I had to step in and regulate.

"Naw Rogue, that's what y'all not gonna do. Go and tell them niggas I said that's exactly what the fuck these pigs want us to do. We're not about to be out here looking like clowns for nobody. What we gonna do is do shit the right way and make an example out of this booty bandit mothafucka. Tell them we gonna bang this mothafucka out tomorrow. Let Ju ju know that I'ma put in the work myself with him as my back up. So, tell him to make sure that he got his banger with him. Hurry up and go tell them niggas before they fuck up my plans."

"Right big homie. You got it Rogue." Tae Tae responded before taking off across the yard to tell them fools what my orders were.

Every time I turn around it's something. Truth be told though, I knew this was going to happen. I guess I was just hoping that things would happen way later, not now. Niggas had too much going on at the moment, but things never work out the way you want. but oh well, I have already warned the scavenger. He did not take heed, so now he'll pay for it. I was not about to let this business with Too Sweet alter or mess up my plans though. It's bad enough that if I get caught, I'm going to sit in the hole for at least eight months. Then, I would mess up any chance that a nigga may have at reeling Sakina in.

I could not be thinking about consequences and shit. It's okay to dream about paradise but right now I was living in the jungle. That meant I had to play by the rules of the jungle. In this jungle if you touch one of mine the devil was coming.

As I walked back to my building, I thought about the irony of it all. When I first came to prison, I was just a regular homeboy. I didn't have any street cred, never made a name for myself. I was essentially a square. Now, I have put in enough work behind these walls for my name to be both known and respected. I used strategical thinking and a lot of violence to rise through the ranks. Now I call the shots for the "Bay Carr". Some dudes look up to me for guidance, teaching and insurance that they will make it up out of here and learn from me how to make a name for themselves.

I was stopped a couple of more times before I made it to my cell to see if I had heard the news. In reality they were just temperature checking trying to see what I was going to do about what was done. I shot them suckas some fake words and kept it moving.

When I got to my cell, I washed my hands and face. I then sat on my bunk and thought about what Dr. Suarez said. Is it possible that Monique's betrayal birthed some sort of subconscious fear inside of me that would prevent me from pursuing a healthy relationship with Sakina? Was I really chasing her, only because in reality, I could not fully have her? Would I seriously want her if I was home and had full access to her?

I mean, I didn't see that as being possible, not the way I've been chasing this woman. I wanted her, fully wanted her. She represented what I was trying to regain my freedom and come home to.

New Beginnings.

Yeah, Dr. Suarez had a good theory, but she was wrong. Monique's betrayal was still hurtful, but it was not consuming me or what I was still capable of.

Which was love again.

Now, it was time to kick things into gear. I went to my tuck spot and grabbed my phone. Catching myself because I was slipping not putting safety and security first. I walked to the front of the cell and grabbed my metal razor and a toothbrush then jammed them into the corner of the door locking it. Then I pulled my curtain and laid on my bunk. I hopped on Google and did my thang. It did not take long before I found an address and a phone number for Sakina's Read and Things.

The next thing I did was locate a florist out her way. One that could fulfill any unique request. Once I found that right florist, I did my *Dougie* and I do mean my *Dougie*. Where I come from, we don't do our thang, we do our *Dougie*. I ordered Twenty dozen long stem freshly cropped roses. Five dozen red, five dozen yellow, five dozen blue, five dozen white and five dozen fire and ice roses. I also made sure that each dozen roses were accompanied by a cute little Teddy Bear. Fuck being nice, I wanted to make sure that I was getting her full attention. On the card, I had them write the following:

The red roses are because blood is our life source and energy along with our essence is in our blood. The yellow

roses are because I can sense and feel your purity. The blue roses because you drifted into my life riding the clouds on the wind. The fire and ice are for the passion that I can feel burning beneath the surface. The five dozen pink roses are because you are my Goddess and delicate. More importantly to me, you are royalty and I will always treat you like such.

With the warmest of wishes and champagne kisses.

Q.

That signature line would become my newest saying.

Yeah, I know I was going all out for a woman that I may never get to meet, but I could not help it. It was as if some kind of powerful force was drawing me to this woman and causing me to act out what came naturally. Just by viewing her pictures on her Facebook page, I could tell she was a woman of class and sophistication, so I was determined to treat her like such. After completing the order and confirmed delivery for tomorrow morning, I felt satisfied with the move I just made.

It was after one in the morning and I could not get any sleep. Finally deciding to check my messages, I grabbed my cell phone in my secret hideaway spot and logged onto Facebook. The red light on the messenger icon let me know I had messages. I clicked on it and there it was. Messages from Sakina.

I sat and stared at the inbox for a while. Excitement was running through my veins like wild mustangs. Deep down, I felt she would respond but I did not know if I was ready for it.

"Well here goes nothing."

I said to myself as I clicked on her name to open the message. I read it twice with a smile on my face.

I'm Listening.... I'm Paying attention.... I'm Seeing....

So.... Keep Talking.... Keep Sharing.... Keep Showing......

Have A Good Night...

Sakina but you can call me Kina

The last two lines of her message had me smiling like the folks on the Colgate commercial.

So... Keep Talking... Keep Sharing... Keep Showing...

Have A Good Night...

Sakina but you can call me Kina

Shittt. She had no idea. I intended on doing just that and much more.

Deciding to reply to her message, I did not even think about my words, I just let them flow:

My beautiful and intelligent Kina, First and foremost, thanks for reaching out and letting me know that I am noticed, it means a lot to me. However, if I may, I do feel the need to clarify my interest and intentions. You are an outstanding authoress and I will always support your career no matter what, because I truly enjoy your work. However, my interest is a completely different story. I have a strong desire for you. My letters are to appeal to your intellect, while my poetry will hopefully reach your heart. Small gestures like sending you flowers are just to let you know that I notice your worth. Sakina listen, as beautiful as you are, I know that you have someone in your life. It would be a crime if you didn't. I'm simply telling you that whoever it is they are completely wrong for you. I know because they are not me. And I am willing to go the distance to show this to you. You just have to give me the opportunity. Something way deeper than my heart is telling me that you are meant to be my Queen. I can only imagine how that sounds coming from a convict trust me I do.

Sometimes you wish upon a star and other times your life is guided by that wish. I've never wished for anything in my life but happiness. Even after my incarceration I prayed and wished for happiness. From the bottom of my soul I know God finally answered my prayers by sending me you. I declare my one-hundred percent interest in you and if you find yourself asking could that be possible, I simply tell you, if you can believe in love at first sight you can believe in this.

Boy I was on a roll, really popping my collar. I know I was laying it on thick, but my gut feeling was telling me that this woman was more than worth it.

Clicking on the blue arrow in the inbox, I sent the message. Strangely, I felt so good with what I've done, that I was able to fall asleep after all. With a satisfied smile on my face, I logged off Facebook, hid my phone in the private spot and closed my eyes with Kina on my mind.

CHAPTER 22
SAKINA

It was Tuesday morning and once again I was exhausted, except this time the exhaustion I felt was from a whole different reason. I licked my lips and slightly smirked at the thought of the late - night freaky session with Lamont. After I returned to my bedroom and climbed into bed last night, he was wide awake. He tried to strike up a conversation, but I was not in the mood to talk.

Between thoughts of Quincy still heavily on my mind and exhaustion taking over, I did not want to be bothered. Really, my wish was for him to retire back to his own house, but I did not want to be rude with such request. So, instead, I opted on falling asleep. For a few moments, the message appeared to be cleared to Lamont. After climbing into bed, silence filled the space between us, that was until I felt his hand on my thigh. I was on the verge of cursing him out until I felt his hand on the boy shorts, I sported. His initiative game was strong, as he pulled them down with finesse. I started to protest as I grabbed a hold of his hand but all that failed when I felt his index finger on my clitoris.

And when he inserted it in, fingering my center, that was all she wrote. His finger game was something else if I must say so myself. In fact, his sex game in all was on the A plus level for sure. From foreplay, to coochie licking, to his dick game, he was on point... So much on point, that round two of our sex-session took place with no thoughts of Quincy crossing my mental.

Lamont took his dick game to a whole other level and I can honestly say I fell asleep, not only satisfied but actually feeling good about him.

But then, morning came, and the sun rised. I opened my eyes at six a.m, looked over to his side of the bed and he was gone. He left no note, no form of goodbye or nothing romantic so to say. I shook my head disappointed. I hated when he did that. His romance skills were limited, unlike his sex game.

I shook my head then confused. There I was, pissed that he showed no kind of romantic gesture, but yesterday I was irritated that he was showing initiative towards me and developing a real relationship.

I shook my head once again and chuckling at the fact that I did not know what the hell I wanted. I pushed my thoughts from earlier that morning to the back of my mental as I focused on my current workload. My desk was bombarded with paperwork consisting of new orders I needed to place from customers and there was no room for exhaustion on my part or anytime for daydreaming.

I let out a sigh as I opted on getting to work when the bell to the store's door chimed, alerting that someone had entered. As soon as I looked up, my eyes landed on a delivery man carrying what appeared to be a bouquet of flowers.

What the hell?

"I have a delivery for a Miss Sakina Michelle," he let me know as he walked over to my desk.

"Uuhm, I'm Sakina Michelle."

"Ok hello, these are for you and I just need you to sign here."

As he placed the bouquet onto my desk, I noticed they were a huge amount of beautiful, multiple colored roses.

"Wow, these are for me?" I just had to clarify because, clearly there must be some mistake. Who would have all these roses delivered to me? Besides the crusage I was given by my prom date back in high school, I've never received any form of flowers from a man before. And I just know Lamont didn't send these. I mean, there could be no way. This gesture was not in him.

"Yes, ma'am," the delivery replied, and I groaned in a partial amused tone.

"Uuugh, please don't call me ma'am. You have me feeling so old."

"Shoot, with all due respect, there's nothing old about you," he responded as he looked over at me with what I could tell was an almost lustful expression. And I could not help but smirk. Unbelievable that he was flirting while delivering flowers to me.

Shaking my head at the nerve of men, despite the fact I was a bit flattered, I reached over for the clipboard he held in his hand and proceeded to sign my name on the delivery paper. After handing the clipboard back to him, he just had to sneak one more glance in my direction and had the nerve to wink at me.

"And there are more of these roses I need to deliver to you. I have a partner bringing some in and I will get the rest."

I frowned at his admission as I stared at him.

"More roses?"

"Uuuh, yeah, twenty dozen to be exact," he shouted out

right before he left out. And a few moments later, he returned along with another deliver guy, carrying more beautiful, multi-colored roses.

"And we have more," the first delivery guy let me know right after I pointed towards a Rectangle shaped table, positioned near my office desk.

"Wow," I said in awe as I stood and walked over to the table. I studied the roses and shook my head.

"I know Lamont did not send these. He does not have it in him to do all this."

Just as the words left my mouth, both delivery guys, indeed, came in with more roses.

"And this last dozen has a card attached to it," the first one let me know as he handed me a dozen of red roses.

"Enjoy and whoever sent all those roses must think you are something special and I don't blame him at all," he let me know and had the nerve to wink at me before he and his partner exit my office.

After they shut the door behind him, I wasted no time, retrieving a small white envelope inserted in the center of the well put together roses. I slipped my index finger inside and pulled out a small card.

Suddenly my heart began to skip a beat as my eyes averted to the bottom of the card.

Damn…

Quincy..

And he striked again…. He was bold with it I must say.

And his bold ways were sexy as hell.

I licked my lips in anticipation as my eyes scrolled up to the rest of the literature on the card.

The red roses are because blood is our life source and

energy along with our essence is in our blood. The yellow roses are because I can sense and feel your purity. The blue roses because you drifted into my life riding the clouds on the wind. The fire and ice are for the passion that I can feel burning beneath the surface. The five dozen pink roses are because you are my Princess and delicate. More importantly to me you are royalty and I will always treat you like such.

Oh, double damn.

The roses had my heart racing, but what he wrote in the card, touched it in a different way. I found my eyes getting moist and before I knew it, tears formed in them and streamed down my cheeks.

Never had a man expressed such an intimate, sweet and romantic gesture towards me before.

No longer able to hold my composure, I stood up and rushed over to my store's door and changed the **Now Open** sign to; **Will be back in Fifteen minutes.**

I needed some time to get myself together. I was losing my cool over roses and a card with the most creative set of words I have ever read, and I did not like it.

Damn you Quincy Norton.

An Hour Later:

"Thank you for your order. You will receive an email once your order ships. You have a great day."

Once I ended the call with another satisfied customer, I let out a sigh of relief. Within the past Forty - five minutes, I was bombarded with calls from customers placing countless orders. I was a bit overwhelmed with the other set of orders from earlier, but I was not complaining because business was booming and I was genuinely thankful.

Deciding to have a moment of relaxation before I enter the new orders in my computer system, I utilized the computer mouse and logged onto Facebook. At first, I attempted to sign into my Author's page, but something directed me towards my personal page first.

Seconds later I was on my page and there it was….

Messages from Quincy Norton…

Damn. He was playing no games. It was bad enough he was invading my mental, but he was now determined to invade my peace.

But…. In a good way.

Bracing myself, since I was still recovering from the surprise of the rose's delivery, I clicked on the messenger icon and once again, my heart skipped a beat.

There was another message from Quincy and dammit it was a long one. But despite that fact, I took to reading with a certain excitement coveting my very being.

Seconds later…

The tears were formed again in my eyes after reading what he wrote, and the last few lines were like whoah…

Even after my incarceration I prayed and wished for happiness. From the bottom of my soul I know God finally answered my prayers by sending me you. I declare my one-

hundred percent interest in you and if you find yourself asking could that be possible, I simply tell you, if you can believe in love at first sight you can believe in this.

"Oh God."

I was stunned and was not sure what to feel. This man... he was like.. coming full force in a way I have never been come for before by any man.

And suddenly, I felt scared. His pursuance was new territory for me, and I did not like the way it was making me feel.

Vunerable and...

Just as I was trying to sort out my feelings, my office phone rung.

Relieved that another customer's call would allow a much - needed distraction, I instantly answered the call.

"Sakina's Reads and Things, Sakina speaking how may I assist you today?"

"Good evening my sistah, I was wondering do you ship books out of state?"

A male's voice on the other end of the phone line spoke.

"Sure, what state?"

"California, my queen. California State Prison Solano to be exact."

And with that response, I was on the verge of passing out.

Could it be?

Hell no.

"I'm ready to order, queen, I don't have much time on the phone. So, can you ship to me or not? I need all of Sakina Michelle's book shipped, like today if that's possible."

Oh God... It's.... HIM.

CHAPTER 23
QUINCY

Ten Minutes Prior:

It was about eight a.m. and I barely slept a wink. I have been up since six a.m. thinking about the mission I had to complete for the day. I had to convert to beast mode in order to carry it out successfully and I planned on doing just that, but I could not stop thinking about Kina. I wondered if she received the roses yet. I started to hop on Facebook and message her but that was not enough for me right now.

Like I said, I could not stop thinking about her and since I was on a roll to get her full attention, I decided to take things a step further.

Reaching for my phone in my hideaway spot, I went on and googled the number to her bookstore and wrote the number down on the same piece of paper I had the address to her shop written. I walked over to the door of my cell and double checked on security. The last thing that I needed was to get caught slipping. Climbing back on my bunk, I looked at the piece of paper again.

I took two deep breaths in attempts to calm my nerves and relaxed my mind. With my eyes closed, I willed my nerves to calm down as much as possible. I thought about her beautiful face, her soft welcoming eyes, and the seductive lips on her face that was a perfect mold.

Before I realized what I have done, the phone was already up to my ear ringing. I don't know why I was nervous, but I was.

"Sakina's Reads and Things, Kina speaking, how may I assist you today?"

I could not help but smile at the sound of her voice. It was angelic.

Finding my voice, I answered her.

"Good evening my sistah, I was wondering do you ship books out of state?"

I was tempted to let her know right then and there that it was me, the man who cannot seem to stop thinking about her and was coming after her no matter what, but I had to stay on point and stick to the script.

"Sure, what state?"

She responded and I decided to toy with her a bit.

"California, my queen. California State Prison Solano to be exact."

There was silence and I smiled. The urge to laugh was strong but I held it in. She knew it was me and I felt it.

"I'm ready to order, queen, I don't have much time on the phone. So, can you ship to me or not? I need all of Sakina Michelle's book shipped, like today if that's possible."

I said to her, breaking the silence.

"I've recently just begun following the author that your store is named after. I've read a couple of her books already and I think she is phenomenal. I'm sorry I don't have my list near me, I apologize for not being ready."

There was more silence and I wanted to laugh, but again I had to keep my composure.

"Queen, are you still there?"

I asked, but I could tell by her breathing that she was in fact still there.

"Uhhm, I'm sorry, yes, I am still here and yes, Sakina is a very strong author and all of her books are great reads. You said you want all of her books shipped?" She asked me warmly making me forget all about not being prepared. I could tell she knew it was me, but she was choosing to play the professional role. And she probably was in shock and in awe of how strong I was coming, and I understood. I decided to play the professional role with her.

"Yes, Queen, I do," I responded.

"Uhhm, okay that's fine, except, I will have to split the orders, since Author Kina has eleven books in total, and from my understanding, most prisons do not allow more than five at a time, per month."

I was impressed with her obvious intelligence and I was also feeling kind of lost. I felt like a shepherd without a sheep. A captain without a boat. I wanted to engage in a personal conversation with her so bad, but I knew once I begun, I would not be able to stop and my time was limited. So instead, I had to keep it professional between us.

"And you're right my sistah and this particular prison does enforce that rule as well," I let her know and added, "So with that said, you can go ahead and ship five of the books to me right away and next month you can do the other five and the following month, you can ship out that one," I instructed her.

"Oh okay, that is great. Do you know which five you would like shipped first?"

She asked me and I honestly did not know. I noticed her catalog on her Facebook page, but I couldn't remember all of the titles. And it really did not matter which five I received first. I owned five of them already, but I did not care. I would buy all of her books a thousand times and read them repeatedly. I was impressed by this woman, so purchasing any of her books was nothing to me. The urge to talk to her more was still strong so I decided to wrap this call before I risked being caught. And while I wrapped up the call, I wanted to mess with her mind a little more and give her something to think about.

"Sistah, I am risking being locked up for an additional four months because I am talking to you on a cell phone that cost me $2,000 to purchase. Every second that I spend talking to you, I run the risk of one of the guards walking up and busting me. Considering that I am calling you from inside one of California's Maximum Facility Prisons, I have no time to break down any titles, so just please send me any five of the beautiful Author Sakina Michelle's titles. Now can I please complete my order?"

Once I spoke those words to her, there was more silence on her end. I smiled because I knew I had her where I wanted her. And it would not be this call, but I knew the next time I called her and yes, there would be a next time, that I would directly reveal myself to her and she will do the same.

"Sistah, are you still there?"

"I'm sorry, yes, I am still here. I was pulling up all of Sakina Michelle's titles to place your order."

I smiled again, because she was quick with the saves. She

THE RIGHT KIND OF WRONG

appeared so in control and very well put together. I was also impressed with her professionalism. I could tell she was hot and bothered on the other end of the phone line, but she was determined not to show or allow me to see that. I was impressed, but I was more curious about her. She almost seemed too in control, like it was a façade.

But I was going to find out, soon enough.

"Okay, so I will choose the five I personally think you should start out with and for these five books, plus shipping and handling, it would be a total of $57.99. How would you like to pay for this today?"

"I'll be using a secured debit card, but please sistah, I need these books in my possession ASAP, so can you please apply a next day shipping and handling fee? Now, here is my card info."

I did not even give her a chance to respond. I gave her my name and card information and secured the transaction she asked me for the shipping information.

"Quincy Norton. California State Prison Solano."

I heard her take a deep breath at the sound of my name. That to me confirmed she knew it was me for sure.

"Um excuse......." She said and let it trail off.

"Yes, can I help you sistah?"

"Never mind it's okay."

Damn we were so close, but so fucking far away. I wanted to talk to her. To tell her... many things.

"Okay, so your delivery is scheduled to arrive tomorrow,"," she confirmed delivery.

I wanted her to say more. I needed to keep hearing her voice. Instead, we said our goodbyes and the phone call ended. With that out of the way, it was time for me to deal with this situation with Too Sweet.

Although I did not want to do it, I knew I had to put sweet Sakina out of my mind. Yes, her voice had my wishing that I was flying first class on my way to Rahway, New Jersey. Instead, the reality of this jungle summoned me, and I had no choice but to answer.

I first said several prayers, asking the Lord to forgive me for my intended sins and to protect me along my journey through the valley of the shadow of death. More importantly, I asked him for my safe passage through. I called on God because that was always who I called on when I did not have the answers or the ability to get myself through whatever I was facing. I called on God because I didn't want to get caught and end up stuck in the body of the beast. Most importantly, I called on God so that he would know that I knew that he had the final say in all matters.

By the time I was finished with my prayers, Casanova was gone and in his place was a Goon! My first order of business was getting to the money. The money was essential to my entire operation. To my freedom and exit out of this place.

J was insulted that I did not include him in the Gangsta shit that I had planned. It took me a while to get him to see the bigger picture. A Captain's job was to keep the ship going no matter what. That is exactly what I was doing.

Once I had the lil homie situated, I placed calls to the safe houses and runners to make sure that they were straight. When that was done, I called JuJu.

"Wh-what's up big homie?" He asked after the third ring. JuJu's been stuttering all his life and most niggas knew not to comment on it.

"You sure you're ready for this?" Now was not the time for

pleasantries. I needed to know that my young Ridah's were ready.

"I wouldn't sign up for the job if I was not ready." His voice was a little quipped, but I shook it off. After all, I just got done questioning his Gangsta.

"Aight look, we gonna have the lil homies bust that distraction thang and we going in. All I'ma need you to do lil homie is keep the lane open so that I can rise back out of that bitch." A dude cannot be too trusting on these phones. Mess around and say the wrong thing at the right time and be facing another life sentence. Code talking is a must.

"Ss-Shits e-easy as pie b-big homie."

"I'll see you at first get down." I replied, telling him that I would see him at first yard release.

"Aight bet!" He did not wait for a response. He just hung up.

The plan was very basic in design but if carried out the right way it was very effective. A few of the lil homies were going to cause a distraction by starting a fight on the opposite side of the yard. Once all the police responded to that side of the yard and everyone's attention was over there, then it was going down. I was going to do my thang and teach that sick fuck a lesson. JuJu was to make sure that I got away from any police who may be straggling and hanging behind. He also was to make sure that Too Sweet did not have any allies that I did not know about, creeping up on me while I was creeping up on him. Everything was set and I was more than ready. I hated predators with a real passion. Why, because they preyed on the weak and I did not like that shit.

I laid back on my bunk and thought about my phone call with Sakina instead of continuing to dwell on the bullshit. The thoughts of her not only calmed and relaxed my nerves but also put a smile on my face. While on the phone with her, I wanted desperately to ask her if she enjoyed the flowers, but as I stated before, I needed to play it cool.

On impulse, I picked my phone back up and sent her a message on my instant messenger:

I hope you enjoyed your flowers. Though their beauty cannot match your

own and their splendor dulls next to you, I still wanted to send you something beautiful just because today is a beautiful day. With warmest of wishes and champagne kisses.

Q.

I looked at her cover photo for a little while longer before forcing myself to put the phone away. But right before that, I realized I left this message on her Author's page, so I decided to go on over to her personal page where I normally messaged her. I was now friends with her on both of her pages and after sending her the same message on there, I logged off.

The moment I disconnected from the internet, the phone beeped, letting me know that I had a voicemail. I pulled up my voicemail and listened:

"Quincy its Sheldon. I'm flying out to see you tomorrow morning. Today is the 15th of May, so I'll see you on the 16th. I have some news that I think you will be happy to hear."

Just like that the voicemail ended. I just sat there for a moment wondering what was up. For him to say that he had some news that he thinks I would like to hear meant that he had some good news for a dude. Could it be possible? After all these years? Was this the phone call that I had been waiting on? It was premature to get my hopes up, so I did not. Nevertheless, the mere possibility of it picked my spirits up.

I put my phone back in my tuck spot and just laid there lost in my head. I must've laid there for hours. My mind going back and forth from Too Sweet and what needed to be done to the information that my lawyer just hit me with. Endless scenarios and questions started to flow through my mind. What if I got caught? Was I sure that I was doing what I wanted to do and not what others were expected me to do? If I killed him tomorrow and got caught, I was for sure going to cement myself behind these walls.

I was putting too much thought into it. What's meant to be, will be, period! Why worry about tomorrow, tomorrow will take care of itself. With that thought, I finally dozed off.

The next morning, I arose with a clear mind and a clear conscious. It was a beautiful day. I'm talking sunny with clear skies with a gentle breeze bringing nice crisp air. It was one of them days when everybody came out to the yard.

Breakfast time flew by without incident. Before long it was yard release and I was walking across the yard to our area. It was game time baby all gas no breaks! When I got to the area I greeted the fellas with some of that G-luv.

"Sup Big brah? How you wanna handle this bitch ass nigga?" Tae Tae asked as we embraced.

"We gone wake his mothafiucking game up!!! That's what the fuck we gone do." I spoke loud enough for all the homies to hear.

I felt a pair of eyes on me, but I knew that was only JuJu somewhere in the cuts playing his position. I laid down on the ground feigning interest in the fight like everyone else. I was only two feet behind Too Sweet. I made one last security sweep with my eyes. Confident that I was cool and no-one was watching, I slipped my knife out from under my jacket. I could feel my heart thumping away inside my chest like a set of African Bongo Drums. Time was of the essence and it felt like mine was running out. The gun tower had begun shooting the little homie with four - inch rubber bullets. A dude could only take so many of them before getting down.

I could taste revenge on my tongue. I said another prayer, took a deep breath and in one swift move I was on my prey. My right hand wrapped around him and covered his mouth. This way he couldn't yell out. I brought my knife up through his back on the left side of his body. He was trying to wiggle free but it was useless. I brought the knife around and stabbed him four more time in front of his torso. His struggles subsided.

After taking the knife out of his body for the last time, I moved over a few feet and shoved the knife as far down into the grass as I could. Once that was done, I began maneuvering my body backwards getting out of the area as fast as I could without drawing any attention to me. I paused momentarily to take off the extra sweats and sweater that I had on, then I continued moving away.

"Q, you's a smooth nigga." I looked to my left side and Jeff was looking at me. He was à cat from Richmond. Jeff was known on the yard as a solid brotha, but when it came to murder, wasn't no telling how niggas would get down. I ignored the comment and just gave him a head nod.

We were on the ground waiting for the police to do their thing for about an hour and a half. The police found Too Sweet and all hell broke out. They got to shouting orders, picking out random people in the area to fuck with. I was out of range so I didn't get bothered. Back in the cell I was thanking God, Moses and some more people for me getting away. I wasn't tripping off of any of the cameras because we were in a blind spot. After washing myself thoroughly I changed my clothes and grabbed my cell phone. I had to check to see what the ramifications of our actions were. Before handling my business, my emotions had me checking my Facebook page to see if Sakina had reached out to me or not. To my disappointment she have not. I shook my head at myself. This woman had me in my feelings and that was the last thing I needed. I had to stay focus while I struggled to survive in this nightmare, I currently called life, but the beautiful Sakina was making it damn hard.

CHAPTER 24
SAKINA

"That nigga is serious!"

"Uugh, can you stop using that word?"

"No Miss Bougie, I can't!"

I laughed and shook my head at Malika. I was currently speaking to her on my office phone and like always, she was her usual loud and dramatic self. I was touching base with her on what has occurred in my life within the last twenty-four hours. With our busy lives during the week, we don't get to see nor speak to each other much which was the reason why we have our weekly girl's night out on Friday nights. But with what has taken place in the last twenty-four hours, Friday night of girl talk could not wait.

I gave her the tea and it was a hot one.

"Like I said that nigga is serious! He had over twenty dozen roses delivered to you and then he called you!"

Malika was laughing non-stop and I just chuckled at her dramatics. She found Quincy's boldness hilarious, while I was experiencing a totally different feeling.

"Is it crazy I'm turned on by his gestures? The man is incarcerated and serving life for God sake. Is it crazy that I'm turned on and wished he wasn't incarcerated? No man has ever gone all out like this to get my attention and I swear I'm intrigued like I've never been before. Am I crazy?"

My admission and questions instantly caused Malika's laughter to cease. There was a moment of silence before she finally spoke.

"Nah, bestie, you're not crazy at all," she replied in a sudden serious tone that was rare for her. Malika was forever joking and clowning but when she grew serious, it was deep, and listening was a must.

"A man doing everything he is doing and coming after you the way he has, is what you deserve and then some and you feeling moved by it is not crazy. When you have a man, who moves the way a real man does, a real woman like you can't help but take noticed. It's what you always wanted and no one else deserves it more than you."

I smiled at her words. Only Malika can give me the truth.

"And if you're feeling interested in this man, no need to feel ashamed because he's locked up. Look at me. When Shawn was sentenced to ten years, my whole family talked their shit and told me to leave him alone and that his life was over. But my heart told me some different shit and I'm glad I listened to it instead of their assess. Shawn is everything that I knew I would never find in another nigga, so when my heart told me to wait for him and ride with him during his bid, I listened and now look at us. Married and running a mini empire together and all my family members that told me to leave him alone are the same ones who are always calling and begging for money and smiling all in his face. My man is the truth and he turned out to be worth the wait."

"Yes, you and Shawn are a true success story."

"Yes, we are, but back to you. I think I like this nigga Q, but we need to know if he's for real," Malika said, and my curiosity was piqued by her words.

"What do you mean?"

"I mean, these prison niggas be on game. Sometimes, they look for anyone to hold them down, so they throw all type of smooth talk and run game. We need to find out if he's genuinely interested in you or if he's trying to do just that, run game," Malika admitted and once again, my initial doubt of him returned.

Is he for real? Or is he running game?

More feelings of doubts crept in as questions crossed my mental.

"Okay, so how are we supposed to do that?"

Silence filled the phone line once again until Malika spoke and expressed herself like only Malika could.

"Message his ass and tell him Thank you for the roses and even though you enjoyed them, tell him not to ever do no shit like that again or call you because it was inappropriate and matter of factly, you have a man, so it's double inappropriate."

"Wait, what?"

I took the phone away from my ear and looked at it with a confused expression. Some folks often questioned Malika's sanity including me. I shook my head and chuckled at my own thought as I placed the phone back to my ear.

"Yeah, you heard me. It's called testing of the will. When a man, a person is genuine with their intentions, nothing you say or do will stop them from going after what they really want."

I sighed and as much as I hated to admit it, she made sense. But then again....

"Okayyy, but what if he is really sincere but decides to respect my wishes. What if he respects that I do have a man in my life," I challenged her, but of course, she challenged back like only she can.

"Heifer, are you crazy? Is this nigga moving like he cares if you have a nigga or not?"

I just had to laugh at her question.

"Yes, he's bold, isn't he?"

"Yeah he is and you like that shit," she pointed out and I grinned.

"Yes," I admitted.

"Okay, well then before of whatever it is that's taking place go any further, let's test Mr. Quincy Norton. Obviously, he wants your bougie ass and he's not letting a prison life sentence stand in his way, so let's see if your protest and rejection will."

I laughed out loud at Malika's jab towards me.

"Whatever, I'm not bougie."

"Uuuh, yeah, you are."

I laughed again as I used my hand and placed it on my computer mouse.

"Now let's go. Get on Facebook and message his ass."

"I'm way ahead of you," I let her know as I logged onto Facebook. I was logged onto my Author's page and went straight to the messenger's box. I normally message Quincy from my other page but he and I were also friends from this page as well.

As soon as I clicked on messenger, a smile formed on my face.

Quincy's message asking if I enjoyed the roses brought it on.

Damn.

"Uuugh, are you typing what I told you to say?" Malika asked in a demanding tone.

"Uuuhm, wait. Are you sure this is a good idea? He messaged asking if I enjoyed the roses," I informed her and went to read the rest of Quincy's short but sweet message.

"Awww, that' sweet, but focus! Now message his ass what I told you to say. Let's see how real Mr. Cali is."

I couldn't help but laugh at Malika again.

"I swear."

"Yeah, yeah. Now type." Malika's laughter matched mine as I proceed to follow her orders.

A part of me was nervous. What if Malika was right and he was all about games?

I sighed as I went on to messaged Quincy with as bluntness as I can muster. I tried to convince myself that if he was in fact a fraud, that it was all for the best. I mean he was serving life. Suddenly I felt foolish for growing excited over a man who was spending the rest of his life behind bars.

Using my current feeling as motivation, I typed the message to Quincy.

Hello Quincy,

Yes, I did receive the roses and the messages attached to each color. They are beautiful and your gesture was sweet, and I thank you very much, but such move was also inappropriate. Although I appreciate your support of me as an Author, I think you should refrain from sending anymore flowers and messaging me. Please make this your last message to me and it will be vice versa on my part. As I stated, it is inappropriate

and unprofessional on my part to interact with a customer. And, with all due respect, I am involved with someone and he would not be too pleased of you having roses delivered to me. Thank you for the gesture once again and I wish you well.

As soon as I completed my words, I wasted no time, sending off the message.

"I did it. Uuugh, I feel torn again. Maybe this is for the best. I mean, Lamont and I are trying to work it out."

"Uuuugh, please don't get me started on his ass. I don't trust him all of a sudden wants to be booed up but I'm going to mind my business. Now back to Quincy."

"What about him?" I laughed as I stared at the sent message. Part of me felt the need to unsend it. If he did respect my wishes, then it would prove Malika correct and it would be the end of his pursuance.

Strangely, that reality made me feel some type of way.

"But uhhm, on the real," Malika's voice broke into my thoughts.

"What did ole boy sound like when he called you?"

Her question caused me to grin suddenly as I remembered the sound of Quincy's baritone voice.

"Let's just say, it's a good thing I have my own business with change of necessities here because after speaking with him, I had to change my underwear."

"And I know that's mothafucking right!"

Malika, I swear.

CHAPTER 25
QUINCY

Three Days Later:

I cannot even lie, I had butterflies in my stomach the entire route to the center complex. I did not want to get my hopes up for nothing, but I could only picture the possibilities if this was the day that I have been waiting on. I silently said a prayer as I crossed the field. I asked God to be with me and give me the strength to accept whatever fate he lays out before me today. I took a couple of deep breaths before stepping to the door.

One of the lieutenants opened the door, checked my I.D. and then let me in. He led me down a hallway on the right side where I could see what I believe were a row of offices that belonged to administration. I knew that I was in here to see my lawyer but that didn't stop me from still feeling a little uneasy. Something about being around all of the brass made me feel like that. The brass were the lieutenants and captains and higher administration.

We stopped in front of a closed door and he knocked gently on it. When the voice on the other side responded, the lieutenant opened the door. Seated behind a standard steal desk-like table was my attorney Sheldon.

He sat with a stoic expression on his face making it hard to read him. I stepped inside the room giving him eye contact. Neither of us spoke a word until the lieutenant walked out of the room. When he left, I finally took a seat directly across from my attorney. Inside I was a nervous wreck but outside I had my poker face on.

"Quincy how are you doing today? " His face broke into a nice smile which melted away some of my uneasiness.

"Sheldon, you know me. I'm just trying to keep my head above water while I focus on getting through another day.".

"Well hopefully my news will help you out a little." He reached down for his briefcase.

"I hope so. Cause I know you didn't fly all the way out here for nothing". I said half-jokingly trying to smooth the rest of the uneasiness out my composure.

He sat his briefcase on the table and searched for a file. Once he found it, he pulled it out with all the theatrics. I could not help but think how he made a damn good trial attorney. I sat back and said a prayer, thinking to myself that I'd said more prayers lately than I had most of my adult life.

"Quincy I'm going to get to the point Rogue. . . " I forgot to mention that Sheldon, a.k.a lil E was from East Palo Alto as well.

"I flew out here because I have good news for you, and I wanted to give you the news in person." He opened the folder and sat back.

I let out a deep breath that I did not even know that I was holding.

"That's the kind of news that a nigga has been waiting to hear." I was excited.

"Last year a senator by the name of Nancy Skinner sponsored a little known Bill regarding accidental murder. It wasn't until the policy director over at Justice Collaborative gave this Bill some support that it began gaining clout. Upon approval, this little - known Bill would make its way to the ballot as SB 1437 or Senate Bill 1437. I sat listening intently while waiting patiently, as he broke it all down to me.

In the gist, what this Bill says is that they can no longer convict someone of murder in an accidental death case. Not first, second, or third - degree murder. Most of us were waiting when the California voters got a hold of the Bill. On the ballot they passed it by a landslide.

"So, the Bill passed last year and just went into action two weeks ago." He sat back and watched me with a smile on his face.

"So, what does that mean for me?" I got the gist of what he was saying yet I needed to hear him in lemans term telling me what he was saying.

"Our appeal is in front of the 9th circuit right now. I filed a Writ of Habeas Corpus to go with it citing the new law. What this will do in effect is give us the ammunition that we need to shoot down and overturn this conviction.

"So, I'm going home?" I finally asked. I couldn't keep playing the guessing game.

"Not right away. What will happen is they will first nullify the conviction which will get you a new trial. The law does allow for them to convict you on a lesser offense such as assault with a deadly weapon or assault with great bodily injury. Honestly I don't see them wasting the tax payers dollar on another trial. Most likely they'll want you to plead out to assault with GBI and offer you eight to twelve years with credit for time served and release you."

I just sat back with a huge smile on my face. I've waited for so long to hear these words I did not know what to say or do. God had finally answered my prayers.

"I- I know...." Damn I was so happy I was stuttering.

"This isn't going to happen overnight so about how much time are we talking about?"

"You should be transferring back to the County in about four to five months. If all goes well you should be on the streets, this time next year."

"Thanks Rogue. A nigga really do appreciate all that you've done. For one, when I get back I'ma send you a payment."

"Don't worry about the next payment. You're going to need it more than me. You just make sure you stay out of trouble. These next few months we don't want to give them no room to get you on anything."

Instantly I thought of Too Sweet and realized how stupid I had been to make the move. I kept my composure and stayed focus. I had to make sure that I didn't put myself in the same predicament or even a similar again. I truly wanted to make it up out this hell hole because my wishes were granted and as the homie said, the rest was up to me. I just had to stay out of the way for four months.

The rest of the meeting with my attorney was a breeze. I can't honestly say I remember it nor do I remember the walk back across the yard to my cell. Yet here I am laid out on my bunk replaying my conversation with Lil E. I was on my way back home. After all of these years of captivity I was finally regaining my freedom.

I wanted to share this news with somebody. It was the best piece of news that I received in almost ten years, I needed to share it. Something told me to fall back though and play my position. Sometimes you have to keep tight to the chest and my instincts was telling me that this was one of them. I thought better of telling anybody my information, at least for the time being.

Instead, I focused my time and thoughts on Kina. I know for sure she'd received my flowers and my last message by now. Hopefully she liked the gesture. I didn't want her thinking that it was creepy for someone that she didn't really know to go so far. I guess before I never really tripped off if she had a dude in her life. I didn't care. Not that I was cold-hearted but I always was the type to go after what I wanted. Plus I know in my heart that I was an upgrade from most men. I was the boss type and I treated my lady like the Queen that she was. Personally, I never understood how brotha's could disrespect and beat on their women like it was nothing and walk around like they feel good about themselves. Didn't they realize that a man's woman was his Queen? She was an extension and representation of him as he was of her. Therefore humiliating and dehumanizing her was in fact humiliating and dehumanizing himself!

See I am a King thus my lady is a Queen and like royalty is how she needed to be treated, especially by me.

You can't expect someone to respect something or someone that you don't respect just because you tell them to. Niggas had the game backwards.

Still feeling myself but electing to keep my news to myself I retrieved my phone from the tuck spot and decided to have a little fun. I pulled up to my soon to be queen's page and began typing:

The day began tragically with turmoil but sun rays appeared through dark clouds.

I was rewarded with a gift, when I saw a pic of your heavenly smile.

Not too often has something so beautified been seen by my personal vision this is why, making you my Queen has become my life's mission. Now if it seem too bold or straight forward please pardon my "G".

Just understand that I'm a King and no King should be without his Queen.

Queen Sakina, royal like none other, one of the few Goddesses on earth.

I, sir Quincy just happen to be, he who knows your worth. Would I be expected to overlook a bar of gold or a rare jewel?

If I let you slip through my hands Kina understand I'd truly be a fool.

Good evening my Queen,

You were on my mind, so I decided to send you a few lines just to inform you that I think you are very special. Hopefully your day was as lovely as you. I also send hopes that your business is doing well and you are enjoying the success of a dream.

With warmest of wishes and champagne kisses.

Q.

Yeah, I was going after her, now with everything I had in me, because I was on my way home… home to her…

CHAPTER 26
SAKINA

"**M**om, can you call him again?"

Silently letting out a sigh, I reached over for my cell phone on my glass kitchen table, utilized my index finger and clicked on Earle's name in the call log. I sent a quick prayer, hoping God would hear me and grant my current wish but I was disappointed when the voice mail picked up for the tenth time within the past hour.

"He always does this! I'm sick of him!"

I watched as Kyle angrily stormed off towards his and Earle Jr.'s bedroom and my heart ached. I wasn't even mad when I heard him slam the bedroom door. The rattling noise only caused tears to form in my eyes. My son was hurt and that only caused my own pain.

I was on the verge of standing up from the kitchen table, with the attempt to see about Kyle when my cell phone vibrated, alerting of an incoming call. I looked down at the screen and instantly sighed.

It was a sigh of relief, where I thought my prayers were answered after all.

"Hello," I answered the call, in a cheerful tone, right after I placed in on speaker mode, however, that feeling was short lived seconds later.

"What's up, Kina. Aye, can you tell the boys that I can't pick them up this weekend, but I got them next weekend."

"Are you serious Earle?"

"Aye, I told your ass about calling me Earle. My name is E," he had the nerve to say and with that, I reached over, pressed the end button on my phone screen, ending the call. One thing I didn't do was argue with any man. Especially, an ignorant, immature one. I barely argued with him when we were together, so I absolutely refused to do so now that we are apart. Instead, I gave him the cold shoulder and avoid any type of communication with him. He didn't deserve any form of my energy.

I shook my head and said a silent prayer preparing for the dreaded talk with my sons. Like many times before, I had to deliver the disappointing news that their so-called father was not picking them up. I just didn't understand how a man, or anyone cannot see their children all week and go two more days without seeing them.

"Of all the men I could've had children with," I mumbled the same line I always did questioning my co-create partner as I stood to my feet from the kitchen table and headed over towards my sons room. After delivering two soft knocks on the door, I turned the knob and let myself in. I slightly smiled at the sight of my best creations.

My eyes fell first on Earle who was seated at a small desk in the far corner of their mediocre size room. His gaze was on a small computer screen. I noticed one of his and Kyle's favorite game was his focus until he turned towards my direction.

"Hi mom!" he greeted me in a cheerful tone.

"Hi sweetie. Are you okay?"

"Yeah, I'm fine, but Kyle is mad that dad is not coming to get us," he let me know and the most obvious thing I noticed that he himself appeared unbothered.

"And you're not mad?" I asked as my eyes briefly averted towards Kyle who was laid in his twin size bed with the bed cover pulled over his frame.

"Nope, I'm used to it. Dad is he who he is, and I learned to accept it," he replied in a mature tone and all I could do is muttered, "Wow," as I shut the bedroom door closed, refocused attention onto him and walked over to the desk and wrapped my arms around Earle Jr.'s upper body.

"I love you," I let him know.

"I love you too mom. Me and Kyle have you, aunty Malika and uncle Shawn. That's all we need," he said and once again I felt tears in my eyes.

I felt a lump in my throat as I was choked up with emotions. No thirteen - year old boy should feel that way about his father. He shouldn't have to accept his father's shortcomings.

No matter what kind of man a male is, he should always step up and be a better man the second he brings a child into this world. It was purely saddening that Earle could never be the man I needed him to be, but it was heartbreaking he was not the father our sons need of him. Often, I dismissed Earle's behavior, appreciating the fact that he was in our son's life at all, since I know of families who have absentee fathers to the fullest, but this was getting old and sad. At this point, I was starting to feel that maybe the boys were better off without Earle in their lives at all. I mean, anything has to be better than the disappointment they endure at least twice a month. It was hurtful to watch the disappointed expression on their faces, especially, my youngest son.

"It will be okay," I assured Earle Jr. once more before I broke our embrace.

"I know it will," he said to me as he looked over and smiled.

I smiled in return. It was ironic how he resembled his father, but was a momma's boy, and Kyle, who was more of a daddy's boy, resembled me. Earle Jr. bore the same dark complexion as his father as well as his eyes and nose. Kyle, on the other hand, shared my pecan tone complexion with my thick eye-brows, sleepy eyes and full lips. As I approached him, I couldn't help but noticed the same emptiness in his that matched my own.

I sighed as I put in my best effort to prevent the tears that were still formed in my eyes, from falling.

"Kyle," I called out to him as I walked over to his bed.

"Did he call back?" he asked me, as he raised the comforter from over his body, and it hurt me to tell him the truth. But it was a must.

Taking a seat onto the bed by his side, I utilized my right hand and touched the side of his handsome face. His eyes bored so much sadness and I knew the answer to his question would only heighten such expression.

"Yes he did sweetie, and I'm sorry but he will not be picking you and Junior up this weekend."

"Oh," was his only response. I studied his face for signs of a possible anger reaction, but to my surprise there were none.

"Are you okay?" I asked him, just to be sure.

"Yeah," he said in a quiet tone. I stared at him for a moment, until he reached over and wrapped his arms around me. I smiled at his warm embrace and with that gesture alone, the tears in my eyes finally fell.

"I love you mom," I heard him say and more tears fell.

"I love you too mom." Earle's Junior's voice was heard, expressing the same heartfelt gesture and my smile through the tears broadened.

My sons. They were the only male species who can bring on my tears and my sensitive side. In the hearts of all hearts, they were the only ones worthy and always will be.

I then felt Earle's arms around my shoulders, and I welcomed his warm embrace as well.

"I love the both of you," I let them both know, and they had no idea just how much I did love them and always will.

Moments went by before Earle Jr. pulled from our embrace. Kyle pulled back as well and laid back onto the bed. Earle resumed his seat at the desk, and I attempted to wipe the tears from my eyes.

"So what do you guys want to do?" I asked them. Often, when their father pulled this usual stunt, I would take them out for a family gathering, featuring the three of us. Although, tonight was girl's night with me and Malika, my sons came first and top priority.

"Can me and Kyle have like two of our friends over and just order pizza and play video games?" Earle Jr. asked, and Kyle immediately jumped up from the bed excitedly.

"Yea mom, can we!"

I laughed at his sudden enthusiasm but welcomed it. I was happy to rid of his solemn state regarding his father in any way I was able to.

"Yes, you boys can," I let them know and the cheering that

followed caused my ears to ring. I laughed again as I stood to my feet.

"Okay, decide which two of your friends you will have over, and I will call their parents and order the pizzas."

"Thank you, mom!" They both cheered simultaneously and hugged me for what felt like the umpteenth time.

"You're welcome," I said to them and added, "And get the sleeping bags ready. Bring them to the living room and I will get blankets from the linen closet."

"Okay," Earle Jr. agreed.

"Okay, but I can't wait until we move into a house, so we'll have more room. When are we getting a house? You said, if your book - store did good and you sold a lot of books on Amazon, that you will buy a house," Kyle chimed in and he was correct.

I did make that promise to them a bit over a year ago and now that my business was in fact a success story, searching for a house was on my agenda immediately. Purchasing and owning my own home was one of my oldest dreams and despite the fact, I always thought I would be married and purchasing one with my husband, I was happy I was finally going to make it happen. And my sons deserved the best and really, I did too. And I did not need a man to make it happen and I was proud of that fact the most.

"I'm going to contact a Real Estate agent first thing tomorrow. It's time we move into our own home," I finally said to them and the cheering resumed once again.

I laughed as I walked over to their bedroom door and opened it, right before I prepared for my exit.

"Hey, is Lamont moving in with us?"

Kyle asked and I silently groaned.

Lately, his questions regarding my relationship with Lamont have been quite frequently and I often wondered why.

"Man, I hope not, because mommy is not in love with him," I heard Earle Jr. voiced as I made my way down the small hallway, leading towards my kitchen. I cracked up laughing in a quiet tone. My boys were wise beyond their years and as I grabbed my cell phone from the table in an attempt to call Malika and cancel our girl's night for the night, Earle Jr.'s comment echoed in my mental.

"Mommy is not in love with him."

It's interesting, hearing the words uttered from a thirteen - year old brought on a certain epiphany.

Later That Night:

"Mommy is not in love with him. I swear I love my Godson."

I shook my head right before I took a sip of the Moscato I was currently nursing.

"Please, don't entertain it. I can't believe he said that."

"Well, believe it cause the shit is true. I think you might have been close to falling in love with Lamont's ass but after a man plays games with your heart and disappoints you over and over again, falling in love tends to get curve. I was happy as hell when ya'll didn't talk for five months. I thought his ass was gone for good but here is back, like he never left. Uuugh!"

I laughed at Malika as I sipped more of my wine.

"Laugh if you want, but you know that shit is true. I spit some real shit."

"Whatever," I dismissed her sentence with a wave of my hand.

"And, plus, you only keep that lame nigga Lamont around because you're sprung on the dick," she spat, and I was too through.

"Oh my Goddddd," I expressed in a hush tone as I tried to suppress my laughter.

"The boys and their friends are in the living room."

"Oh please, they not paying us no mind," Malika waved me off as she, herself took a swig of a bottle of corona she held in her hand.

She and I were comfortably settled in my home office as my sons entertained their friends for the night. After calling her earlier and attempting to cancel our weekly Friday girl's night ritual, she decided to grab some drinks and some fried shrimps, which were our favorite, and have our girl's night at my home. After indulging in the seafood and enjoyed some laughter with the boys, we retired to my office. The space was enough room for relaxation and lounging. I was seated in my office chair while Malika was settled in a plush chair near me.

"Sooo, anyway, enough about that nigga Lamont. I know when you're sick of his corny ass, you'll send him on his way."

I looked at her and sucked my teeth as she grinned my way.

"Or get a better dick," she added, and I laughed.

"Speaking of better dick, you heard from the King of Cali?" she asked, and I immediately groaned.

"Uugh, noo and you were right. I guess he was a fraud. I've been checking since Tuesday and the message has remained unseen. He never been back in the inbox. But he did leave me a message which was sweet but he never responded " I vented to Malika and after I took another sip of my wine, I noticed she bore a rather puzzled expression on her face.

"What's wrong?"

"What page did you send him that message?" she inquired, and it was my turn to wear a puzzled expression.

"Uuhm, my Author's page. I mean that's the page I was already logged on that morning and I've been on here all week," I answered her question and suddenly, a sort of an epiphany crossed my mental.

"Oh waittttt," I said, and Malika finished my sentence for me.

"Yeah bisssh. Don't he usually message you on your personal page? That's probably why he never answered you, because you sent him that message on your Author's page."

"Oh my God," I voiced, and Malika quickly stood to her feet and swiftly walked over to my desk.

"Uuuuh, uuh. Let's see."

I leaned forward and watched in anticipation as she used the computer mouse and clicked on my computer screen.

"Your password for your personal page is still Kyle and E.J.'s birthday, right?" she inquired.

My eyes remained glued to the screen as I watched her logged onto my Author's Facebook page and when she clicked on the messenger, my eyes widened in disbelief.

"See that shit. He didn't respond because he never received that message from Tuesday. Ain't this some shit," Malika voiced, and I felt the same way.

"Oh my God. So does this mean he's legit after all?"

I wondered out loud as I read the short but sweet message from earlier.

"Don't know. Not sure if he's legit just yet. Let's wait and see how he reacts to the message. Sooner or later, his ass will come on this page since he stalks you on both pages, so let's just wait and see,"

Malika replied and I was too through. I laughed at her crazy ass while thoughts of Quincy stayed on my mind.

"But he did send you a cute little message earlier or whenever so let's read it."

I heard Malika voiced as I wondered more and more what Quincy's reaction will be when he does read my message. And as I did so, I silently prayed for the best.

CHAPTER 27
QUINCY

The Next Day:

After sending Sakina that brief message on her private page the day before, I decided to go back to her Author's page since she posted more of her flyers on that page. It was eight am, California time, on a Saturday morning when I went on Facebook. I was excited the same way I always am when I'm leaving her a message, that was, until I came across her last message to me from four days ago, based on the date inside of the inbox. When I first read her message, I did not know what to say or think. I had already told myself and prepared for the fact that she might have a dude. Yet, I completely miscalculated her response.

For over an hour, I analyzed, and dissected her message. I am not even going to lie; I even went as far as to write it down on paper. They say it helps to compose the things that you visualize and to get a better feel and understanding of things. That's exactly what I needed.

While I was digesting all of this, I had to question myself. Was I right with my assessment of her to begin with? Is she the woman that has constantly graced my dreams? The one whom my spirit feels so comfortably with? Or have I gotten things all mixed up? Has this time gotten to me so much that I was willing to devote myself and my life to the first woman that I interacted with?

The more I read the words in her message, the more a clear answer began to form. First off, if she were confident or happy in any relationship, she would have mentioned it. As would anyone who was in a happy relationship. Because they would want to represent the relationship to the upmost.

So, if she was in a relationship, it must not be a good one. She must not be happy or content. Telling me that she thinks it is inappropriate as an author for her to receive messages and flowers from me may very well be accurate if I was a fan. Since I am not familiar with the moralistic side of the writing world, I would have to concede that perhaps she is right or would be right if I was fan.

Although I read her work, and incredibly pleased with it, I am not one of her fans. If she would open and let me in, I am the man that is going to change her life. Therefore, that rule did not apply to me. Not in the least, and with me being me, all I could do was turn it up. I have never been the type to give up easy and I damn sure was not going to start now.

I grabbed my note pads off my shelf and searched for the number to the same florist that I had used before. When I finally found the number and called, the shop owner laughed at my request. She asked me why I did not just hand it to her myself.

After explaining to her that I was all the way in California and explaining to her that I was the same person that placed the large order last week, she told me that she would help me. She also told me that whoever the young lady was that I was going through all this trouble for must have been special.

"Like you wouldn't believe," was my response.

Once my order was placed, I thought about my next move. I had to double check and ask myself, was it indeed my best move. Each time I asked myself the answer was the same. Yes!

The shop owner ensured me that my single long stem fire and ice rose along with a card would be delivered within 30 minutes. As I sat there waiting for the time to relapse, I thought about the words written on the card, "I can't stop what fate has placed in motion."

Now that was Gangsta, if I must say so myself. Simple yet divinely prophetic. I needed to let her know that this was out of our hands. I needed to let her know that this was out of our hands. This was fate, the main ingredient on the recipe of love. If we tried to interject our personal desires or fears, things could go wrong. Yet if we just let go and allow nature to take its course, we will both nurture a love like non other.

Seems rather farfetched now considering we've yet to formally introduce ourselves to each other. But fate is a very powerful thing.

I looked at my watch and noticed over forty minutes had passed. It was time for me to finally face reality. Time to roll the dice. Or as my football coach used to say, "It was time to shit or get off the pot!"

My heart rate began to race as I started getting nervous. I had to laugh at myself. What was I getting nervous for? I was just going to talk to a female. Something, I used to prize myself on doing with ease all my life. Suddenly a niggas mind started playing tricks on him. All sorts of weird thoughts popped into my head like; what if she is really not interested? What if she was serious about her message? What if I messed up my opportunity by saying the wrong thing?

I put the phone down and rolled a cigarette. I felt like a high school kid getting ready to ask a girl to the prom but trying to work up his nerve. While I smoked my cigarette, I forced myself to get out of my head. Instead of the negative thoughts, I replaced them with positive attributions such as: She is only testing me to see if I really want her. She is actually waiting for me to respond. Sakina was meant for me. Those thoughts and a few more went through my head.

I decided right then and there that I was going to man up and go for what I know. Since I had to either man up or man down, I chose to man up.

My fingers did the dialing without my recollection.

"Thank you for calling Sakina and Things, this is Sakina speaking. How may I help you?"

Oh my God her voice was magical. Like the soft sounds of Heaven.

"I hope the rose was almost as beautiful as you are."

What? That is it? I have waited all of this time to openly speak to her and that was the best thing I could come up with?

She was quiet for so long that I thought she had hung up.

"Uh..... Excuse me .... Quincy is that you?" She sounded a bit puzzled. Yet, I thought I heard some excitement.

"Your voice sounds like birds singing in the early spring morning." I closed my eyes and imagined her right there in my face. She was so beautiful.

"Yes, Sakina its Quincy. I hope you liked your flowers and the rose.

The line was silent for a long time again. I held my breath waiting to see what she would say. If she would respond or not. Hopefully, she would not hang up the phone on me.

"Yes Quincy, I did receive your Roses from Monday and the rose just a few moments ago and card. They were both beautiful. But I thought I told you that we can't do this....."

"We can't do what? We haven't begun to do anything." I cut her off not waiting to hear her say anything negative.

"We can't be sending each other messages and you can't keep sending me flowers. Although they are beautiful, I am a professional Author. It wouldn't be appropriate for me to become intimately involved with a fan." I could hear uncertainty in her voice. I was correct with my assumption. She did not want me to fall back. Even though she was telling me to.

"Believe me, I understand your morally-related concerns regarding your career. I assure you that you do not have a thing to worry about. Although yes, I have read some of your work and I believe you are indeed fabulous, I am, however, not a fan. I am a man who is interested in a remarkable woman. A man who is following his heart. When I read your first book, I just knew I had to get to know the woman behind the pen. I know it's going to sound crazy, but I felt a special connection to you as a woman, not as an Author and hearing your voice on this phone only confirms those feelings." I pictured her in my mind with a smile on her face, I could not let up now. It was all or nothing. Everything was right here. I had to put it all on the line.

"Kina listen, I know from my current standpoint that it may seem like I don't have anything to offer. I promise you that could not be further from the truth. First and foremost, I am not spending the rest of my life behind bars. I guarantee you I am coming home. So, do not let my current incarceration be a deterrent. As far as attributes, my first and greatest attribute is the fact that I know how to treat you. I treat my woman like the queen she was rightfully born to be. I eternalized the mantra "Happy wife happy life." Secondly, I respect your independence. I am not one of them brothas who are so insecure that they do not want you chasing your dreams. I am going to support you chasing your dreams while I work hard to chase mine. Because I am old fashion enough to believe that a man is supposed to protect and provide for his woman. I hope that I am not overstepping my bounds, but on your personal page I see that you have children. I love children and believe me when I say they love me. Now I would not expect you to just introduce me to your children. I am just letting you know that I get along very well with children. I do not smoke weed or use drugs of any kind. My one flaw is that I smoke cigarettes, but if you want me to quit, just say the word and its done. I'm rambling on because I need you to see that I am one hundred percent serious and I need you to see me as a man instead of as a convict. And not just any man, but the man who can promise you that I can, and I will make you happy, if you just let me. Before any of that, I just want to be a friend. I want us to openly communicate. Kina, let me into your life just a little and let nature take its natural course."

There it goes, I shooted my shot. I took a deep breath and waited on her response.

CHAPTER 28
SAKINA

Ten Hours Prior:

"With warmest of wishes and champagne kisses. Hell yeah, that nigga is smooth as hell," Malika laughed, and I just shook my head.

"How many times are you going to say that?"

"Bissh! That's my new motto! Ooh you need to make that a book title! That's some romantic shit for real!"

"I swear." It was my turn to laugh right before I finished off my fourth glass of Moscato. I was feeling nice, so nice, that I almost wished that Malika's loud behind did not decide to spend the night. Lamont called and texted me approximately five times since she and I have been relaxing in my home office, but I opted on ignoring him, since I knew Malika would act a fool. She did not care for Lamont and she made no apologies for it. In fact, she never cared for him since day one. From the minute I introduced her to him, she voiced her opinion like only Malika could.

"That corny nigga ain't it," she let me know three years ago and I must admit, although he was considered a good catch on paper, he's proven her right as time passed. He truly was not it and I hate to admit it, but my thirteen - year old, oh so wise son was correct as well. I was not in love with Lamont and Malika was also right. After a man toys with your heart repeatedly, any love you bored for him, tend to deteriorate.

And…a man who a woman never had to give a million chances to, was the one who can win a woman's heart. Especially my heart. I swear all I want is a man who does not disappoint. A man who cares about my heart as well as me and one who will give me his with ease. No games, no difficultly, no second guessing.

Unfortunately, that man was not Lamont, no matter how much he has been professing his love as of lately. All of a sudden, he has a desire to do right, and although, I should be happy, the vibe was off.

I just wasn't sure why, exactly. Or maybe I did?

"So, what are you going to do? Are you going to respond to his message or you're just going to stare at it like you've been doing for an hour now?"

Malika's question suddenly had me on overload. Instead of replying to Quincy's message, I chose to simply stare at it. Yes, the message was sweet, but the truth remained a mystery as far as I was concerned. Was he for real or was he just gaming? Thanks to Malika, I'm wondering more than ever, since he has not come across my other message.

"No, I'm not going to respond. I decided you're right. Let's test him and see if he's for real. Let's wait to see his reaction after he reads my other message. He will go on that page sooner or later."

"And you're not convinced he's for real after all those damn roses he sent? Which is also smooth as hell."

I thought about Malika's question for a second and I finally replied, "No. I need more confirmation."

"Okay, then, let's wait for Mr. Cali's next move after he reads the message."

I nodded my head to Malika's response in agreement, but then something dawned on me.

"But wasn't this your idea even after he sent me those roses?"

"Uuuh, hell yeah it was my idea, but this message he sent to you today is some sweet shit. I don't know about you, but Mr. Cali gained some cool points with me. He kind of remind me of Shawn."

I partially smiled at Malika's admission until her next set of words.

"But, let's just say his ass is for real for real. Then what? The nigga is doing life."

I let out a sigh and the reality of this situation is indeed bittersweet. Here is this man, who can be the men of all men, but he's behind bars for life.

"I don't know," I admit sincerely.

"I just never been pursued like this before, so it feels good and there's something about this guy..."

Before I could finish my sentence, I noticed Malika was grinning at me.

"What are you grinning at?" I just had to ask her.

"Your ass smiling that cheesy smile when you talk about

King of Cali," she replied to my question, and that was my cue to call it a night.

"Whatever," I waved her off as I stood to my feet.

"I'm going to bed," I announced as I headed towards my office door.

"You can either sleep in my room or take the boys room," I let her know.

"And you sure you don't mind staying with the boys and their friends for a few hours while I go into the office in the morning to receive my inventory? Normally I wouldn't go in on a Saturday or I would just take the boys with me, but I have to be there for my inventory. I received an email that it was arriving Saturday morning."

"Bissh, I don't even know why you talked all that shit. I already told your ass an hour ago that I would stay with my Godsons and if their friends even think about disobeying me, that's their asses."

I laughed at Malika as we both prepared to leave my home office.

"I swear, you shouldn't even be thinking about having kids with your mindset," I joked.

"Whatever, I want to give my hubby some kids and some gotdamn warmest wishes and champagne kisses," she shot her subliminal joke towards Quincy and I almost fell out laughing.

Present Moment:

I was sitting at my desk making note of the inventory I just received for my business when the door to my store chimed. I suddenly looked up and in walked the same delivery guy from Monday with what appeared to be a single wrapped rose in his hand.

"Oh boy, another flower delivery?" I quizzed and couldn't help but notice a card in his hand in addition to the rose.

"Yes ma'am. Someone sure thinks you're special," he replied with a slight grin curving his lips.

"Uuugh, I told you about calling me that." I groaned.

He laughed as he handed me a clipboard with a delivery sheet, indicating for my signature. After I signed it, I handed the clipboard back to him and retrieved the rose as swell as the card.

"Have a nice day," he said to me before he walked over to my office door and made his exit.

My eyes quickly examined the beautiful single rose and averted towards a small card placed inside of a white envelope. Just as I was on the verge of removing it to read, my office phone rung.

I was almost tempted not to answer since I'm normally closed on Saturdays, but something told me to go ahead and answer.

"Thank you for calling Sakina "N" Things, this is Sakina speaking. How may I help you?" I managed to say as in much of a cheerful tone I can muster. I was exhausted from staying up late with Malika and did not have much energy in me so I'm sure it was obvious in my voice.

"I hope the rose was almost as beautiful as you are."

As soon as the voice spoke on the other end of the phone line, my heart instantly started skipping beats. Small bead of sweats formed on my forehead just as quickly. I swallowed, in attempt to control my breathing.

I wasn't sure what was happening until I realized....
Damn....

I was excited.

But, wait, it can't be. Then again, how would he know I just received a rose.

"Uh..... Excuse me .... Quincy is that you?"

I managed to finally ask, even though I already knew it was him. Just like I knew it was him the first time he called a little over a week ago.

"Your voice sounds like birds singing in the early spring morning," he said and....

Damn.

"Yes, Sakina its Quincy. I hope you liked your flowers and the rose," he added, and I was speechless.

His voice...His words... His lingo...His energy..

Just everything about him so far. Excluding his prison bid, but the man he was before he landed in prison, the letters and poem he wrote, his messages, his roses delivery and now his phone call. Well, his second phone call, except this time he was beyond bold with it.

He dared to identify himself and let me know it was in fact him and I would be a true fibber if I did not say that the way he moved wasn't the sexiest thing in the world. I was turned on to the fullest in that moment. He wanted me and he was coming for me full force.

But.. then Malika's words from a few days ago echoed in my mental as well as our conversation from last night. And of course my own words. So, as intrigued as I was with Quincy Norton, I needed to see how real he was. Was he just some bored perverted inmate toying with me because he thought he could or was he a real man coming after what he truly wanted.

Closing my eyes, I silently counted from ten to one and composed my breathing, for I was about to put on my Oscar winning performance. I was indeed impressed and intrigued by his, smooth, handsome, and sexy self but I needed to know just how real he was. Just how much he wanted me...What was he really made of...

Here goes nothing....

"Yes Quincy, I did receive your Roses from Monday and the rose just a few moments ago and card. They were both beautiful. But I thought I told you that we can't do this....."

I started to say, even believing myself, but received a true shocker.

"We can't do what? We haven't begun to do anything."

He cut me off and I instantly realized he did so to keep me from saying something he did not care to hear.

But I had to stick to my script because I just knew he was going to back off and put an end to this crazy cat and mouse game he was playing.

I took a deep breath and gave it to him....

"We can't be sending each other messages and you can't keep sending me flowers. Although they are beautiful, I am a professional author. It would not be appropriate for me to become intimately involved with a fan."

I mean, my intention was to give it to him, but something happened in that moment. Deep, deep down in my soul, I did not want this beautiful man to be a fraud. I did not want him to back off. I wanted him to be as real as he was coming and maybe, just maybe, be my knight and shining armour... Be my prince Charming. The kind of man, that most little girls don't even know or ever become accustom to.

Yes, God, for once, I needed him to be the kind of man I only read about or witness in movies. And as I uttered the words I just did; I couldn't even hide my uncertainty. I'm sure it was in my voice and I wondered if he could detect it..

And then he spoke.... And after he voiced the first line of words,

"Believe me, I understand your morally-related concerns regarding your career. I assure you that you do not have a thing to worry about."

I became lost in his voice.. his words.. the sincerity in them. The words he spoke were so beautiful and when he reached the end and said his final peace...,

"Not just any man, but the man who can promise you that I can, and I will make you happy, if you just let me. Before any of that I just want to be a friend. I want us to openly communicate. Kina, let me into your life just a little and let nature take its natural course."

And I knew right then and there that I would indeed let him in. He just past Malika's test and I silently thanked God, for sending me the realest man that I have ever met.

"Yes," I found myself saying. Suddenly, I felt intoxicated by this man's energy, his aura. I almost felt, submissive even, and that was one word I was not, but he felt like such a man, man.

"Yes, what, beautiful," he challenged me in that baritone voice of his and I, oh God, I felt weak in that moment. Weak.... I wasn't sure what that felt like, but this must be it, because at this present moment, I just wanted to take a trip to California and break him out of prison, or at least go to the judge that sentenced him and plead for his case to be overturned.

"Yes, I'll let you in," I replied honestly, clarifying my response.

"Thank you beautiful," he said, and I felt myself melting. I just love the way he spoke. Suddenly, I realized if I was going to let him in, then I needed to be totally honest with him as I expected him to be with me. So, I decided to put it out there for him.

"So, if I'm going to let you in and we start a friendship, then I want it based on complete honestly," I let him know.

"Of course, beautiful. I wouldn't have it any other way."

Oh god, I wish he would stop speaking that way.

"So, to start our friendship based on honesty, I must tell you, that I have a man in my life," I started to say until he cut me off.

"Do you now," he said in an almost questionable tone and the sarcasm wasn't missed either.

I suddenly found myself laughing and he laughed along with me. I had a feeling Quincy Norton was something else and was going to be a force to be reckon with.

"Okay, Quincy, if I'm going to let you in and we build a friendship, we need to learn each other's world as well as respect it."

"I hear you beautiful," he said in once again that seductive tone.

"Quincy," I said his name in an attempt to tell him about Lamont and the complication of my situation when the unthinkable happened.

"What's up baby?"

Oh God. I looked up towards my office door, and Lamont entered my store. I was in such a mini trance speaking to Quincy that I did not even hear the chime sound off.

"Tell him what's up, baby," Quincy voiced in my ear in an amused tone and I just shook my head.

"Damn, who the hell bought you all these flowers?"

Lamont question and I internally groaned. Today was the

first day he has been here to my office since Monday, so this was his first time viewing them.

"Yeah, baby, tell him who the hell bought you those flowers."

I almost smirked at Quincy in my ear. Oh yeah, he brought the capital B to the word bold.

I slightly exhaled before I attempted to defuse this situation. As a matter of fact, what was I doing? I should've been ending the call with Quincy, but it suddenly dawned on me, that I did not want to end our conversation.

Oh God, what was happening?

"Uhhm, Lamont, can you grab a seat and I will be with you in a minute," I called out to Lamont and I was thankful he simply nodded his head. He then winked at me and blew me a kiss and strangely, his gesture put me in a bad headspace.

He made the number one mistake any man can make which was, give another man a chance to pique his woman's interest.

Quincy Norton has done just that, and I could not stop what was happening, even if I wanted to.

"Hello, yes, I completely hear what you are saying and yes, we can definitely do business together. I normally do not come into the office on Saturdays and I am about to leave, but how about you give me a call this evening and we can finish discussing business further. My business calls will be transferred to my cell phone. Please call at your earliest convenience."

I held in my breath, hoping Quincy would oblige and go along with the obvious, until I can figure out what was really taking place here.

I heard Quincy laugh once again before he finally spoke the words that were like music to my ears.

"Okay, beautiful, as your new friend, I will go along with this for now, but just know, I'm not the kind of man who plays games. So remember that for the future. I will call you later this evening so we can continue our conversation. Warm wishes and Champagne kisses."

And with that, he ended the call and I sat there for a few seconds speechless.

Damn.

Finally, I placed the phone in its hook and Lamont's voice caught my attention.

"So, who the hell send those flowers?"

CHAPTER 29
QUINCY

Two Days Later:

My lawyer's predictions were starting to come true. I received word just yesterday that my Writ of Habeas corpus had been granted. I was going back to jail where I would await a new trial. Therefore I needed to be in tiptop, A1, pristine health.

The sweat was running down my body, but I had to push myself. My normal workout was done, but I continued doing sets of pushups. The more I could feel my muscles burning, the harder I pushed. Up and down, I continued to push out my sets. Before I realized it, I had knocked out an additional ten sets. Yeah, I was feeling good.

Once I was finally done, I grabbed my stuff and took a bird bath in the sink. All the while I had nothing but positive thoughts on my mind. I know the old saying about getting your hopes up. It did not pertain to this though. I was actually going home.

After my attorney's visit I did my own research on SB-1437. This was not some kind of wild goose chase or a scavenger hunt. This was the real deal. This senate bill was everything that my lawyer said it was. If the murder were accidental, then you could no longer be convicted of first degree nor second degree murder. At the most they could drop it down to aggravated assault.

Now, I am not exactly sure how much time aggravated assault carries but I know it is not life. I will have time to research it and find out before it is all said and done. For now though, I believe it could not carry no more than six to eight years. Which mean I would have enough credit for time served and I will be released. I could not believe it but God does answer prayers. I may have been doing the devils work since I have been down, but throughout this entire incarceration I have been calling on God. He was finally answering me now.

I finished washing up and cleaned the sweat off the floor. Next, I turned on the television to catch the prison news channel. It has been a while since the shit went down on the yard with Too Sweet. I still had to keep my ears to the streets though. I had to stay one step ahead of the game and one step ahead of the police if I did not want to get caught up.

The good thing about the situation is, Too Sweet did not die. So even if things went south and they came and snatched me up, it would not be for murder. Even though attempted murder or assault with a deadly weapon are both serious, they are both better than murder.

Not finding anything on the station that pertained to what I was looking for, I decided to channel-surf. When I got to the news channel I stopped. Unfortunately, it was only Donald trump giving a press conference about trying to secure some extra funding for that foolish ass wall that he was having built along the border. I was not feeling Donald Trump and I sure as hell did not give a rat's ass about no damn wall. I turned the channel faster than a New York minute. It did not matter because there was nothing on worth watching on any of the channels.

Right then they announced yard release. This was like the second- or third-yard release. Yard had been open for some time already. Initially, I was not going to hit the yard, but boredom had me putting on my boats and walking out of the door.

Before I walked out, I made sure to grab my Sony CD player along with my headphones and my Messy Marv's Hustlinaire CD. Normally I would not take my CD players and headphones out to the yard. I like my full attention on everything around me, being on my safety and security hype. Today it was different, I was in a good mood and it was a beautiful day, so I brought it out with me.

No matter how beautiful the day was, when you are locked up, there really is not a such thing as a beautiful day. So even though the sun was out, and a nice spring breeze was blowing, shit was always gloomy inside of these prison walls. So I kept my focus.

Since I did not have a destination in mind, I just turned on the CD player and let my feet do them.

I had traveled about two thirds of a lap and was on the last verse of "Rising Star" listening to brah talk that shit when I heard a familiar voice call out to me. When I looked in the direction that the voice came from, I saw the little homie J approaching me.

"What's up Ridah?" I hit him up as he approached me.

"You know me, big homie I'm just mack'n and mobbin. I saw you with your head - phones on so I thought you were slipping but I guess I was wrong". J told me as we embraced in a one arm gangsta hug.

"Nah Ridah, you know I ain't neva got to get ready because I stay ready but I leave the illusions for the clueless." I pulled my head - phones off to show him that I had one of the speakers removed yet I left the speaker box intact.

This gave off the illusion and appearance that the speaker was still inside of the headphones, allowing me to still hear as I listen to music.

"I should've known your old ass was on point and up to some crafty shit". We began walking continuing along the track.

"On the real Rogue, what you doing on the yard? Today ain't a holiday."

"Shit Ridah, today was just one of them days. You know when a mothafucka just need to get up out the cell and get some air. Them walls were starting to close in on a nigga." While we walked, I placed my headphones around my neck.

"Oh yeah Rogue I feel you. Every now and then a nigga get a feeling like I'm suffocating, or some shit up in that bitch. On them days I don't care what it's for, I just got to get up out of my cell."

"What's going on with you though Ridah? How you looking with them books that I dropped off to you? Are you reading them okay?" I asked just as we rounded the far corner of the track.

"You know it Rogue. I gotta stay up on my studies so I can get up on my higher learning. Speaking of which, I just had my girl butterfly drop a donation off at the local library in our area." Even though we were outside, we still talked in code.

"That's good, ain't nothing wrong with giving back to the community. Speaking of which Ridah, imma bout to fall completely all the way back and leave the community in your hands".

"You serious big brah? Rogue don't be playing games with me!" The shock in the little homie's voice was priceless.

"J, Rogue you know I'm not about to play with you especially about something like this. It's time for me to fall back Ridah."

"Rogue, I ain't neva gone look a gift horse in the mouth so I thank you fa'real fa'real. But why the change now? Shit is going good as hell for us. Niggas don't just walk away from shit like what we got Rogue. So tell ya boi Rogue, what's up?" I could sense through his suspicious voice that J felt something was wrong.

I thought about how long I have been known the lil homie and all of the shit he's done for me. The shit we have done together. I did not want the yard to know that I was leaving to go back to court. I wanted to slide on out of here. But I had to let the lil homie know at least. It would not be right if I didn't.

I turned my head behind us making sure no one was trailing us too close, trying to hear what we were saying.

"Look Ridah, now I'm not trynna make no big deal out of this or nothing like that. I'm telling you only because you the homie, Rogue and you have the right to know. I saw my lawyer recently. This bill just passed so they are bringing me back to the County. Rogue, I should be outta here in a couple of weeks. A nigga might be going home Ridah. But I don't want to leave and have you stranded in this bitch like Gilligan on Gilligan's Island so I'm in the process of turning everything over to you. I already knew you would want the keys to the city, so I'm putting it together already without you having to say anything."

"Damn big brah, a nigga ain't even bout to lie, I'ma be happy as fuck to see a real nigga make it back to the streets. I'm tired of always seeing suckas and bitch niggas catching all the breaks. As far as the city goes my nigga, that's a good look and I'ma make sure shit is ran in a way that things will only get better never worst."

I knew young wolf was more than capable of carrying out exactly what he said he would do. To make sure that was possible I was passing J my invisible security team as well. These were cats that he did not even know about that would put in work and protect a nigga at the drop of a hat. J and I continued to talk until he knew everything that he needed to know, such as why he was about to all of a sudden receive a job change from where he was to a.m. cook. He would soon be finding out that our boss was indeed the connect. He needed to know this and some more things before it was all said and done. We walked laps and talked for the remainder of yard time.

Back in the cell, I was staring in the mirror while washing my hands. I truthfully did not recognize myself, these years behind these walls had taken a toll on me. I could see the wear and tear all over my face. Not to mention the stress of wearing the multiple hats that I wore. With one hat, I was shot calling. With the other I was a prison drug king and then there was the actual hat of the man I really was. No one would believe how easy it was to go from your average working Joe to full pledge gangsta. Though it was stressful, I pulled it off well.

C.O. Johnson told me when I walked into the building that I

had about a thirty - minute wait until it was time for my shower. I was tempted to call Sakina so I could hear her lovely voice, but I did not want to take the risk. Instead, I put my blockers in the window like I was sitting on the toilet. Then I sent her a quick message.

Queen Kina,

Hello beautiful, I was just sliding through your inbox to remind you that you are a very remarkable woman and you should be very proud of yourself. Thank you for giving me a chance and letting me into your life. I know I still have some hoops to jump through, but I told you I would not disappoint you. Continue having faith in God because I see him working miracles. Remember the saying; when praises go up, blessings come down. I have been receiving good news all month beginning with you letting me into your life. I just pray the good news continues. If you are available, I will call you tonight. I love hearing your sweet voice. It is like honey to my soul.

With warmest of wishes and champagne kisses... "Q"

CHAPTER 30
SAKINA

Good morning Q. Aww you're so sweet. I swear, your words. Lol. But I hope you will share your good news with me, and I hope it's regarding your case. I know you told me your lawyer had some lead that would work well in your favor. And yes, I will be available tonight. I'll look out for your call. I have some good news myself. Two goods news, actually. Hope you have a good day and I will talk to you later.

I could not help but have a huge Kool-aide smile on my face as I sent my message to Quincy on Facebook messenger. In that moment, I wished he was online, but the messenger time clock showed he was inactive and have been for over an hour now. Yes, I was feeling quite good about him. We have been indulging in some pretty deep and at times, intimate conversations within the past two days and I must admit, our vibe and connection was something out of this world. Thank God that I allowed myself to let my guard down and let him in. He was one hell of a man.

He was intelligent, funny, a true gentleman and something else that was hard to find in a man…. he was spiritual.

Last night, right before we ended one of quite a few of our conversations, he asked me to pray with him.

I must admit, his request caught me off guard. Never, in all my years of dating, have I had a male ask me to pray with him nor have anyone prayed for me.

Last night was a first and that alone, put Quincy Norton on a whole other level. He truly was the kind of man who ruins it for all the rest of the male species. He's the type of man, once you go Quincy, you could never go back. Any other man after him, would have to step his game up because Quincy was everything.

I mean there was one attribute I wondered if he did possess but Malika debated that it shouldn't matter. She made me realized that was part of my problem with men. My requirements were and had partially always been on the superficial side.

A man either had to look good, have a great job with money or must be well-endowered or sex me good. I put up with Earle for as long as I did because of the sex and for the fact he had a bit of money. He was a terrible boyfriend and family man, but always kept a job and made good money. The one thing he did well was help take care of our sons financially and that partially made up for his fatherly and family shortcomings.

Speaking of short comings, Lamont as well fit the criteria of my superficial attraction. He was a great status on paper and one again, the sex was outstanding, but strangely, the more I've gotten to know Quincy, the more I'm starting to realize that I am surely settling with Lamont.

The more Quincy and I are getting to know each other, the more I have been comparing the two. Really, Quincy was in a class of his own, but there was still the small doubt that lingered deep within that he can still be a fraud. Behind the keyboard and all of his romantic gestures, he appeared to be amazing, but what was he like in real life? I often fantasied what he was like in person and how it would feel to see him, embrace him, perhaps kiss him.

Damn.

Suddenly, I felt the sudden need to view his pictures. I exited messenger and moved the computer mouse onto his page.

The first thing I noticed was his status he posted an hour ago.

A true Queen deserves a true King. You my Queen deserve to be treated like Royalty. For a while now, I thought of myself as the one nigga a woman would never meet a duplicate of, but since you've entered my life, I now know I am the one man, the one King, not that nigga, but that King you will never find again.

So now, my Queen, I ask you...
Will I be your reality or just a fantasy?
Q... Cali's own.

Damn.

And seconds after reading his beautiful words, I then noticed that he tagged me in the post. And not only tagged me, but my Author's page as well. He also posted a few new pictures of himself I've never seen before and tagged me in them as well.

Wow.

He was sending a message and I heard loud and clear. But of course, the other women on his friend's list did not get the same message or they just didn't care. The lustful and seductive comments were flowing in, however all I could do was smile.

He wanted me and only me and was letting the other women know and that's all I could focus on.

Damn. I guess now it was my turn.

I sat in place at my store's office desk, contemplating my next move. Then my thoughts traveled to Lamont. Status wise, he was everything I needed in my life as I took my writing career to another level.

I was contacted by Essence magazine earlier that morning, to be interviewed and featured in their next issue as an up and coming Author and I was beyond excited. Like wow. This was one of the news I wanted to share with Quincy, but the news was a bit bittersweet. The Administrator from Essence who contacted me, informed that I was referred by Rahway Police Officer Lamont Tracer.

Lamont. He was stepping his game up, but I did not know how to tell him that he was in fact too late.

My heart.... It was with Quincy Norton.

Incarcerated Quincy Norton my inner conscious suddenly echoed, and I suddenly felt torn again.

Later That Night:

Lamont: I've been trying to call you all day and evening but no answer. Did Essence magazine reach you?

I sighed as I read Lamont's text message. I did see his calls all day and evening once I arrived home from work and picking up my sons, but I opted on avoiding him. I knew what he really wanted. I also felt he referred me to Essence magazine as a way to prevent me from leaving him. Since he discovered the roses in my office on Friday, he has been questioning me non - stop. He wanted to know who sent the countless roses, and despite the fact I told him one of my customer's sent them, he insisted otherwise. He expressed he felt I was not telling him the truth, which he was in fact correct. But, I refused to admit the truth.

I did not feel he needed to know. As far as my heart was concerned, he was halfway out of the door. I was preparing to end our relationship, but I was unsure how. And a part of me was afraid of making the wrong choice. What if I let Lamont go at the peak of him trying so hard to make us work, and Quincy never makes it back home. What if his lawyer's lead in his case is a dead end?

Uuugh. I was feeling torn again.

Suddenly, my cell phone vibrated. I viewed the screen and read another message from Lamont.

Lamont: Look I'm sorry I pissed you off all weekend. I miss you. You shut me out and I hate that shit. I just want to know who really sent you those roses and that rose. But fuck it, you don't have to tell me. I know a customer didn't send them, Kina. Please don't insult my intelligence. But you know what, it don't matter. I now realized it's my fault if another man is trying to get at you. Baby, I love you. I love you, Kina, please don't leave me.

Ugggh. God Help me.

Separating myself from this man was not going to be as easy as I thought. I mean, was I supposed to? Maybe he wasn't so wrong for me after all. Maybe Quincy was all wrong for me and Lamont was the right one.

But…..Talking with him. Vibing with him…And earlier he let

me know on Facebook, in front of a billion of folks that he wanted me.

But……he was still incarcerated. So he was the wrong one.

At least I tried to convince myself.

But… He felt so right…..

Lamont: I love you Kina.

Smh. Lamont texted, confessing his love once again and I just shook my head.

Lamont: Can I come over after I get off work at eleven? I can be there in two minutes. You know the station is only minutes from your place. Please baby, I need you.

Uugh. I knew what he wanted and needed. I exhaled and closed my eyes.

God please send me a sign

I was unsure on what to do in that moment as I sat on my bed. I simply stared at Lamont's text message for a few moments.

Moments later, I was still contemplating on what to do when I heard a knock on my door.

"Come in," I called out.

"Mom, here." I looked up to the sound of Earle Jr.'s voice.

He walked over and handed over his cell phone and I knew exactly who was on the other end of the phone line.

"Thank you, sweetie," I gave him a faint smile. He smiled back and quickly left my room. He asked no questions and I loved that about my children. They knew how to stay in a child's place.

I exhaled before I placed the I-phone to my ear.

"Yes, Lamont."

"Baby, I'm sorry. I know you hate when I call Junior's phone, but you weren't answering me," He instantly started to plead his case and I was just......

"Okay, you can come over when you get off work," I simply replied and ended the call.

I closed my eyes and counted to ten in attempt to calm my nerves. Me and my love life were always so complex.

Sighing once again, I laid down on my bed with my eyes still closed. My eyes felt sleepy the second my head hit the pillow. I decided to rest for a few before eleven which was only two hours away.

I was also waiting on Quincy's call and I hoped he called before eleven.

This was crazy.

Two Hours Later:

The vibration of my phone woke me out of a deep slumber. I looked at the time on my phone screen and noticed it was approximately eleven p.m. I also noticed a text message from Lamont.

Lamont: I'm on my way, baby. I'll be there in two minutes.
Uuugh.

I instantly groaned but Lamont's text wasn't the reason.

Incoming Call: Q

That was the reason. Quincy chose then to call. I ended up dozing off after I never received a call from him. Now he was calling when Lamont was on his way over. And strangely, I now wished I never told Lamont to come over. Strangely, I felt as if I was cheating on Quincy.

I shook my head at my current dilemma as I just watched the screen until the call attempt ended.

I instantly felt guilty. And even guiltier when I read his message.

Q: I guess you're busy, sweetheart. Message me on Facebook when you can. Hopefully I can get back on. There are new guards working tonight so the risk of me being the phone are high. If I don't speak to you tonight, I will talk to you tomorrow.

Warm wishes and Champagne kisses. Q.

And after I read his short, but sweet message, here came another incoming text message.

Lamont: Baby, I'm at the door.

Uuuuggghhhh. Help me.

CHAPTER 31
SAKINA

Four Months Later:

"Happy Birthday! Bish!"

"Thank you!"

"Wit your old ass."

I laughed at Malika's comment and waved her off.

"Old my ass. This is what Thirty-six looks like."

I twirled and did my little two step dance, as I modeled a cute, black, laced, two-piece top and skirt set with a pair of black, Michael Kors, strapped, stiletto heels. My shoulder length hair was styled in a doobie style with streaks of Burgundy highlights. I was looking great if I must say so myself and for my thirty-sixth birthday, I felt great.

"Sit your drunk ass down!" Malika shouted and laughed out loud.

I laughed along with her as I resumed my seat. I reached

over on the table and sipped on my second glass of Apple Martini for the night. Yes, I was borderline tipsy, but nowhere near wasted. Leave it to Malika to over exaggerate. I was, however, feeling down, but not because I was not happy about my birthday, but for a couple of other reasons. Such reasons suddenly crossed my mental and I reached over for a shot glass, placed on the table, which consisted of my favorite dark liquor, Hennessey.

"Happy Birthday, huh?"

Malika watched as I downed the drink and for a second, the look in her eyes resembled one of concern. I tried to ignore it as I swallowed the drink and bared the burning sensation.

"Shamille still didn't put you on her visiting list?" She questioned trying to find out the source of my obvious current state.

Instead of answering her, I shook my head, reached over on the table and grabbed a hold of my second shot and downed that as well.

I briefly closed my eyes shut as I gulped the strong liquor.

Drinking it straight burned my throat, but it did the trick and help suppressed my pain.

"Kina," Malika called my name, but I stopped by then taking a sip of the Apple Martini I was still sipping.

"You haven't heard from Q?" She asked another question and that time I could hear the concern in her voice loud and clear and there it was. One of the reasons for my sudden solemn state, but I opted on doing what I did best, which was pretend otherwise.

"I don't want to talk about him!" I shouted over a sudden reggae jam which soared through the lounge's speakers.

"Kina," I heard Malika call out to me once more and once again I was determined to pretend that everything was all well in my world. Appearing perfect was a must to me and no one understood that better than Malika but still, the look in her eyes pulled at my heart string. Her sensitive side did not make an appearance too often but when it did, it had me concern as well.

"I'm going to dance," I announced, before she was able to protest. I grabbed another shot glass filled with Hennessey and headed over to the dance floor where I was the only one on it. I didn't care to talk about my sister. And no, I did not want to talk about Quincy. But, yes, I was hurt. We have not spoken for four months now.

Yes, four whole months and as silent as it was kept, I was sick over it. My relationship with Lamont finally took a toll on him and he let it be known one day when he called while Lamont was over. He stated his feelings and things took a turn for the worse after that. He hung up on me before I could barely get a word in. And that was the last I've heard from him. His phone calls cease as well as all Facebook interaction. I wanted to reach out to him plenty of times, but my pride would not allow me to do so. He hung up on me and I did not allow any disrespect from no man.

But all in all.... I missed him; however he will never know. He knew of my situation when we first decided to start our friendship, and if he chooses to be stubborn now then so be it.

But, again, I could not help but miss the hell out of him.

The phone calls.... The intimate and deep conversations.... The poems...His words....

He just ended all that with no warning...and I was sick...literally.

And here it was my birthday...and still no message on messenger.... I knew he was fully aware of my birthday since

I've been receiving countless birthday wishes since midnight last night.

But still, no phone call.... No roses.... Nothing....

A wave of depression suddenly washed over me, and I quickly suppressed it as I brought the shot glass to my lips and swallowed the strong drink.

Fuck Quincy. He was all wrong for me anyway....

My inner conscious tried to convince me, and I opted on believing it. Instead on dwelling over a man I couldn't be with anyway, I decided to get my mind right tomorrow and forget Quincy Norton and the fact he ever existed.

Instead, I decided to enjoy my birthday to the fullest.

Malika, Shawn, who was arriving soon, minus Lamont who was working, and I were out celebrating at one of my favorite Caribbean club and lounge establishment in the heart of New York City. I loved it for it's grown and classy atmosphere, great DJ and outstanding cuisine. Especially my favorite, which was Haitian food.

We were seated at an open table right next to the bar which was Malika's favorite spot. She had ordered three bottles of Moet with several shots of Patron for her and Hennessey for me. She loved white hard liquor and dark liquor was my choice. The rectangle shaped wooden table was adorned with drinks and assorted Haitian dishes. You named it and it was positioned in front of us. Drinks were included.

Despite my current state, I was having the time of my life and I had Malika to thank. Every year since the year we met all those years ago, she opted on celebrating my birthday in style and this year was no different. She rented out the whole lounge area just for us and I was amazed she was able to pull it off. It was a Thursday night, one of the busiest nights for the popular establishment and we had it all to ourselves with the exception of the staff members. And really that was fine by me. I didn't have any friends. I had associates and a few females I refer to as acquaintances. Malika was my one and true friend and I was content. She was actually more like family and she definitely made up for the absence of my own sister.

My sister. I missed her and events like my birthday, I missed her the most. And this morning, just like I did every birthday, I reached out to the women's facility she was incarcerated in and checked to see if she by any chance placed me on the list and just like every other year, she did not and my heart broke all over again.

Another birthday without my sister. Another birthday without my mother. Another birthday without my father.

And now.... another one without my true heart desire..

To hell with it....

I continued to dance alone to the unidentified reggae jam as I became lost in the beat of the music.

CHAPTER 32
MALIKA

This was the bullshit. I hated to see my girl, my sister hurting, and it was time I stepped in and do what I did best, which was be a true friend and family to her.

Sakina. Her ass was my heart. From the day, all those years ago I rescued her from being almost attacked and raped by some wanna be thugs at Rutgers University, where we were both students, I bonded with her. And that lead to a true sisterhood.

I loved her more than I loved my own two biological sisters and that was because her love for me was pure and real. She loved and accepted me for who I was…No questions…No judgements…. I know I was rough around the edges and she accepted that shit to the fullest so of course, I chose to return the favor.

Outside looking in, she appeared to be the poster girl for perfection, but she was as complex as they came, and no one understood her like I did.

And with that said, I knew she was full of shit.

She was hurting and I should mush the hell out of her head

for trying to play me, but instead, I'm going to let her make it since it was her birthday.

Instead, I was going to do something I've never done before.

Our sisterhood was based on mutual respect and with that, we respected one another's decisions, so we never got involved in each other's love life and that has worked for years. I hated her choice in men. From the jerks when we were in college, to her whack ass baby daddy to that corny nigga, Lamont, I couldn't stand none of their asses, but I must admit, there was something about this negro Quincy that actually had me feeling that he might be the one.

Yeah, I was skeptical when he first reached out to her months ago, because I know first - hand a lot of these niggas locked up be up on game, but I must admit, Mr. Cali has gained some cool points with me.

I loved a bold nigga but in a good way. He knew what he wanted and went after it and wasn't letting his current situation stop him and I loved that shit.

And what I love the most is his great taste. He sees in Sakina what I know to be true and that she was one hell of a woman and person.

So hell yeah, I've been rooting for him, despite the fact his ass was still doing life. Sakina have told me of the new lead in his case that his lawyer had informed him of, and I was now rooting for him more than ever. I knew if he was to come home, him and Sakina would be one hell of something special.

But first, he had to make it home.

In the meantime, I was all for their friendship and the fact that they were building a bond, but now this nigga wants to be in his feelings over that cornball Lamont, fucking with my girl's emotional state and I wasn't having it. He haven't contact her in four months and the last time they talked, he hung up on her. I wanted to give his ass a piece of my mind then, but as I stated, she and I respected each other's boundaries. But after four months of my girl hurting, I had to do something. Not to mention, it was her birthday and this nigga still didn't reach out? Nah, he got the game fucked up.

It's time I stepped in this shit.

So, while Sakina was dancing on the dance floor, I decided to grab a hold of her cell phone which was rested on the table. I hated to do this, but this was necessary.

Acting quickly before Sakina returned to the table, I went straight to the contacts and was thankful Quincy's name and number was still programmed in.

Her ass wasn't that mad at his ass

I chuckled at my own thought as I clicked on Quincy's number and dialed his number. I was pissed when I received his voicemail, but instead, I decided to leave him a voicemail with a quickness. My eyes stayed glue to Sakina on the dance floor lost to the beat of some Haitian song that was now playing.

"Aye, check this shit out, Mr. Cali, you know who this is and just in case you don't, this is Malika, Sakina's best friend. I'm going to get straight to the point. This is not really my business, but it's fucked up you hung up on her the last time you two spoke when your Mr. lover, lover ass was the one who chased her and initiated this friendship, but what's even more fucked up, is that you don't reach out on her birthday or even wished her a Happy Birthday. I know your ass know it's her birthday since you're still Facebook friends with her. I know your ass could see on both of her pages. Now get your mind right. You knew she had a nigga when she started this with you. Even though I don't like his ass, that is still her situation and she was completely honest with you about it. Now, your ass convinced her to let you into her life despite your situation, so now be the man you told her you were and deal with this shit."

And with that, I hung up. The ball was in his court, but if he knew what I knew, he better throw that mothafucker right.

Now, I needed a drink after playing matchmaker and shit.

CHAPTER 33
QUINCY

Down, out, push up, push up, push up, push up, push up an up count, seventy-seven. I was covered in sweat. I started my workout today with one thousand push - ups, twenty sets of fifty. Then I jumped right into thirty-two counts of burpees. I was too pissed off to feel the burn of the workout. I mean I was hot! It takes a lot to get me fired up, but I was there. When I hit one hundred-seventy-two, I started to feel an intense burn in my chest and my upper thighs. I pushed myself even further. Since I was so close, I had to make it to two hundred, before I stopped. The floor to my cell was covered with sweat. In all actuality, I don't know how many burpees I did. I kept losing track of the count because I kept thinking about Sakina.

I thought about her every day, but today was one of those days she was heavy on my mind, because it was her birthday. It has been four months since we have spoken, and I was missing her something serious. Her voice, our late - night talks and the way she said my name.

Damn, I missed her. But after all the sweet thoughts, the memories of our conversation from four months ago replays in my head, which brings on my anger. And the only way I'm able to calm down is by getting my work out on. Today I was heated so I went extra hard. By the time I finished, the cell was stuffy and humid.

I walked over to the window in my cell and blocked it with a towel, before walking over to the sink located in the corner in my small cell and washed the sweat off my body.

In that same moment, I tried to take my mind off Sakina, but I was not able to. Walking over to my bunk I laid down and closed my eyes. And that's when the memory from four months ago came to mind like a bad nightmare.

Deputy Trujillo's partner had walked off somewhere, and she was writing a report, so I figured it was safe to make a phone call. The first time I called Sakina's phone, she didn't answer which I found odd because she always answered my calls except for the night before. I thought about putting the phone away, but something told me to call again. As soon as she answered, I wished that I hadn't.

At first, all I heard was laughter, but then, I heard the bullshit. "Hahahaha Lamont, you are so crazy. No we are not about to do that!...." It sounded like she had answered the phone before putting it to her ear.

"Hello?" She finally spoke into the phone in a cheerful tone.

I felt some type of way, but I tried to control my feelings. I knew she had a man in her life but to hear her playing around like she all in love with the next nigga, I did not like the shit. No matter what, I was still a man.

"I was calling just to see how you were doing but since you got company right now and it sounds like you're about to be busy, I guess I'll just hollar at you whenever."

Damn! I was caught up in my feelings fo'sho.

"Q-Quincy? Oh my God, Quincy I didn't know that it was you. I'm so sorry." She lowered her voice and that pissed me off even more.

"Sorry that I heard you or that you picked up the phone?" I could hear that nigga in the background talking but I wasn't paying attention to shit he was saying.

"No it's not like that at all. I just never looked at this caller I.D. before I answered the call."

"So, what are you sorry about?" I was wondering what she was sorry for. Sorry that I overheard her? I cannot lie, my feelings were actually hurt. I was jealous that I was not the one there with her.

Her next words fucked all that up, though.

"Look Lamont can you just please call...." I cut her off.

"What the fuck did you just call me?" I was livid!

That was the ultimate disrespect to have a woman call you another nigga's name.

"Oh my God! I am sorry. I didn't mean to do that please.........." I cut her off again I was more hurt than pissed.

"Kina, listen. You're fucking up because you are nervous. You really don't have anything to be nervous about. It ain't like we're together. Plus you did tell me you had someone in your life, so you're not in the wrong as far as I'm concerned. However, I do have to tell you this........." This time it was her who did the cutting off.

"Look Quincy can we please talk about this later?" She sounded like she was pleading with the teacher not to give her detention.

"Naaw, I'm sorry but you're going to have to hear me out on this one. Up until now I've been the absolute perfect friend. Always listening and never questioning you about anything, but along the way,

I've expressed my feelings towards you, while showing you that I most certainly know how to treat a woman. Especially my woman. I need you to hear me on this because I can never sit back and play second fiddle to any nigga. That's not me, I never done it before and I'm not going to start now. I know this is going to be tough given my situation. I also realize that I might even miss out, but I got to do me . Something's got to shake. Either you are going to be true to dude or you're going to go out on a limb and give us a try. The only thing I want you to realize is dude was in the picture long before me. If things were the way they were supposed to be between the two of you, I wouldn't be on the phone with you now. So the way I figure it, he is not what you want. So you need to let me know if you want to try giving us a shot. Point blank."

After I spoke my peace, I did not wait for her response. A part of me didn't want to hear what she had to say because with dude there, she wasn't going to keep it real with me, so I just hung up on her. But I did hear o'le boy saying some slick shit, pissing me off more.

I shook off the memory and reopened my eyes. I reached over on the desk in my cell and grabbed another one of the books that D-Lo gave me, which was book two of Gorillaz in The Bay. It was written by one of the homies named De' Kari.

The book was hard as hell. Plus, since I was from Menlo Park, I knew about some of the people mentioned in his book and the shit that he was talking about. When I got up to use the bathroom, I realized it was almost nine p.m. I kicked myself mentally because I was supposed to call Cynthia earlier. That was not me, forgetting to contact my lil sister.

I decided to call her any way. We talked for about thirty

minutes. My sister was always the one planning things which naturally meant she had already started planning what we were going to do when I came home. I loved her enthusiasm, but I was more of a let's wait and see what happens before we plan kind of guy. But I let her have her way and do what she wanted to do.

Needless to say, I made sure to tell her to make sure she included Sakina in our plans because she was fa' sho going to be right by my side. This was a minor setback. I am sure... no I'm certain that she will open her eyes and see that I am the best choice for her.

Cynthia and I hung up the phone promising each other that we would talk in the morning. I fought the urge to call Sakina after I hung up with Cynthia. My will power held out in the end and I placed the phone back inside the breathing machine. I proceeded and brushed my teeth before hitting my knees and saying my prayers.

After I laid back down, I started thinking about life and what the future held. Just when I began to get nervous about my upcoming hearing, a warm feeling came over my body. It was a sweet warm calming sensation. I don't know if this was going to sound crazy or not, but I think it was God. I believe he was calming my fears and telling me everything was going to be alright.

My eyelids grew heavy, I was in fact sleepy, but thoughts of Sakina haunted me as well as the last day we spoke. Thoughts of the days that turned *into* months also crossed my mind. Then I thought of how I finally swallowed my pride and called her. Then the final thought of how she hung up *on* me without giving me the chance to say hello. I knew she was aware that it was me due to the 650-area code. I mean, how many niggas she had calling her from a 650-area code number.

I started to call her back, however, I took it that she had chosen o'le boy instead of me. As the days went by, I was torn between calling her and not calling. Something wasn't sitting right with me. I knew damn well she was feeling me. I wanted to know why she was willing to throw it all away, but I was too hurt, and my pride was wounded, to make that call. Occasionally, I would look on her Facebook page just to see what she was up to. I felt like a stalker but couldn't help myself. I fell in love with this woman whom I never met. Hell yeah, I was in love, I silently admitted when I started dozing off.

I guess Sakina was on my mind heavily because I was dreaming about her and all of a sudden, I woke up. I kept thinking about her, so I decided to grab my phone to check her Facebook page again to see if she had posted anything for her birthday. I reached over and pulled out my phone. Looking at the screen, I noticed a miss call from a Jersey number. I was not sure who it was, but unless they called back, they wouldn't talk to me tonight, because I really wasn't in the mood to talk to anyone. Instead, I decided to look at apartments online just to get a feel for things and where I would want to move once I was home.

A few minutes later, I noticed I had a voice message. Listening to the voicemail message, I was heated all over again. Sakina's best friend Malika left a message, and I was convinced she was crazy for real. She had talked so greasy on that message that had she been a man I would've went upside her mothafucking head.

I have always been the type of man to address a situation

head on. So I called her back immediately. When she picked up the phone, I fed her both barrels.

"Now I don't know how them niggas in Jersey get down, but lil mama, I'm not with the games nor the disrespect. If you wanna get my attention, get at me on some real shit, because coming at me on some ratchet shit is the fastest way to bring a side of me out that your little ass don't wanna see, trust me. Malika you don't know me, if you did, you would know that I am a grown ass man not one of them little boys that let you talk to them like that. Now, do yourself a favor and don't ever call my phone with some bullshit again."

Though I was heated, a part of me wondered why she was calling, but I was too piss to care at that moment.

I started to hang up the phone when I heard her voice yelling out to me.

"Wait! Wait! Wait! Quincy, damn I'm sorry okay! I knew you were different than most men and I should not have come at you like that. It's just that my girl is hurting, and I don't like seeing her in pain!" She blurted out.

Her admission tugged at my heartstring, but I had to hold my composure.

"How is she hurting when she is the one that had the nerve to hang up on me?"

"Quincy, first off, from what she told me, you hung up on her first. And second, Kina would never do that. She told me, she think Lamont was messing with her phone, because she walked in on him holding it in his hand. So if you were hung up on, that nigga did that. Kina would never hang up on you," she pleaded and proceeded to explain things to me. Damn, could it be true? All this time I have been tripping for nothing.

"So, where is she now?" I asked, ready to talk to my Goddess.

I could hear music playing in the background like they were at a party. Most likely her birthday party.

"Hold on," Malika said to me and minutes after that, I heard the sweet voice I've been missing these past four months.

"No Malika I don't want to talk on the phone with nobody! What? No, who is it?" I could tell she had an attitude but finally grabbed the phone and said hello.

"Hey lil Goddess."

I heard her gasp at the sound of my voice.

"Q-Quincy?" She asked sounding like a little girl.

"Kina, you know I'm the only one that calls you Goddess," I said to her and wasted no time getting straight to the point.

"Kina, listen, I got to tell you something. I knew what the deal was with dude, so I guess I must take some blame. But you got to understand that it isn't my fault that my feelings for you have grown way beyond the platonic phase. Kina I'm laying claim to what is mine. Baby, I am willing to give you any and all of me. But Goddess you got to give me the same in return. It's got to be all or nothing."

There it was. I laid it out for her and waited for her response. I hope she knows that I meant what I said. This time around, it was all or nothing. I found myself holding in my breath as I waited for her response.

CHAPTER 34
SAKINA

Moments Prior:

An pran on ti rendevou, ti rendevou lanmou
Pou nou ka we doudou- ann pran on ti rendevou lanmou

I was lost in the sultry beat and lyrics of one of my favorite Haitian love ballads better known as Konpa. Konpa was a genre in Caribbean music and this song; **Ti Rendevou** by a group called **Zin** was one of my all-time favorite.

Ti Rendevou... Ti Rendevou lanmou..

The lyrics soared and I was lost...I had my eyes closed as I stood in place and slowly gyrated my waist and hips to the beat.

Ti Rendevou.... Cherie Mwen anvi fe lanmou

The words soared through the club's speakers as the lead singer sung in Creole requesting for a love making session and for a second, I felt as if he was singing to me.

And seconds after that.... I felt his presence.... except... it wasn't the lead singer Alan Carve's body suddenly glued to mine.

"Warm wishes and Champagne kisses" his words and signature phrase to me suddenly echoed in my mental. He felt so real.

Mmmmm. Yess. He felt so real.

Quincy... I felt him...

Ti Rendevous... Ti Rendevous...

And as the lyrics repeated, I wished it was Quincy requesting for a love making session.

Mmmmm... I continued slow grinding my body to the beat and I was just about gone.... Gone into my own secret fantasy world filled with nothing but thoughts of Quincy Norton. His conversations alone used to bring on an - orgasmic trance that I've never experienced before and now I craved beyond comprehension. God, I missed him.

Plenty of times, I wanted to call him and apologize to him for what took place four months ago...Plenty of times I wanted to message him on Facebook. Plenty of times I wanted to confess to him, I think...

I think I've fallen in love with him....

But...me and this pride of mine...

So, instead, I chose to simply secretly dream and long for him.

This current moment as I continued to dance in place, was the best time as ever, as I wished he could've sealed my birthday wish with his presence...

I was in the middle of fantasying just that, when I heard Malika's voice over the loud music.

I heard her calling my name until she was then in front of me shoving her cell phone in my face.

I reopened my eyes, halted my dancing and noticed she was lip-syncing something to me. At first, I protested that I did not care to speak to anyone, until she placed the phone directly onto my ear.

"Hey lil Goddess."

For a second, the sound of his voice caught me off guard.

What the hell?

"Q-Quincy?" Finally, I uttered his name, stuttering, still in mini shock.

"Kina, you know I'm the only one that calls you Goddess," he said, and I partially smiled. He was indeed and I missed that as well.

After he voiced those words, he went on to confess what was exactly on his mind. As I listened to his heartfelt words, I made eye contact with Malika who stood in front of me.

She was mouthing for me to tell him how I felt about him. And I intended to do just that, when I heard he concluded his speech with his final words of plea.

"But Goddess you got to give me the same in return. It's got to be all or nothing."

I heard him loud and clear and my heart wanted it all and to give him all...

But... And in that moment, my eyes landed on a familiar figure by the front entrance of the lounge.

In walked Lamont, still sporting his Police Officer uniform. It appeared he came straight here after getting off work.

See, when Quincy hung up on me and cut off all contact, Lamont begged for a commitment. He even asked for me and my sons to move in with him.

Unlike me, he owned his own home. He suggested that I could save money by moving into his home instead of purchasing a whole new one. He even offered to add my name onto his house deed.

At the time, I was pissed at Quincy, so I told Lamont I would think about it and as the months, days, minutes and seconds passed and I heard nothing from Quincy, I figured he was all wrong for me after all and that Lamont was indeed the right man for me, but…my heart ached for Quincy every minute of every day symbolizing that he was the man I wanted and fallen for.

And as I stood there, with him on the other end of the phone line waiting for my response I knew what I wanted.

But… I needed one request of my own.

"Q, I love you and I want it to be all, but I need to end this chapter with Lamont, first. Second time around, I want us together as a real couple. And whatever support you need with your case to get you home, I can give it, but first I need to end this thing with Lamont, and I promise it will be all for us. I will be all yours."

And there it was. And as Lamont made his way towards where Malika and I stood, holding a dozen of red roses, I knew getting rid of him was not going to be as easy as I wished it would be, but I was determined to make it an accomplished one.

And I knew right then and there I was indeed in love with Quincy, because I stood and listened to his response as Lamont halted in front of me. Malika gave him the evil eye but all I cared in that moment was what Quincy had to say.

"Kina I hear what you're saying. I don't have a problem letting you handle your business, just don't take advantage of a good nigga's heart. And don't take your sweet little time in handling your business because you and I have some serious business that we need to handle. Just know this, I am glad that you have finally made the right decision..."

CHAPTER 35
QUINCY

Two Weeks Later:

"Look at you, I missed that laugh, Goddess."

We have been on the phone for the past thirty minutes and she had me laughing non-stop and vice versa. Her laughter was contagious, and I realized just how much I truly did miss her.

These past two weeks have been sort of a make-up time for us after not communicating for months and despite my situation, I felt as if I was in Heaven.

Who would've thought, I would connect with a woman I never met before just by reading her words. And from that moment on, I have slowly been bonding with this woman spiritually. Our connection was too powerful for me to ignore and now that we have reconnected, I was happy that I chose not to ignore it. Folks always say love happens unexpectantly. With no schedule, no appointment, no warning.

When I told her it was all or nothing, I meant that from the heart. But, after her confession the night of her party, I also understood the reality of it all.

I believe that what she feels for me is in fact love, but I also believe in a woman's heart. In Sakina's heart. A woman like her needed assurance. She needed confirmation. She wants to be sure that she is finally choosing right after choosing wrong for so long. And the truth was... The reality of it all.. Until I was a free man and able to show her that my walk matched my talk, there would always be doubt.

Finally, the possibility of going home was closer. Earlier this morning I received the call telling me to transpack my property. I would be on the bus back to San Mateo County Jail in the morning.

I did not mention it to Sakina, though. I simply told her that I was going back to take care of some small formality. I did not want anything to jinx the possibility of my getting released.

Plus, I wanted her to focus on her current situation. When I agreed to give her time to work things out, I had to look at the situation from a realistic point of view. She had two boys who experienced disappointment from their biological father constantly, according to Sakina and as much as I hated to accept it, the dude Lamont has been some sort of father-figure in her sons' life. So, ending things with him needed to be handled in a delicate way.

I was man enough to accept that.

"Freestyle a poem to me." She said suddenly, and I smiled. This was our regular routine. She would request a poem from my heart. No pen and paper, just right on the spot and I always honored her request.

"After me, to love any other man would be senseless," I recited to her.

She was silent as I waited for her response and finally, she expressed in an amused tone, "Boy, that's not yours. Does L.L. Cool J know you're stealing his shit?"

I busted out laughing.

"You owe me a poem, Q," she said, and I smiled again. I loved when she called me Q. The way she said it was sexy as hell. I suddenly felt a feeling of lust taking over and just like every other time I experienced this feeling, I suppressed it with my other talent, which was telling jokes.

"Boy, your ass is crazy. There's no way that Bernie Mac was funnier than Kat Williams and I don't care how many impressions you do, it's not going to change that." She said after I did my Bernie Mac expressions.

"You're only saying that because you like hearing me say, *Do something to make me feel good*.." I imitated St. Louis from the movie Players Club making her laugh even more.

We continued with our conversation until she placed me on hold to let her boys know it was time to shut off their PS4 and prepare for bed. It was the middle of September and they just returned to school.

"I'm back," She let me know a few minutes later.

"Is everything good?" I asked her.

"Yes, everything is good. And thank you again for purchasing that PS4 for them. It's like pulling teeth to tear them away from that thing for the last three days since it arrived here."

"You're welcome, Goddess. You do not have to keep thanking me. I just wanted to do something nice for them since they were upset after their dad canceled on them again."

I do not understand how a nigga could keep standing up his own sons, but I chose to keep my opinions to myself. Instead, I decided to just show Sakina the kind of man I could be to her and her sons and buying a game is just a preview. Of course, they were unaware the PS4 came from me and we both felt that was for the best.

"By the way, how do you have that kind of money Q? I mean, I don't mean to pry but A PS4 is kind of expensive."

She asked the one question I was not ready to answer. I was not prepared to share with her the activities I had to involve myself in order to survive and secure an attorney to fight for my freedom. Yes, I was sitting on a nice amount of money and if I make it home, I may have to explain it to her, but, right now, I wasn't ready to have that conversation with her and maybe when or If I do, I will never tell her the complete truth.

Once, I do return to life in the real world, I plan on closing this chapter of my life and never reopen it again.

"How do you have that sexy body? You work out?"

I asked her, switching the tone of the conversation and subject altogether.

The van was travelling down highway 580. I could not believe that I was finally back in the Bay Area. California alone was a beautiful place, but the Bay Area has a beauty all of its own. The buildings, the music, the streets, hell even the air smelled different. Because of all the traffic, the air was a little polluted, yet to a Bay Area native, the air was sweet.

The van exited the freeway. It had to drive down the streets through the city of Hayward for a little while and connect to interstate 92, which leads you straight to the San Mateo Bridge.

So many things were different. I couldn't believe how foreign everything looked. It seemed like we caught every green light on Jackson Street in Hayward. Before I knew it, we were driving on the San Mateo Bridge. *Messy Marv's "Black Jesus"* popped in my head and I rapped it to myself. After that song played in my head I thought about his song *"Shackles"* and let that play next.

The Bay water under the bridge fueled my soul and really welcomed me back home. Although I was headed to the county jail. I was indeed home.

Before I knew it, we had already pulled off the highway into Redwood City. I was back in Redwood City jail.

I sat in intake for two and half hours after I was processed. I didn't mind because I was locked inside of a holding tank that had phones with free calls instead of collect calls. I used the time to call my little sister and Sakina. Both were all over me with questions. Was I okay? How long would I be there? And a bunch more.

I eased their minds by answering a few of their questions, letting them know I was okay. Some I sidestepped and the rest I just told them that I did not know the answers.

They finally took me to a cell. I was sent to 6-W-3. I was tripping at first because before I went to prison, 6-W was the pod that they housed the P.C. (protective custody) inmates in. When I mentioned this to the deputy that was escorting me, he informed me that they had switched things around and all the P.C.'s were located at another location they had just built. Including, adding new staff.

When we walked into the pod, I saw that he was telling the truth. All the deputies were new, and they were kids. I am talking 25, 26, 27 years-old's running the facility. To me this was a sign that it was a new day. When I got in the cell, I cleaned it from top to bottom, then made my bed and laid down. The only piece of personal property that I had was my breathing machine for my sleep apnea. That was all I needed. After a while I drifted off to sleep.

CHAPTER 36
SAKINA

"Oh God, please, I know I don't talk to you often, but I promise you, if you grant me this one wish and make this negative , I promise I will do right and leave this man alone because the fact that I'm feeling like this tells me this is the wrong man for me. Please God."

"Girl, if you don't calm your ass down. Why do people beg on God when they want to get out of some shit?"

I couldn't help it as I laughed through my tears. As distraught as I was feeling, leave it to Malika to make me laugh even when I'm not up to it.

But despite what she pointed out, I continued to say a then silent prayer as she stood up from where she was seated next to me on my bed and exited my bedroom. Seconds later, she returned, and I was scared to look up into her face. I wasn't prepared to hear the worse and I knew her expression would tell it.

"Uuuhm, you can look at me and relax. Your ass is not

knocked up," Malika announced and with no hesitation, I dropped down to my knees and thanked the almighty God.

"Uuuuh huh. Go ahead and thank God and don't forget what your ass promised him. If the test is negative, you will finally leave Lamont's whack ass alone."

I laughed once again at Malika's outspoken ass but what she said was beyond factual. I did promise the man up above and it was about time that I did what was right. When I have been vomiting for the last couple of days and my time of the month was late, I feared the worse and thought I was pregnant, despite the fact I recently was placed on birth control pills by my Oby-Gyn.

And the fact I could be carrying Lamont's baby brought on a panic attack like never before. And I knew right then and there it was time to let Lamont ago.

Truthfully, I was holding on to him for several reasons, but the main reason of all was due to fear. Fear of the possibility of ending up alone due to another fail relationship, fear of making a wrong choice again. I mean, what if Lamont was really the right one for me and Quincy was......

But then again...and in that moment the very thought of Quincy crossed my mind. Suddenly, a warm feeling coveted my body.

Quincy.......

If you thought you were pregnant by him, you would've never reacted the way you just did moments ago

My inner conscious spoke to me and I also felt as if God himself was speaking to me as well. It's ironic, I wasn't the most spiritual person in the world, but as soon as Quincy entered my life and had me indulge in daily prayers, I felt a whole new connection to the higher power and yes, Quincy was the reason for that.

And in that very moment, I knew, I just knew that the man who reached out to me all those months ago, who's very first letter to me, I discarded, who I deemed as nothing more than just a convicted felon who was serving a life sentence was all wrong for me was the right man for me after all. A man who I felt God sent just for me.

Suddenly I started crying again as I remained on my knees. But this time, such tears were ones of joy.

Seconds later, I felt Malika's arms wrapped around my body as I transformed to the fragile mirror of myself that no one else get to see but Malika.

CHAPTER 37
QUINCY

I was moved last week from six-west to five-east. It did not bother me too much, as far as I was concerned, jail was jail. But when I got here, the first thing I did noticed, was there were a few more homeboys in 5-east than there was in 6-West.

This was a good thing, I didn't have to worry about anyone trying to start any shit with me. My focus was on my upcoming hearing so keeping clear of any drama was a must. I was currently laid up on my bunk when I had the sudden urge to get me something to eat. I got up and made a plate of sausage and chicken nachos. I did not eat the food they served; it was straight trash. I could not understand how some dudes ate that shit.

As I ate my food, my mind drifted off to Sakina. Things have been pretty good between us, except, I had a feeling something was bothering her for the last couple of days. Something was off in the tone of her voice. I could tell some shit was wrong and each time I questioned her, she assured me everything was great, but I knew she wasn't telling me the truth.

I tried to convince myself that she was good as she was saying, but my gut told me otherwise. In fact, I had a feeling that she was not always all on the up and up about a lot of things regarding herself. She always appeared to be so composed, happy and reserved but I sensed it was bullshit. No one was that well put together.

Yeah, I had a feeling there was more to her than what she was letting on and she wasn't letting me all the way in. I felt a little hurt, because I thought we were on the right track to connecting as a couple, but how can we if I don't know the real Sakina. After all, I told her everything about me. Everything, except details regarding my life as a convict, but as far as I was concerned, the person I was in prison was irrelevant to who I will be once I touched down back into society. The man I was once before. So all she needed to know was who I was before this conviction and who I will be after.

And in that moment, I felt the urge to pull my phone out and give her a call. I was once again concerned with what was going on with her, but truthfully, I couldn't risk it. A C.O. by the name of Garcia was working our pod today and he was an asshole. I'm talking Robo-Cop by the book ass dude. I respected him, but I just did not like him. However, by the time I had finished eating I said fuck Garcia. After I washed my bowl, cup, and fork out, I decided that I wasn't going to let Garcia stop me from doing me. I needed to speak to my Goddess. I pulled out my phone and laid in bed with my courtesy sheet pulled. I turned towards the wall and adjusted my cords on my breathing machine so it would look like I was asleep. Then I did my thing.

When I turned the phone on, my intentions were to call

Sakina, but my notifications let me know that I had quite a few messages from Cynthia. I decided to call my Angel.

"Hey brother how are you doing?"

She asked me and I noticed right away from the tone in her voice that something was wrong.

"Hey baby sis, I'm good how you doing?"

There was silent for a few seconds and she hesitated before speaking. "I just miss you brother, I wish that I could get on a plane and come home but instead I'm stuck way out here in Pennsylvania, away from everyone I love and I'm lonely."

She suddenly started crying. That right there, bothered me, but I just allowed her to cry for a minute and let the pain out. Knowing there was not anything I could do to help her, and it hurt. After letting her cry for a minute, I spoke.

"Baby girl it's okay. You are my little sister and I love you more than anything in this world. But right now, you need to focus on your education. You will get to come home soon and visit." I tried to console her.

"If you love me so much then why are you lying to me?" She asked and I became alarmed.

"What do you mean lying to you? Cynthia what are you talking about?"

"Quincy, I am your little sister. I can tell when you are lying to me and you are lying about why you are back in Redwood City Jail. If you don't love me enough to tell me the truth what does that say about our bond?"

Damn, what she was saying hurt because it was true. We have been through so much shit, it was unbelievable. I know that I was only trying to protect her from false promises or getting her hopes up. I had to ask myself if I should just open up and tell her or hold back from telling her the truth.

After thinking it over, I decided to just tell her.

"Lil Angel I would never intentionally destroy our bond or trust by lying to you. I was actually just trying to protect you from getting your hopes up for nothing." I paused to take a deep breath and while I was doing so, I checked to make sure no deputies were walking around.

"Cynt," I said, addressing her by her long-time nickname, "I came back to the County because a new law just passed that says if you kill somebody by accident, then you can't be convicted of first- or second-degree murder."

"Okay brother so what does that mean?" Cynthia questioned and I explained further.

"Well, if my attorney can prove that the murder was accidental, then they would have to lower my charges. If that happens, then they will have to let me up out of here. Then, I'm coming home sis."

Damn, it felt good saying those words.

I could hear Cynthia breathing, momentarily before she spoke.

"Brother what's the likely hood of that happening?" She sounded like she was asking the doctor if I was going to live or die.

"I believe I'm coming home sis," I let her know and she let out a loud scream. I was almost afraid the deputies heard her through the phone.

"Damn sis, what are you trying to do, let the entire jail know I have this phone?"

"I'm sorry brother, I am just so happy for you. I cannot believe after all this time, you are coming home." She expressed to me and I could hear the sudden joy in her voice.

"I know but let us not get our hopes up too high. At the end of the day these white folks still have the last say so," I admitted to her, risking upsetting her again.

Right then, I heard mumbling coming from the speaker. I told Cynthia to hold on and went to check it out.

"Norton?" Trujillo, the main deputy on our pod, called out.

"Yeah!" I responded.

"Your attorney called, he wants you to call him," he let me know.

"Alright, let me put some clothes on."

I whispered to my sister that I had to go, before I ended the call. Then I placed the phone back in its spot.

After I dressed, I walked out of my cell over to one of the phones and called my attorney. When he answered, he told me a bunch of shit that I did not want to hear. There were some issues with the calendar and my hearing was being postpones for a few months. I was not trying to hear that shit, but there was nothing I could do about it.

For the first time in a while I was feeling down. As I walked back to my cell, I decided to call Sakina. Before I called her, I hit my knees and said a prayer asking God to give me strength because it was his will to be done not mine.

After my short prayer, I took a seat on my bunk and reached for my phone. I dialed Sakina's number and waited for her to answer.

"Hello."

"Hey lil Goddess how are you doing today?" I greeted her after she answered.

"Heyyy Qunicy," she answered in a cheerful tone. At least that's what she was trying to sell me, but I don't know why I was able to catch the bullshit. I think me and this woman were like kindred spirits of some sort.

I could feel she wasn't okay.

"How are you doing?" I asked her and silently prayed she told me the truth. I hated being lied to.

"I'm doing great. How are you?"

And I heard it, despite the fact she tried to disguise it. She was not great, and I was feeling pissed that she didn't trust me enough to let me in and tell me what was wrong.

I did not like the sound of her voice, so I decided to forget my problems and support her with hers. At least I wanted to support her. So I decided to try a different angle.

"Kina, baby, you sound like you got a lot on your mind and I could hear it, do you want to talk about it?

"Thank you, Quincy, but I told you that I was fine."

I didn't believe it, but I decided to leave it alone. I was hurt that she was keeping something from me and once again.. I knew ole boy was still in the picture, so the fact she won't talk to me, tells me that whatever was wrong concerned him.

"Okay, Kina, I was just checking on you. Let me holler at you later." I said to her.

Before hanging up I decided to let her know, that no matter what she was going through, I was there for her.

"I love you."

"I love you too, Q."

She replied, back to my surprise, and the fact she finally called me Q instead of Quincy caught my attention.

And I smiled a bit. Yeah, I hated that she would not open up to me, but I decided to give her the space and time she needed. I was sure she would eventually tell me.

"I'll talk to you later," I said to her.

"Hey, wait. Are you okay? What's happening down there? What are they saying?"

She asked and I wanted to express to her that I was not okay, but I decided against it. Call it petty or otherwise, but if she was holding back, then from now on, I would do the same. "I'm good, Goddess, always. I have to get off this phone now since there is an asshole officer on shift, but you take care and I will call you when I can."

CHAPTER 38
SAKINA

"Okay, Sakina, the pregnancy test is negative."

I was so happy by my doctor's words I jumped off the examination table in her office and hugged her.

"Oh, okay, then," she laughed as she hugged me in return.

I laughed along with her as I pulled from our embrace.

"I'm sorry, I'm just soo relieved."

"I can imagine," she said as she took a seat in her office chair. I myself, grabbed a hold of my purse from her office desk, preparing for my departure.

"Even though the home test said negative, after the nasty break up with Lamont last night, I just had to come here this morning, to make sure I wasn't pregnant for sure."

"That's understandable," my doctor agreed.

"I swear, Dr. Callahan, I'm never having sex again, uugh."

She laughed once again at my statement and I joined in with her. And this time, unlike yesterday, when I laughed, I felt the ultimate joy. Yesterday, I panicked when I experienced a vomiting episode along with extreme fatigue and when Malika had me realized that my monthly cycle was off schedule, I went into panic mode.

An unwanted pregnancy for a man I wasn't in love with was the last thing I wanted and needed and that opened my eyes to what I really wanted and needed and unfortunately, for Lamont, he wasn't it.

It was time to put an end to this façade of a relationship and last night I did just that. After calling Lamont and telling him I couldn't do this anymore, he did not take it too well.

After a few disrespectful slurs, I was forced to block him on my phone, Instagram, My sons' phones and out of my life.

And for the first time in months, I never felt so free. Free indeed.

"I'm so serious, Dr, Callahan," I said to my long time Gynecologist.

"Well, I don't know about never again, but practicing celibacy until you find the right man is never a bad thing," she advised and not I only did I hear loud and clear, but I also fully agreed.

"And you're soo right. Starting today, this love box is on lock," I said, probing laughter from Dr. Callahan, who was not only my long - time doctor since my teen years, but it was safe to call her a friend.

"So, I guess that means you don't need a prescription for a different birth control pill."

"Oh, no I'm good," I protested with no hesitation.

"Plus, I think those things caused my nausea and my off cycle. That never happened to me before," I pointed out.

"And that is a great possibility. Different birth control pills have had some negative effects on women. There have been acme issues, weight gain and even hair loss."

"And that is exactly why I've never asked you for those things before," I let her know and she nodded her head in agreement.

"Yes, well, but we're clear, that you don't need a new prescription, right?" she asked for assurance and it was my turn to nod my head and I answered with a quickness, "Right with a capital R."

She laughed at my mini dramatic as I prepared to make an exit.

"Oaky, Sakina, you take care and I will see you for your next check - up."

"Thank you and same to you," I returned her farewell as I pulled opened the door to her office and exited.

As soon as I took small strides towards the front entrance of the office building lobby, a feeling of contentment and peace took over me. And as natural as our connection took place, none other than Quincy crossed my mental. Suddenly I had the sudden urge to hear his voice. Plus, I needed to have a much - needed talk with him.

I was ready. Yes, it was time to let him know that I was all in. Earlier, when I spoke to him, and he questioned if I was okay, I lied, like I've done so, quite a few times prior. I wasn't always okay, in fact there were many layers to me and for the first time ever in life, I was ready to allow a man to see every inch of those layers. And I felt in my soul that no man was more worthy than Quincy Norton.

Smiling, I exhaled as I pulled out my cell phone. My attempt was to send him a message on Facebook, requesting for him to call me. I'm never comfortable with calling that cell phone, especially with him in the County where there were more security.

So, as I held my phone in hand ready to scroll to my Facebook page, a familiar voice halted my movement.

"You're calling your new man?"

Halting my steps, momentarily, I sighed and whispered a silent prayer. I turned where I was then facing Lamont. As I looked into his eyes, I suddenly wondered what I've ever seen in him.

No, such thought was in no reference to his looks, but his eyes. Folks always say the eyes are the windows to the soul and for the first time, I noticed the man who I've spent three years with, possessed a tainted one.

Something was not quite right with him, which was more than likely the reason he was never fully able to do right by me. Even with his attempts months ago, it never felt real or sincere and as I stood there and eyed him in his Police Officer Uniform appearing to be the image of a Mr. right, I now understood the meaning of it all.

The lord worked in mysterious ways and when he sent an inmate, serving life, in the form of what appeared to be the wrong man into my life, he was rescuing me, delivering me, rebirthing me.

I now understood fully. Quincy Norton.

The Right Kind Of Wrong.

"You have a nice life, Lamont," I simply replied to now my past as I walked away with nothing else to say to him.

"You can forget the Essence magazine interview. They don't fuck with bitches who deal with convicted felons," I heard him call out.

I had a feeling I knew how he was aware of Quincy and I silently cursed that my interview with Essence magazine would no longer be, since he did in fact made it happen, but I kept walking with my head held high. He did not deserve a response and that was a given.

CHAPTER 39
LAMONT

Traumatic experiences can change a person into a carbon copy of someone that was total opposite of who they really were. Have you doing shit, exercising behavior and messing with lives you wouldn't normally do.

Was it wrong?

Hell yeah, but I've accepted my reality a long time ago.

I wasn't a good person. At least not anymore. July of 2008 changed that.

The night a drunk driver turned on the same one way street I was traveling and hit my car head on, causing my wife and three year old daughter to die instantly, was the beginning of living life with an I don't give a fuck attitude.

Prior to that, I was Lamont Pacer, the all - around nice guy with a heart of gold. I was raised in a two parents family home with morals and good standards. I was raised to do everything right. My parents sent me to the best schools, so I achieved the best grades. I was accepted to an Ivy league school, so I attended and graduated with honors. I was told by my parents that it was time to settle down, so I married the school of dean's daughter. I was told I should follow in my dad's footsteps and become a cop, so I did that.

All my life, I lived life by the books, and I was actually happy.

But the night I lost my family was the night I no longer gave a fuck.

It's as if I've been bitten by an evil spirit and no one was exempt from feeling my raft and they have. I've done some fucked up shit in these last ten years, however, with Sakina, I tried to change. I tried, yes, I fucked up along the way, but compared to other victims who's been on the receiving end of my raft, Sakina had it the best.

From the minute I laid eyes on her, I wanted her and the day I came across her book at a local bank, presented the perfect opportunity for me to approach her at her bookstore. I asked her out on a date and things took off from there. Shortly after, I knew she wanted a relationship and grew to care for me, but I just wasn't right. I played many games and her affections were my main target.

But, after I slept with a co-worker, who Sakina caught me talking with outside my house, I realized Sakina was who I wanted. After five months of us separated, I wanted her. I tried to do right. I did, but then her whole behavior changed. She didn't want me like she once did and I had to find out what was up so, I placed a mini camera in her home.

And eventually, I found out the truth. Another man caught her attention and that shit was a no in my book. I conducted some researched and found out exactly who she was playing me for, and I was insulted. I would've been more impressed if he was a white-collar man or one with a higher status than me, but a convict?

And despite that shit, I still tried with her. The fact she was still with me, I thought she chose me, but she was on the phone, every day, chopping it up with a fucking murderer. I even picked up her phone one day when he called, and I hung up on his ass. And still, I stayed, and was willing to try with her. I was even bonding with her boys more.

But none of that seemed to matter to her. She finally called and ended our relationship and I felt played for the last time. Yes, I let her know exactly what I thought of her and I had no remorse.

Calling her some names and pulling the plug on her Essence magazine interview was actually me being nice. I can do a lot worse, but I decided to allow her to make it.

But, of course, no matter how hard I tried to be good and nice, my evil side always seem to prevail.

My cell phone suddenly vibrated in my pocket and I grinned, for it was just the call I was waiting on.

"Yeah," I said to the caller on the other end of the phone line.

"Eleven months is the longest you could have it pushed back?" I asked the caller as I clenched my jaw. I was pissed that my wish was only going to be granted for a temporarily basis, but my connections as a Police Officer can only go so far.

"Alright thanks, and next time I'm in Cali, I will contact you."

And I ended the call.

I smirked as I thought of Sakina. She didn't have to be with me, but she wasn't going to be with her criminal boyfriend anytime soon, either.

I wished I could tamper with his case and keep his convict

ass in there indefinitely, but the hook up I had in the California court system could only do so much.

But I was content for now. Yeah, some might say I was dead wrong, but I could care less.

I was actually trying to be good just for her, but that wasn't good enough. Moving in with me in my house that I owned wasn't good enough for her, having my baby wasn't good enough for her and me trying to be there for her sons were not good enough either.

No, she wanted a fucking murderer. A convicted felon. I don't give a fuck that he used to be a well - respected citizen and top Real Estate agent in California. His ass killed someone and had lived as an inmate for almost five years, so that made him a criminal, a felon. He was all wrong for an upcoming Author and I couldn't believe she has fallen in love with this guy.

So yes, it's fuck her from now on until she comes to her senses and choose right, which was me. A well respected, Police Officer, with a clean criminal record and high connections within the professional world. I can help her reach her ultimate goal as an Author, starting with the Essence Magazine interview but first she needs to get her mind right and choose me. Yes, my mental was fucked up, and has been but, she can make me right and I'm hoping while her convict boyfriend's hearing have been pushed back to almost a year, she would get her mind right as well, and come back to me, the right man for her.

I needed her to make me right again. And I'm willing to do whatever it takes to make her see that.

CHAPTER 40
QUINCY

August of 2019

I cannot believe that I have been back in this damn County jail for about eleven months now. It was now August of 2019 and finally my court date was here. I had a little time before I left for court, so I laid on my bunk and called my baby. She answered on the second ring.

"Damn, I was just thinking about you and wondering if you were going to call me," Sakina said, sounding very happy. I swear to God her voice was like sunshine after a mighty storm.

"Goddess, you know I can't begin my day without hearing your voice."

And that was the truth. She and I have been talking every day for the last eleven months and despite the fact I was upset over my court hearing being pushed back so far which was a still a mystery as to why, I still managed to stay in good spirits. And that was mainly due to Sakina. Our bonding reached a whole new level all these months.

Slowly, she started letting me in. I still felt she was holding some things back from me, but the fact that ole boy Lamont was finally out of the picture, was good enough for me not to pry. I was unsure of the details regarding their break up, but when she told me she loved me and only me, that was like music to my ears and enough for me to leave the subject alone, unless she chose to confide in me in the future.

I was content for now with the fact, she was unattached. For how long? That was unclear.

My case was still up in the air and, was I coming home for sure? That was unclear as well. The answers to those questions were still up in the air, but her friendship, her loyalty meant the world to me. She definitely made this time much more bearable.

"You are so sweet. Are you ready for your hearing today? I have been praying all night that things go favorable for you. I know you deserve a break, and I can feel that God is going to give it to you," she said, and I smiled.

Her words, her encouragement, were reminders why I fell in love in the first place. I knew she was something special just from the words she's written in her books and after getting to know her, I can honestly say, second time around I picked the right woman for me. Now I just needed to make it home to her. I would say this; until we were physically together.

"Thank you, I believe God is going to work in my favor and give us some good news. My attorney told me that he felt confident and believes we are going to win this hearing."

When Sakina told me, she was no longer with Lamont and confessed her daily love to me, I decided to give her a little something to look forward to. I told her that I was in the County to see if they would take the life sentence off. This was partially true. I did not tell her the rest.

THE RIGHT KIND OF WRONG

"I hope he is right," she replied.

"Goddess, I'll call you as soon as I get back to let you know what happened. Let me get off this phone and get ready."

"Okay, I will continue to pray for you."

"Thank you, Kina." I hung up the phone and put it away.

About ten minutes later, Trujillo came over the speaker in the cell and told me that it was time to go. When she popped the door, I stepped out and walked to the area in front of the officer's station. This was where they put the waist restraints on. As I was waiting, a few of the homies who were standing at their doors looking out, wished me luck.

There were only three of us going to court this morning. One was this white dude named Phil. He was in here for stalking. It seems he was in love with this gal that works at Heidi's pies on El Camino Real in San Mateo. The second cat was this dude they called big D. The dude stood about six foot six and weighed over 400 lbs. I did not know what he was in here for, but I knew one thing, his big ass better stay out of my way. I do not need no Looney Tunes nor no stress cases messing up my day.

Trujillo escorted us to court or at least to our first pit stop. The other two guys were doing their court via Zoom video, so we dropped them off on the sixth floor. I was in live court, so she had to walk me across the catwalk to the court waiting cell.

Once we were inside of the elevator, she asked me," So Norton, what are you going to court for today?"

"I'm having a motion and resentencing hearing today." She was cool peeps, so I answered her. Trujillo looked to be about twenty-five. She was a slim goody with killer looks but I kept that shit professional.

"Well hopefully everything works out for you today. You

seem like a nice guy so hopefully you get a break." She sounded genuine when she said that.

"Thank you, Lord knows I could use just a pinch of good luck and some things to go my way for a change."

"How long have you been down?" She asked, walking behind me on the catwalk. I had to turn my head slightly to hear her.

"Over five years now."

"Five years?" She repeated in astonishment.

"Yeah," I replied as I continued to walk in a steady pace.

"Well, I hope you get some good news, because over five years is a minute."

"Thank you," I said to her.

"No sweat," she said. Afterwards, we walked the rest of the way in silence. When we got there, they had me wait in the holding cell. The moment I got inside the holding cell I said a prayer. My palms got sweaty and my breathing quickened. It was time.

The deputy in charge with escorting me into the courtroom came and picked me up about ten minutes after I got in the holding cell. He was smart enough not to try to talk to me. I had to go into one last holding cell and wait to be called.

A couple minutes after I got there the deputy came to the door.

"Norton, your attorney is here for you." He walked me to a hallway with chairs lining the wall.

My attorney was sitting in one of the chairs and I took a seat next to him. Once the deputy left, my attorney spoke.

"How you feeling?"

"I am good. Just hell a nervous." I admitted as I wiped my sweaty hands on my pants.

He leaned into me and began whispering.

"Well, there is no reason for you to be nervous. I crossed my T's and dotted my I's; this motion is basically a walk in the park. I briefed the judge a little while ago and he understand that there is virtually nothing that can prevent us from winning this motion."

He then reached over and patted me on the back.

"Quincy, you're going home son," he said suddenly. I looked over at him, witnessing the genuine smile on his face. I was speechless. Actual tears began forming in my eyes. Those were the words I have been waiting to hear since this ordeal began.

"Damn," I said, still in awe.

"Let me go in here and let the judge know we are ready. Oh, did I tell you the D.A. was pissed?" He chuckled as he stood up. I watched him walk away wondering if he was correct.

The deputy's cold stare did not even phase me. Nothing he did could take my joy away. Not now.

When I went inside the courtroom and all the formalities were finished, the judge shared that he already previewed the transcripts from my trial. Now it was the D.A.'s turn and he fought his ass off. He pulled out all the guns trying his best to come up with a reason why the motion should be denied. But everything the D.A. threw out, my attorney shot down. Towards the end, the D.A. got so desperate, he began yelling. It was like a verbal spiral for the heavyweight championship.

In the end we prevailed. God truly blessed me. As soon as the judge ruled, my attorney had another motion, asking him to resentence me right away, which he did.

My life sentence was overturned along with the guilty conviction. I was found guilty of aggravated assault and assault with a deadline weapon. The judge sentenced me to nine years and six months, gave me credit for time served and ordered my release.

All of a sudden, I felt lightheaded, then fell to my knees. The only thing I remember is thanking God!

CHAPTER 41
QUINCY & SAKINA

Quincy

When I told Cynthia the news, she screamed so loud I was shocked that she did not shatter any windows. She screamed over and over for almost five minutes before she started crying. That moment was priceless.

I thought about telling Sakina but then decided against it. I needed to do something big to get her attention. I had the perfect plan in mind. Once I got back to Solano, I placed a call to her best friend Malika. After putting her in check last year, she and I have been pretty cool since.

I laid everything out on the table, and she was stunned. And after getting to know her, I can say that her shocked reaction did not happen too often. Malika was a trip but she and I had one thing in common and that was our love for Sakina. Needless to say, getting her to help was a piece of cake.

I stayed in Solano another month before I was finally

released. It was the best day of my life. I had to argue with Cynthia tooth and nail over not allowing her to pick me up. I had plans but she was not having it. In the end I relented.

The whole year that I was gone, in County, J kept things running smooth. He made sure he kept his word and gave me my cut out of every move he made. Since my attorney, lil E stopped taking payments from me, my money stacked nicely. I was sitting on a sizeable chunk of money. My thoughts instantly went to the brief conversation Sakina and I had regarding my finances. I had to offer her some form of explanation, because once she realized how much money I have, she would have questions for sure.

But I decided that I would just cross that bridge when I come to it.

In the meantime, I was on a mission to finally come face to face with the woman I have fallen in love with. And what was ironic, is the fact that I was released on none other than her birthday. Just last year on this day, I was behind bars and she was celebrating her birthday without me, and now here we were. I was a free man. Free to do whatever I wanted and all I wanted was to finally be in the presence of my Haitian queen, Sakina Michelle.

First thing first, Cynthia took me to this store called K&G in Oakland and I bought a whole new wardrobe. All suits and casual linens. Since she was away at school, Cynthia told me that I could stay at her place until I figured things out, which was cool with me. I kicked it with Cynthia for two days, then I had to take care of my business. Within those two days, I booked a flight to New Jersey and prepared for my trip. After Cynthia dropped me off at the airport, I boarded my flight and made myself comfortable.

I slightly smiled a short time later as the plane took off. I never thought I would ever board an airplane again, let alone be taking a flight to New Jersey. I honestly thought my life was over when I received that life sentence years ago, but now here I was on my way to not only New Jersey, a state I've never been before, but to meet an incredible woman who has captured my heart. Never thought I would love again after Monique, but here I was, head over heel. Life was truly something.

I shook my head at the irony of it all as I closed my eyes, leaned my head back against the seat and enjoyed the flight.

Four and a half hours later, I was landing at J.F. Kennedy airport in Queens, New York. After retrieving my luggage, I took quick strides through the terminal and shortly after, I reached the front area of the airport where the taxi cabs were stationed. I instantly located the car service I reserved to pick me up. So I headed in that direction.

"Gold Star Car Service, here to pick up a Quincy Norton," a short stocky, Hispanic male called out.

"Quincy Norton right here," I let him know. I raised my index finger and he made his way over to me.

"Welcome to New York, sir," he greeted, and I returned the sentiment with a head nod as he grabbed a hold of my luggage.

"Are you here for business or pleasure?" he asked as I followed him towards an all-white stretch out Mercedes limousine.

I smirked as I thought of Sakina in that moment. The anticipation to see her was then greater than ever.

"Pleasure, my man, pleasure," I replied to the driver as I climbed into the back seat of the decked - out luxury vehicle. The first thing I noticed was a stereo system. After I looked through it, I noticed one particular song that was Sakina's favorite and an idea came to my head.

"Where to sir?"

He asked and it dawned on me that I had no idea where the hell I was going.

"Start driving and stop at the nearest flower shop and by then I'll have an address," I instructed him, and he followed suite.

I planned on picking up a dozen of long stem white roses and a box of chocolates. I took two deep breaths, closed my eyes, and leaned my head back against the seat. After a five count, I released my breath as I pulled out my brand new Apple XR I Phone 10 from inside of the pockets of a pair of the grey Armani slacks I sported.

I used my index finger and tapped on the message log. I clicked on Malika's name and sent her a text, letting her know I was in the car service and was on my way to Jersey from Queens. I requested for Kina's address and sent the message.

"We've arrived at the flower shop, sir," the driver called out right after and I climbed out and proceeded inside of the store.

Forty - Five Minutes Later:

I watched through the windows as the driver turned on a quiet street with modern size houses.

Right then, the driver lowered the partition and told me we were close to our destination, based on the address Malika sent.

I decided then to place my call to Malika and let her know that I have arrived.

"You here? Are you out here already?" Malika sounded so excited, folks would have thought she was my girl.

"I'm less than twenty-minutes away, sis." I said to her.

"Okay just wait! Just wait! I'm going to call her on 3-way right now."

And before I could even get a word in, she switched over to the other line. I put my phone on mute so no mishaps would happen. Moments later I could hear Malika.

"Girl, don't be questioning me like you the police or the FBI. You do not need to know how I got the limo. All you need to know is I am pulling up to your house to pick you up because we're about to do the most for your birthday! Can you say stretch Mercedes?"

And just then, my baby's voice came on the phone.

"Malika this better not be some sort of joke. You're telling me you are riding in a stretch Mercedes limo heading to my house?"

"I'll be there in ten minutes bissh! so you better be ready. Bye!"

A few seconds later, Malika's voice came back on the phone.

"Q? hello?"

"I'm here, I just had the phone on mute," I answered her as soon as I unmuted the phone.

"Okay, I'm speeding over there. I jumped in my car the minute you called. I should get there a couple minutes after you."

Just then, the driver called out to me.

"I'm turning onto her street now."

Hearing that made me realized how excited and nervous I felt.

"Okay it's a peach house with white trimming," Malika said to me.

"We're pulling up in front of it now," I let her know as a modern size house with peach and white coloring came to view. I smiled then. My baby did good for herself. She finally went ahead and purchased her own home in the beginning of the year, and I felt proud as hell. Not only was she beautiful and smart, but she was about her shit.

"Hold on, let me call her," Malika said, and the line clicked again.

"Do you see this big mothafucka parked right here?" I heard Malika say and I muted the phone for a second time.

"I see it, but I don't believe it girl. How much did that thing cost?"

And I smiled again. That was Sakina. Always worried about the cost of a dollar. I guess it was a great thing, the way she was. We could balance each other out, because I was the total opposite. I was always a big spender and I felt no shame. Shit, you can't take money with you when you go, so you might as well live it up.

"Why are you asking me all these weird ass questions instead of bringing your ass out here? " Malika spat out and I almost busted out laughing.

"Okay, okay. Shit, hold your horses. Girl I'm on my way, damn. I have heels on, you know, and it's those expensive ass Prada heels you gave me for my birthday!" I heard her say before she hung up and I smiled for the tenth damn time. Just then, a vision of her legs up in the air with nothing but those heals on crossed my mind and I felt my man down below getting just as excited as I was.

Damn.

"Q, I am right around the corner. Shit I got to see this!" Malika shouted, through the phone, shaking me from my almost wet dream.

Damn, I had to get my shit together.

But then, the front door opened. Sakina appeared in the doorway and me getting my shit together went out the window.

My God, she was even more beautiful than her pictures. As she walked down the pathway, it looked like she was gliding instead of walking. Heaven could wait because my angel was right in front of my eyes. As I gave her the once over, I was more intrigued with her than ever. I loved her style of dressing from the countless pictures I've seen of her, but to see it in person was on some other shit.

She was my kind of woman in every sense of the phrase, and the more I'm getting to know her, the more I realized she possess qualities I didn't even know I admired in a woman until now.

As I studied her, I saw a fire red Infinity truck pull up in front of the house. Sakina stopped in her tracks. A look of confusion came over her pretty face. I swear Malika's timing was impeccable.

When she stepped out of her vehicle, Sakina took a step backwards in shock. She was only four or five feet away from the door of the limo and the windows were tinted, so she could not see who was inside.

"Malika, what the hell is going on?" I heard her ask as I studied her from head to toe. She was definitely classy with it, but sexy wise, damn.

She wore a pair of black, form fitting dress pants, with a black, laced material, strapless top showing off just the right amount of skin. And to top off her look, she indeed was sporting a pair of strapped, open toe heels with her pretty, manicured toes in full view. I noticed her nails were the same color as her toes and I was then more turned on like a mothafucker. And her hair. A doobie style, framing her angelic, round, shaped face. Simple, but beautiful.

She was elegant, but simple. Sexy, but classy.

Yeah, I chose a winner, for sure.

And in that moment, I decided it was time. I checked my charcoal grey Armani suit and my black Mauri Alligator's, making sure I was on point. Now was the moment of truth.

"Malika, what kind of games are you playing out here?" She asked as Malika approached her.

And that was my cue to show her that this right here, was no damn game at all. Reaching over to the stereo system, I pressed a button and music began to play. I took a deep breath, grabbed the box of chocolates, the roses, and opened the door to the limo.

SAKINA

Thirty Minutes Prior:

"It's in his kiss. If you wanna know if he loves you so, it's in his kiss."

My favorite oldie, **"It's in his kiss"** soared through my home stereo system and I sing along with **Betty Evertte** as I completed my birthday ensemble. It was my thirty-seventh birthday and I was feeling good. I had just finished completing my birthday look as I prepared to head on over to my brand – new book - store to handle some paper - work, when I received a call from Malika. And as usual she was with the dramatics.

Her crazy ass rented a stretch limo for my birthday and I swear...

But that was Malika. Every year she did it big for my birthday so why should this year be any different.

I smiled before I applied some clear, Mac lip gloss onto my lips and made sure my hair was on point. After checking my reflection in my dresser mirror, I went on over to my bed and took a seat. I took that time and meditated as I welcomed the peace in my newly purchased home. My boys were with their dad and I was alone, so I made the best of it. After some much - needed meditation, I closed my eyes and suddenly thoughts of my heart invaded my mental.

Quincy.

I heard from him earlier, but strangely, within the past five hours, he has been quiet.

I started to wonder what was going on with him, when my phone suddenly vibrated and I noticed it was Malika calling.

I answered her call and she was with the craziness as usual, asking me to check out the limousine from my living room window and head on outside. I wasted no time honoring her request as of course, I shook my head at my crazy best friend.

As soon as I opened the door to my home, I gasped.

I could not believe her ass rented a limo for sure and not just an average looking one, but a very, chic, luxurious, Mercedes limo.

Unbelievable this chic.

I was all smiles as I started to walk on over to where the vehicle was parked, when suddenly, an Infinity truck halted in front of my house. Malika climbed out and I was now confused.

"Malika, what the hell is going on?" I asked her.

I watched as she walked on over to me. I turned and looked towards the limo and wondered why she was in her own car and not the limo. Over the phone she made it sound as if she was already riding in it.

And as I tried to figure out what was happening, Malika approached me.

"Malika, what kind of game are you playing out here?" I asked her.

And in that moment, music appeared out of no - where, but then I realized it was sounding off from inside of the limo.

And not just any ole music, but my favorite song, "**Love Riddim**" by my fantasy husband, singer, **Rotimi**.

> **Wish I could start it over: Baby I need you over**
> **Wish I could taste**
> **kiss you down by your waist**
> **He treats you wrong**
> **And as the song played, the door to the limo suddenly opened and ……sweet Jesus…….**
> **Wish I could show you love: Wish I could make you know it**
> **Baby you need to know it**
> **Where do you go every time I touch you there? (yeah)**
> **Whispering love, ain't nobody gotta hear**
> **He lost control, does he even know you here?**
> **Nobody knows, I just keep it in my head**

The lyrics solidified the moment as my heart was beating so damn fast…. And when he stepped out of the limo, Malika had to indeed catch me for sure.

Standing before me…in the flesh… was….

Quincy…

"Does this look like a game?"

He asked and I was frozen in place. Sudden tears formed in my eyes as he towered over me looking like a true….. King.

The lyrics to the song played, and I was then taken to another dimension as he wrapped his larger than life, strong hand around my waist and pulled my frame, away from Malika's reach and towards his solid built.

He then lowered his face down towards mine and when our lips touched……I was a goner………………………………………..

Make it rise, make it rise: I don't say too much
(Baby baby, yeah)
I'm just here to touch
(Baby baby, yeah) baby
I don't say too much

S TAY TUNE!!!!!! FOR THE EXPLOSIVE FINALE!!!

SPRING 2021!!!!!

MONA'S CATALOGUE

Catalogue by Authoress Mona:

My Brother's wife
My Brother's wife 2
A Man's heart
My Brother's wife 3
After the Honeymoon (Desmond & Angeline)
A Speical Valentine's Romantic Getaway (The Aeikans & Family)
When We Touch (A Novella)
Forbidden Love, Unforbidden heart (Novella)
Love or Lust: Sho Me Right
Why Me: A Novella
The Right Kind of Wrong (Collaboration with Author Khatari)

MORE BOOKS BY MONA

NEVA DIE
PUBLICATIONS

PRESENTS

THE RIGHT KIND OF
WRONG 2
THE FINALE
BY AUTHORS:
KHATARI & MONA

RELEASES BY KHATARI COMING SOON...

NEVADIE PUBLICATIONS PRESENTS
KHATARI

If It's Meant To Be
Love Shouldn't Hurt

RELEASES BY KHATARI COMING SOON...

Made in the USA
Middletown, DE
28 May 2023